Origins of a D-List Supervillain

by

Jim Bernheimer

Visit the author's website at www.JimBernheimer.com

First Printing: June 2014

Print ISBN: 1500107727

Print ISBN-13: 978-1500107727

Dedication and Acknowledgements

For this novel, I have to start with the fans. If you hadn't bought *Confessions of a D-List Supervillain,* there would be no prequel. Thank you for all your support.

As always, I want to thank Kim, Laura, and Marissa. You are the reason I keep at this.

I would like to thank the efforts of the following people with this particular book: David Bagini and Graham Adzima for being my primary test readers, Todd Osborne for *almost* reading the whole thing, Raffaele Marinetti for the killer artwork, Jeffrey Kafer for what I'm sure will be an awesome audiobook, and David Wood for the assist on the cover with the lettering and so forth. Janet at Dragonfly Editing gets special thanks for making my keystrokes slightly more readable.

I also want to thank "the real" Joe Ducie for being awesome and providing the bucket list for Joseph.

Origins of a D-List Supervillain

Chapter One

Object Lessons in the Mirror are Closer than They Appear

Honestly, I don't think anyone starts out wanting to be a supervillain. Well, villain might be a little too strong of a word. To be certain, I was a criminal, but a villain, I don't know about that. Let's just go with a super powered criminal for now and see how things develop. My only goals involved the two P's—paycheck and payback.

I'd taken precautions. I'm no fool. I knew which jewelry stores had security cameras and which didn't. Even the ones that had them weren't much of an issue because they were pointed at the display floor and at the front window. I wouldn't be coming in that way. No, not me. I had my own version of a key. I'd even invented it for someone else. His company wouldn't put my name on the patent and that kind of started this whole mess.

The harness was a little on the bulky side. Promethia's industrial powercells weren't exactly light. That's why most things using them would also be using Promethia's synthetic muscle. In industry, that's known as a win-win situation.

I didn't quite have the coin for that, yet. Even if I did, I would try and steal it anyway, calling it compensation for ex-employee harassment and stealing my other invention—a power compressor. Fortunately, I had a spare prototype hidden away when their goons showed up and took my computers and the other prototype with their warrants and court actions.

They'd get theirs eventually. I'd be the one to ensure they did it.

Without my power compressor, I'd have had to carry two more powercells to make my force blasters do anything more than make a pretty light show. At fifty pounds a pop, that would have cut my mobility down to nothing. Good thing I'm an engineer, and a pretty effing brilliant one, at that. Even so, fifty for one cell and ten for each manacle left me toting around seventy extra pounds.

Dad always said I should exercise more. This was my way of taking his advice to heart and wallet.

The control mechanism was a simple dial on a belt—cheesy I admit, but I'd only been at this two weeks so far...two delightfully profitable weeks. The hardest thing had really been making the decision to become ManaCALes. It was a play on manacles, which my setup sort of resembled. I figured turning the knob to fifty percent would get me through this building's walls; constructed in the early eighties. The brick, like everything else in Mississippi, seemed substandard. At fifty percent, the cell and compressor combination would give me a dozen shots. No more than two to make a Calvin sized hole and one or two more for the security cameras.

The pressure stud on my wrists activated and I let the wall have it. This was one of those chain owned stores and, considering my background, I didn't possess an ounce of sympathy for someone in an office somewhere looking out for their bottom line. Besides, someone would have to repair this wall and they'd have to hire a local construction company. In a way, I was creating local jobs. It's not exactly Robin Hood, but I'm not in it to be some kind of legend. After all, who in their right mind would want to read a book about me?

"Add another count of grand larceny to my tally," I said and stepped through the opening. "With a cloud of dust and a hearty 'Let's go get some silver'."

A pulse from the left wrist-mounted force blaster took out the nearest camera and the right put a hole in the ceiling next to the other. My aim still needed some work. I corrected and finished the other off, before blowing open the locked areas below the display cases. Immediately, I started in on the trays where they kept the rings, necklaces, and earrings. The little light on my belt went off and it indicated that an alarm had been activated.

"Guess I don't have time for the safe today," I muttered and picked up the pace. I didn't have a beef with Johnny Law and I'd rather keep it that way. It was an easy fifty grand. After my fence took care of it, the haul would be thirty, but that broke down to ten grand a minute. It was a good wage when you can get it.

Not wanting to push my luck, I hoofed it back to my nondescript white van with stolen plates, with my ill-gotten, but still-gotten, goods and called it a day. Opening the back, I tossed the two bags into the magnet surrounded cylinder and fired up the degausser.

"Did they really think I wouldn't spot tracking chips? Nice try though."

I climbed into the back and my "getaway driver" pulled away. Self-driving technology has existed for decades. I might not have the resources to be able to build my own robot yet, but I could rig up a laptop and some control circuitry. Throw in an inflatable sex doll with a wig and I had my own semi-autonomous van. I called her Tracy, after the woman who'd made it all possible.

"Too easy," I said, removing my, mask, cape, harness and force blasters. "Maybe I should man up and try a bank job? One big score and I'd be able to finance my powersuit."

Grabbing a can of beer from the cooler, since I wasn't driving, I smiled and remembered all the stupid shit that I'd put up with before I finally made the right choice.

• • •

Thirty months before

"Mr. Stringel, I need to speak with you. Do you have a minute?"

Checking the clock on the wall, I answered, "There're three hours left in the work day, so you can have all one hundred and eighty. Well, technically I need five to finish packing up my desk."

"Very good," the chunky white dude in the suit said. "Let's take this down to my office."

Tossing the going away card the team had given me at the luncheon into the clear plastic tub, I followed the man through the maze of cubicles in Restricted Area B. I caught Joe "the Tweaker" Ducie giving us an odd look and shrugged at him. The Aussie engineer, who endured countless green card jokes from me, mouthed something that looked suspiciously like, "Watch your back."

Frowning, I tried to dismiss Joe's warning. He was a decent enough fellow with a fine taste in scotch. Joe and I worked fairly closely together on *the project*. Joe's job was Chief Diagnostician. He kept Lazarus Patterson's mobile money pit running at peak condition, running a series of never ending checks, and having the nightmare of adapting all the prototypes everyone else came up with. His job did have one nice perk: he was the only person, other than *the man*, allowed to wear the suit.

My job was much easier and came with fewer headaches. I made stuff go boom. When I first got here, Ultraweapon flew into battle and used a plasma rifle as his main gun. While fairly cool, the boss kept getting it knocked out of his hands during a fight, usually at the most inopportune time.

My predecessor had tried his best with that rifle. His best effort was a magnetic locking system mechanism, which sometimes interfered with the weapon's targeting and alignment during actual combat. Let's just say he was let go after a rather messy hostage incident that left Promethia paying for the UN Secretary General's facial reconstruction.

That's when I was called up from the bullpen and given the go ahead for project force blaster. It required Ultraweapon's arms be expanded, but my directed energy emitter was now built into the suit, making it considerably more durable and harder to knock out of alignment.

Lazarus Patterson, himself, came to my desk to thank me in person after his first fight with them. The guy was a colossal jerk, but even he was impressed by my design, said I'd be "going places."

Fast forward six months and he was right.

My stroll down memory lane ended at an office, complete with an attractive secretary. I glanced at the name on the door to see who I was dealing with.

F. Randall Barton, Vice President Intellectual Property Division.

Okay, I thought, imagining what his first initial stood for. *An I.P. Nazi. Nothing to worry about, Cal old buddy. You've got your robotic ducks in a row.*

"Please sit," he said and waddled around to the large leather high-back chair. My chair wasn't nearly as impressive, or comfortable for that matter—one of those schlocky mind games, I assumed.

I decided to play it cool and not immediately demand to know what I was doing here.

"So, Calvin," he began. "You're leaving us."

"Yes," I said. The two week notice and the going away luncheon must have roused his suspicions.

"May I ask why?"

Being an engineer, I didn't really care for beating around the bush. "I've been over this with the HR people, and I am sure you already know exactly why I'm resigning. Unless you want me to believe that people get to be division heads in this company without being prepared?"

"Yes," he admitted. "You want us to attach your name on the patents for the projects you assisted on."

"Assisted on? Exactly who was I assisting?"

He ignored my questions and blathered on, "It has been the company's policy, since long before your employment began, to attach Mr. Patterson's name alone to our patents. I can produce your signed employment contract, if you'd like?"

"Already seen it and I get it. He's never going to allow anyone other than himself an iota of credit."

Shaking his head while tapping his left middle finger on his desk, the man replied, "The policy is for your protection, Mr. Stringel. Suppose, for a moment, that your name is attached to a component on the Ultraweapon armor. You do realize the majority of our chief executive officer's enemies have the mental capacity to execute a patent search. Have you ever met a supervillain, Mr. Stringel?"

"No," I said. "I don't think I ever will either."

"If we put your name on a patent, I can pretty much guarantee that you not only will, but when you do, it will result in your rather messy and painful death."

"Fair enough," I conceded, not very warm to the ideas of pain or death. "You've got a perfectly acceptable answer for why you won't give credit where it's due. And...that's why I have chosen to leave."

I didn't want to add, "Like so many others." I was set to be the fifth person in two years to leave *the project* and was reasonably certain the turnover would continue after I'd left this facility in the dust.

"Are you familiar with the Compton-La Guardia Core National Defense Asset Act passed last month?"

He had me there. My reading list usually consisted of tech manuals, game manuals, shit I found on the net, and letters to the editor that began with the phrase, "I never thought it would happen to me."

"No, I am not." In fact, the only vague recollection I had of it was hearing Joe make a joke about a law that he called, "Corned Ass." To me, it sounded like something that involved diarrhea and bad Mexican food.

Somehow, I didn't think F. Randall there would have appreciated our interpretation of this law.

"Then allow me to familiarize you with the parts that may concern you, Mr. Stringel. There are certain things that qualify as a National Defense Asset under Compton-La Guardia. The Ultraweapon Suit just happens to be classified as one of them."

Processing his statement, I replied, "Well, since you're not going to credit me as being part of the team that works on it, I don't see a problem."

"But I, and, by extension, Promethia do, Mr. Stringel. The law restricts foreign access to intelligence on National Defense Assets. You have unique knowledge of a particular asset. Therefore, Promethia will challenge your employment by any corporation that has a foreign bureau or offices in other countries."

"Promethia has foreign offices, dipshit! You sell combat robots to nine out of ten governments on this planet."

"Yes," he admitted. "And we would have to submit and approve a waiver with the NSA if we wished to transfer you to a different division."

"So, Ubertex can submit a waiver. I still don't see the problem. I'm not going to be working in directed energy weaponry there."

He leaned forward and leered at me. "But as the releasing authority, we reserve the right to reject any waiver for a period of time up to three years from your separation—five if Promethia files for an extension. You will not be employed by Ubertex or any other defense company for the foreseeable future."

Taking a deep breath, it occurred to me that my row of robotic ducks might be lined up in front of a firing squad.

"All right," I said. "Why exactly would you do that? I haven't been a troublemaker. What's with the thumbscrew treatment?"

"As you have no doubt noticed, you're the latest person to leave your team. Mr. Patterson has expressed concerns about this technical drain on our company's resources. Compton-La Guardia now gives us a vehicle to combat this, Mr. Stringel."

That's when the light came on in my mind. "You're going to jack me over just so the rest of the team sees what will happen!"

"It did say in your file that you are a fast-learner," F. Randall commented.

"New twist on the Company Store, eh? Digital style," I said. "Last time I checked, Lincoln freed the slaves."

"A good analogy, young man," he replied. "However, President Lincoln also suspended portions of the Bill of Rights that interfered with his ability to win the Civil War, just something for you to consider."

"We'll see about that, you pompous bastard!"

The sack of shit shrugged, having probably been called much worse, and replied, "I suspect you will."

• • •

After a slightly panicked call to the HR manager at Ubertex, and a "what can I do" conversation with Joe, I went back to F. Randall's office and waited with my tail between my legs while his secretary announced me.

Opening the door, he didn't bother bringing me into his office. "Yes, Mr. Stringel?"

As much as I wanted to wipe that smug expression off of his face, I sucked it up and said, "I'd like to withdraw my resignation."

He shook his head. "Unfortunately, we can't risk having a disgruntled employee working on the most important project in the company. I'm afraid we cannot return your resignation, Mr. Stringel."

"Why the hell not?"

"Well," he said, sounding like a father confiscating his kid's college fund, "I'll put it simply, in a manner even the brilliant, but naïve can understand. You've been judged to be the most expendable on the project. Everyone who is on that project statistically has one revolutionary idea in them. You've already delivered yours, Mr. Stringel, and we thank you for that. That law has been on the books for a month now and no one moved to stop you when you turned in your notice. That should be telling you something, but you still don't get it, do you?"

Finding myself running out of options I said, "So, you're just going to screw me over anyway. That was the plan from the start."

"Someone needs to be the example, Mr. Stringel. We've decided it will be you. It's nothing personal and I could say something along the lines of, 'It brings me no pleasure,' but that would be a lie. I take great pride in my work and I'm quite good at it. By the time I'm through with you, you won't even be able to flip burgers at a fast food restaurant if they have a franchise in another country."

Losing, and badly, at that, wasn't something in my twenty-five year old vocabulary. I'd been a whiz kid and my talent had always kept me on top. I took a step at him, but stopped, figuring that it would make things that much easier for him. Turning, I saw the secretary with the phone already off the hook, looking like a deer caught in the headlights. She'd heard the entire exchange and would sell me out in a heartbeat for that son of a bitch!

Face it Cal, he's got you by the balls, I thought and walked back to my desk. Security was there to escort me out of the building, which was probably Barton's plan, anyway. Even so, I walked out of there with my head held high. I was down, but I wouldn't be out.

• • •

"I'm sorry, Calvin," the voice on the other end of my prepaid cellphone said through the poor reception. "The judge decided not to hear our appeal. I wish I had better news for you, but it looks like it's over for good."

There wasn't enough fight left in me to scream at him. The suit wasn't the bad guy here. He'd taken the case pro bono, looking to tilt at a few windmills. Unfortunately, Promethia's slick legal team was three steps ahead of him at every turn. Hell, the day he was finally able to depose

Patterson was the same day the tin-plated tyrant saved a bus full of senior citizens from going off the highway into the Pacific. Lazarus Patterson might as well have been kissing a baby during it.

"No other options?" I asked. "They're just going to take my invention, like that?"

My free lawyer said a few more things that fell on deaf ears before I let him go and started planning my latest pity party. Barton was wrong. I'd had two revolutionary ideas in me. Even so, they'd protested my patent application for a power compressor and had said it was derivative of my work there. Despite power containment and directed energy weapons having about as much to do with each other as the electricity in a house and an appliance plugged into an outlet, the judge agreed with the moneybags and Promethia won again.

I'd played the game to the best of my abilities. My first lawyer filed complaints with state and federal labor boards. There was a nicely worded one that brought the wrath of OSHA down on Lazarus Patterson's company, at least for a day, but Barton's virtual blacklisting had stuck like a case of vocational herpes. The high tech companies on both coasts wanted nothing to do with me. Promethia had stepped in when I wanted to go work for a university in South Korea and now I was on some kind of International Travel Watch list with no passport.

A child molesting, white supremacist had a better shot of landing a decent job than I did. Only one of Promethia's competitors brought me in for something resembling an interview, but it was mainly some kind of spat between rich men who had too much time and money on their hands. By that point I knew I was just leverage in a corporate version of the game chicken. I tried grad school, but my applications invariably got lost or I'd get rejected by a university that suddenly received new grant money.

Facing less opportunity than a known card counter trying to get into a casino, I took whatever I could get, which was how I ended up in a small town in Mississippi.

"So," Dougie Walters said as he invaded my personal space. "I know you like to tell people how you used to work on Ultraweapon's suit and all that inventing stuff, but what I really need from you, Mr. Engineer, is that brake job on Mrs. Conroy's Caddy before she takes her money somewhere else. Think you can do that, or have you got some supahero bidness that's gonna interfere?"

Dougie was the manager at Chism's Brake and Muffler Shop, where my skills weren't exactly being tested, and the salary was a drop in the bucket compared to what I used to make.

"I'll get it done, Dougie," I said, not wanting to lose the only job I'd been able to hold for more than six weeks since Promethia decided to make my life a living hell.

Dougie stood there, spitting his chew into a styrofoam cup, like the stereotype of every redneck mechanic all rolled into one. I glanced away at the trickle of black liquid that dribbled down the side of his mouth. He must have taken that as a sign that I accepted his superiority, instead of my abject disgust.

"Well, then," he said, satisfied that he was the alpha male, or maybe the fattest pig on this farm. "Don't let me keep ya. Also, since you're some kinda fancy electrician, take a look at her 'lectrical system and see if you can find what's draining her battery."

Nodding, I ignored the slight to my electrical engineering degree and thought, *Good thing this place only works on American, or as Roscoe P. Butthole over there would say, 'Merikan, cars. Otherwise, F.Randall's lapdogs would probably find a way to get me fired from here as well.*

"It's got dealer tags on it, why isn't her husband's dealership working on it?"

Dougie answered, "Word out in town is that she and Mr. Moneybags are pretty much through. She's all paranoid his boys'd cut her brake lines or something."

Argos Mississippi didn't count as much of a town. It should have been named Hour Away, because it was at least an hour away from anything remotely interesting. Then again, it could also be Rock Bottom, because here I was—renting a doublewide trailer and daring the powers above to come and finish me.

F. Randall Barton probably laughed over cocktails with Lazarus Patterson about how completely screwed I was.

Sadly, the man had turned my fate over to a group of overzealous brown-nosers. With the exception of stealing my patent, I wasn't worth his time anymore. My fall was now officially complete and I was more nuisance than nemesis.

I was still fuming about the sad state of affairs when I reached the caddy to get it up on the lift. The inside put the filthy in filthy rich. The disposable paper floor mat was used more for my protection than anything else. Driving into the bay, I had to roll the window down. It smelled like the aftermath of a damned frat party in there.

Dougie sauntered back forty-five minutes later. "I don't 'spose you're done already?"

"With the brakes," I said. "I haven't even started on the electrical problem, yet."

He hemmed and hawed for a minute before I said, "What is it?"

"Well, it's like this," he said. "She's out there raising hell, so I'ma gonna give her our loaner and when you finish with her caddy, you can drop it off and come back in the loaner."

"I don't even know what's wrong with it yet," I said looking over at the battered clock on the wall. "Even if I do, there's no guarantee that I can get whatever part might need to be replaced."

"Yeah, that's the thing. I told her you'd stay 'til it's done."

"So, you're going to pay overtime?" I said to the notorious tightwad.

"Shit, naw! I'll make it up to ya down the way. 'Sides, you're such a hotshot that you should already be done insteada flappin' your yap with me."

That was "Dougiespeak" for "Don't count on it and be happy you have a job." I knew he'd fleece the woman out there for the extra work, but I wouldn't see a dime of it.

Three months ago, I would have laughed at him and walked out the door. I still had some self-respect back then.

"Sure, Dougie," I said digging a few more inches farther into my rock bottom. "I'll take care of it."

By closing time, I'd learned a few things about Tracy Conroy. She was first and foremost a mess and on her way back to being named Tracy Jeffries. Under the driver's seat was a monument to prescription drug abuse. The empty pill bottles under her seat with addresses from pharmacies in a three hour radius told me she coped with her personal problems with the support of her three close friends Xanax, Ambien, and oxycodone. The bleached blonde pill-popper was also pretty careless of her possessions as well.

Wedged into the crack between the seat and the console, with the flotsam and jetsam of someone who was rich enough to drown their sorrows in legal drugs and booze, was a pair of bank envelopes with three hundred dollars inside and a really expensive tennis bracelet.

Call me paranoid, but I immediately considered the possibility that this might be a setup. Repeatedly getting the shaft had influenced my disposition. I set the valuables on the passenger seat and began working on the short in the seat heater, which appeared to be at the root of her electrical problem.

"Because having a seat heater in southern Mississippi is so damned important," I muttered knowing I could probably just disconnect the stupid thing and be done with it, but it wasn't that difficult of a repair—more time consuming than anything else.

Pondering my situation, I found this moment was dangerously close to defining me—in the middle of nowhere repairing something that isn't even necessary. Was this what my life had come to?

• • •

Three hours after the shop closed, the seat was back together. The same couldn't be said about me. I locked up and read the directions Dougie left scrawled on a piece of paper and drove out into the hot night in search of Tracy Conroy's house.

The caddy was a decent enough ride. When I was still hauling in buckets of money out west, I'd had a mustang and wouldn't have considered something like this. I had been all about speed and performance. This was a vehicle for dudes in their fifties who had the money, but were out of the game, or for guys who had lost their nerve.

Maybe that's why I was starting to like it.

According to the directions, she lived about thirty minutes outside of town. Rolling down the windows helped air the odor out and make the drive a little more bearable. My eyes kept drifting over to the bank envelope with the money and the tennis bracelet inside. The bit of sparkling jewelry was probably worth more than I'd see this year and my lawyer mentioned that Promethia's goon squad might be considering suing me for legal costs; to add insult to injury. I'd never considered being a criminal before, but the temptation was there in spades.

After a few minutes of searching through the stations for anything to listen to, I gave it up and started singing some of my old standbys. I was halfway through a rousing rendition of *Just a Friend* when I spotted the cluster of emergency vehicles and the sea of brake lights on the two lane highway ahead. Eventually, some of the rubberneckers began making three point turns at the urging of the police. One cruiser pulled up next to me and the man inside said, "You're gonna haveta turn around. The road's going to be closed for a few hours."

"What happened?" I asked, filled with morbid curiosity.

"Some fool went off the road and wrapped her Camry around a tree at about sixty miles an hour."

"Camry?" I said, getting an odd feeling. Our loaner was a Camry. "Was the Camry white and the driver a woman?"

"Yeah," the officer answered. "Ya reckon ya know who she was?"

"I work at Chism's Brake and Muffler," I said. "We loaned our white Camry to Tracy Conroy while I stayed and fixed her caddy. I've got keys for the loaner here. They've got the plate number on them."

I read him the tag number while he radioed to the accident scene for confirmation. It didn't take more than a minute before he said, "I don't think you'll be getting that loaner back anytime soon."

I'd already set the useless spare keys to the loaner back on the passenger seat—next to that small envelope filled with cash and a very expensive tennis bracelet while a scheme began to form in my mind. F. Randall Barton, Lazarus Patterson, and their Armani wearing choirboys weren't going to let me make an honest living. What had being the nice guy and playing by the rules ever gotten me? Tracy Conroy's drug and alcohol-binge fueled death was a sign of what happens when someone spends too long at rock bottom.

That wasn't going to be me!

With the officer following me back to the shop, where I'd call Dougie back and have him confirm my account, I slid that bank envelope into my pocket. Tracy no longer needed the contents and her widower owned three car dealerships. This bauble probably meant squat to him and he wouldn't care.

As for me, a whole new group of possibilities were opening up. All of them sprouted from a single idea I'd had several times, but never when I was stone cold sober. I did build Ultraweapon's force blasters after all, and that power compressor would allow one powercell to do the work of three. It was there on a two lane highway, driving a dead woman's car that I decided I could make my own version of the Ultraweapon suit.

After a couple of rudderless years where I let people with more money and power get the best of me and push me around, I had a purpose. This time, I'd be the one doing all the pushing.

Chapter Two

ManaCALes is Not a Stupid Name

"Hey, Cal, how are things?"

"As well as can be expected, Dad," I said into the receiver. "How are things with you and Mom?"

As chit chat goes, it was pretty much how we started every conversation. Dad managed a bowling alley several hundred miles away which was about as close as I liked my parents to be.

"Oh, the same," he replied. "Your mom's probably going to have to get her hip replaced in the next few months."

"That's not good," I said. "Tell her that I'm thinking of her." My mother and I had a complicated relationship. Well, actually it was pretty simple. She doted on her brilliant son and bragged to all her friends about how much better I was, as opposed to their crotch droppings. My whole blacklisting from any high tech position in this country appeared to have hurt her social standing, and accordingly, she blamed me. At least, that's what I could surmise. For her part, she pretty much just stopped talking to me.

That's me, I thought. *The big disappointment. I'd be her least favorite child, if she had any other.*

"I'll do that, Calvin. Don't mind her, she's just being difficult. Sorry about your court case. Is your lawyer going to try and appeal?"

I took a deep breath and said, "No. I think it's over at this point. The rich get richer and the little guys get the shaft. Seems like that's the way it's been done and that's what's happening now. It'd be nice if Barton got hit by a truck, but with my luck he'd have left instructions in his will for his flunkies to keep harassing me while Lazarus gets to keep playing hero in his shiny suit."

Dad paused for a few seconds before saying, "Doesn't seem fair, though. Any time that sonnuva bitch is on the news, I just flip the channels. I keep hoping someone's going to whip him good."

Considering all he watched was bowling and the cable news channels that really said something. Dad wasn't a brilliant man. He worked hard and I'd like to think I inherited his determination. As for my mom, she had the brainpower and the acerbic wit. Had she been born a decade or two later, I'm certain she'd be in a powersuit as an executive in a fortune five hundred company. Instead, she worked in accounts receivable for a furniture wholesaler keeping their books balanced.

If I was being brutally honest, Monica Stringel probably thought that she had "settled" for the life she lived and tried to live vicariously through the accomplishments of her son. When my professional life took a hard left and dived into the dumpster both my dreams and apparently hers were shattered.

Hell, all it took was four weeks of being back home after I'd abandoned California for me to wear out my welcome and decide to hit the road and look for any place else—even if that landed me in Argos, Mississippi.

"I'm sure they'll get what's coming to them in the end." I said, thinking it might be sooner now that I'd reached a decision.

"You know what they say about karma, Cal?"

"Let's hope so. Well, I hate to cut it short," I said, lying. "But I've got to get going to work. Let me know when Mom plans on having that surgery. I'll try to make it back or at least send flowers."

"You take care," he said. "It'll all work out in time."

"Thanks Dad. I'll talk to you soon."

Hanging up, I shook my head. I looked at the round trip bus ticket in my hand. My beat-up, old Hyundai probably wouldn't make the trip to and from Miami. Some kind of vacation was in order, plus I knew a pawnshop owner down there, who wouldn't ask too many questions about a certain bracelet I possessed. Joey Hazelwood had the misfortune of having the same name as the captain of that tanker that dumped all that oil into Prince William Sound, and the equally dubious distinction of being my roommate for four years at UCLA.

• • •

"So the woman is dead and the husband has already moved on with his new girlfriend," Joey said. "You better not be shitting me, Cal."

He'd packed on the pounds and was fighting a losing battle with his hairline already. The truth was that Joey Hazelwood had gone to shit, but I'd beat him there by a country mile.

"I'm on the level, Joey. He'll probably assume she hocked it for money," I answered. "You could just as easily say it was a blonde in here and no one would be the wiser."

"Yeah," he said. "I can move this. Damn, Strings, remember when I was going to be a marketing genius and you were going to invent the things we were going to sell? Where did we go wrong?"

"Well, I think it was when you inherited this place from your uncle and switched coasts and I decided that Promethia would look nice on my resume. That'd be my guess. So, what's it worth and what can you give me for it?"

"It's worth about twenty five," he said. "I'll give you eight for it, because I'll have to send it to a guy up in New York to sell it, which means I'm only going to get fifteen."

Frowning, I wanted a bit more, but knew Joey wasn't going to be able to go much higher. "I'll take two and some store credit if you have any tech."

"What do you need?"

"What have you got in the way of powercells?"

I'd been working with some class A "home use" powercells when I'd built my prototype compressor, Promethia and the US Marshals had confiscated those. The likelihood I'd ever see those again was about the same as Lazarus showing up at my trailer and delivering a personal apology. Along with my spare compressor, I still had one class A, but that wasn't going to cut it.

"I've got a half-dozen A cells and two class B industrials. How about two grand and two A cells?"

"What about the B cells?"

He scratched all three of his chins. "Both of them need serious reconditioning and either one is out of your price range. I got them damaged from a construction accident."

"I can recondition a powercell, Joey. How about I recondition both and you let me walk with one?"

It was Joey's turn to frown. It was the second time today I had asked him to skirt the edge of the law. To own a class B powercell, you had to have some kind of paper trail. Class C and above required government clearances.

"Just write off the one as being unsalvageable and sent for destruction. Bust up one of the A cells and turn it in in its place."

Smiling, I knew I had him. True, I was offering to do several thousand dollars' worth of repair work for him at cost, but he'd hardly paid retail for them to begin with.

"Strings, my man," he said. "You got yourself a damned deal!"

Instead of three days of Florida beaches and wasting my money chasing tanned bodies, I spent it hunched over a workbench in the back of Joey's shop, but all that work scored me an industrial powercell, well, at least one that could hold eighty percent charge, but beggars can't be choosers.

• • •

In one of my more paranoid moments, I bought a bulletproof vest. Fortunately for me, Barton wanted me humiliated and destitute instead of dead. Joey would have been awfully suspicious if I had asked him for one.

"Hey, Stringel," Dougie said. "Anything going on?"

"No, I'm good."

"Oh, it's just that you haven't been such a whiny little bitch lately."

It was his way of giving me a compliment. Somehow, I doubted he had any training in spotting changes in employee behavior and linking that to criminal intent. His idea of profiling consisted of watching women walking by and seeing how big their racks were.

While building a pair of force blasters, I'd kept a low profile. That meant none of my usual outbursts at work for over two weeks running.

"I've accepted that there is nothing more to be done," I replied.

"So, no more calls from lawyers and suppahero bidness?"

"If I never see another superhero again, I'll be a happy man."

Dougie grinned, giving me a look at how badly coffee and chewing tobacco can ruin tooth enamel. "That's good. I just wanted you to know that if you keep this up, you're in the running for employee of the month."

"Thanks," I said, hoping that I didn't sound sarcastic. That honor would go great alongside my magna cum laude from UCLA. In a shop of seven mechanics and two women working the front office, competition for that coveted distinction, and the parking spot accompanying it, was positively cutthroat.

"Anything else, boss?"

"I've got a Durango that needs an oil change, flush and fill, and the rotors either need to be turned or resurfaced."

Nodding, I told him I could take care of it. The job would consume the rest of my day and required only enough attention to make certain I didn't forget to put the drain plug back in. That way, I could spend the rest of the day on my mental chalkboard designing my super powered crimesuit. Although, I will confess to a five minute interlude while I fantasized what my blasters could do to this place.

My high school guidance counselor always stressed the importance of having goals. If I ever go to my ten year reunion, I'll have to look her up and thank her for that advice.

The class B cell was heavy, checking in at fifty pounds. Without my power compressor, I would have been forced to carry two or three to power my blasters, which would have left me virtually immobile without some kind of Waldo or synthmuscle exoframe. That was the beauty of my invention. It was really a lightweight capacitor and if my calculations were correct, I could squeeze eight full power shots before running the cell and the compressor dry.

Using a thrift store backpack, I crafted a harness that would carry my power supply. With the weight restrictions, I was pretty much limited to what I could carry in the deep pockets of a set of black coveralls. A red, insulated ski mask, from when I used to be able to afford that form of recreation, would cover my face along with a pair of those yellow tinted, light enhancing glasses. For the control interface, I had a belt with an oversized dial on it. It went beyond crude, but often the easiest solution to a problem was the ugliest. The dial had five settings. On the lowest, the blast would toss an average-sized man about ten feet and smash through most regular glass windows. The next settings up carried enough force to bust a door off its frame and seriously injure a human. Anything beyond that and they'd be scooping the body off the ground into a black bag, since three through five were meant for walls, bulletproof glass, and safes.

I had no plans to be a murderer, though I could convince myself to make an exception for a certain lawyer. From my point of view, it'd be justifiable, but I wasn't sure the judicial system would agree.

My lack of carrying space left me with two options: banks and jewelry stores. Banks always meant federal agents and possibly superhero involvement. It was higher risk with greater reward. One big score could net me enough to build my powersuit. It also meant human interaction and I wasn't interested in that. Jewelry stores meant more trips to Miami or other pawn shops to unload the goods. That path would add lengthy delays to my plans, but Dad always used to say that "slow and steady wins the race."

At that moment, all I had was time.

• • •

Second thoughts? Yeah, I started having them as soon as the force blasters were finished. Up until then, I was just planning crimes. The day I test fired my blasters was when shit got real. The first place I decided to knock over was a chain jewelry store, figuring they would be insured. I toyed with the idea of robbing the pawn shops, but, considering I might need them to fence my goods, that seemed problematic. Also, I could easily be distracted by all the other shiny objects inside a place like that.

From the amount of sweating I was doing, I worried that the police would be able to track the water trail back to my trailer. Somehow, I doubted a double wide could ever be considered a criminal lair. It was around two in the morning, when the cops would be camped out by the bars and looking for easy ways to make their ticket quotas. Dialing the belt controller up to level three, I blew open the back door and scrambled through the opening. A second burst from my left hand took out their server closet. Unless they sent their security feed offsite, I'd just rendered their cameras useless and destroyed the recorded data.

Most crooks down this way wouldn't even consider that, I thought, mentally patting myself on the back. I blew the power panel for good measure, but the alarm had already been triggered. It was more for the sake of not listening to it while I broke into the drawers below the display cases and poured rings, necklaces, and earrings into a pillowcase.

Yes, I was using a pillowcase. Don't judge me. Given my costume, I looked like a trick or treater, so it seemed to work. "Function over form" was what I always said.

At the two minute mark, I lumbered back out to the red Hyundai and tossed the pillowcase onto the floor of the passenger seat and then dropped the backpack assembly on the seat above my haul. It was a little uncomfortable with the cables running to the wrist mounted force blasters and the wires going to the belt controller assembly, but I pulled away before the fourth minute had elapsed. My route took me away from the direction the police cars would be coming. It was a twenty minute drive back to Argos.

Several times one of Barton's legal thugs implied to the judge that my acts were criminal in nature. At least now, I'd given them cause to say that.

"I need a criminal name," I said aloud, basking in the joy of my first heist. "Blasterman? Ultrathief? Nah, that one would be a dead giveaway. The blocky powercell, almost makes me look like the Hunchback of Notre Dame, maybe I should use Quasimodo."

Since I didn't have the synthetic muscle to make a pair of gauntlets, my force blasters were mounted on my wrist instead. The way the cables ran off of it made them seem like those shackles they make prisoners wear.

"Powershackle? Closer. What about Manacles? I like it. Almost sounds like my name. I've got it! ManaCALes!"

It didn't seem like a stupid name to me.

● ● ●

One of the things I always found amusing about my time working with Patterson and his supersuit was that after he fought in a battle, especially the times he'd gotten beaten, the entire project would gather in an auditorium and watch every piece of footage of the battle—like we were a damned football team watching game film.

It was fun watching everyone trying to deflect the blame.

"If the offensive systems performed better, the shields wouldn't have taken such a beating." I patently ignored the comment from Owen, because he was full of shit and offensive systems wasn't the reason Lazarus was resting in a hyperbaric chamber at that moment.

"Don't look at maneuverability! Ever since the latest upgrades were installed, the suit is quicker. Maybe internal structure could work another shield emitter into the skeleton."

Derek probably kissed a picture of Patterson's ass every morning before he kissed his wife. He was the scientific equivalent of a cockroach—ready to scurry at a moment's notice.

"There's no wasted space in internal structure. If we cram anything else in there, we'd have to amputate one of the pilot's limbs. Feel free to pitch that idea to the boss."

Owen wasn't done. "Maybe ATAI could have done a better job predicting Mistress Magma's attack patterns."

Rita took offense to that. "She shoots flames from her hands, it's not rocket science! Her temperature exceeds the current rating of the suit shielding and armor. Block it, shoot her first, or dodge it."

Todd's response was a bit more succinct. He gave Owen the finger.

"Okay," Ducie said, cutting off the bickering. "Mr. Patterson is recovering and we have forty-eight hours to get the suit back up and running and come up with a winning strategy against a five foot three she-volcano. I need ATAI to run simulations and determine a minimum safe distance, if Ultraweapon runs into her alone again. I also need team scenarios because I'd rather have the rest of the West Coast Guardians with him."

Four members were responsible for the Adaptive Threat Assessment Index. It was a database of supervillains, and oddly enough, superheroes. Yeah, Lazarus Patterson was that paranoid. The ATAI team were a fun bunch; Todd, Rita, Matt, and Brad. They were a fountain of knowledge when it came to super powers. They ran simulation after simulation of Ultraweapon versus everyone else.

Whenever we upgraded the suit, they ran it against the "Imaginary Larry" test first. Larry was an insanely powerful telekinetic, with equal emphasis on insane and powerful. By all accounts, he was the strongest person on the planet. In over two hundred simulated battles, Ultraweapon only beat him twice in a stand up fight. The first time came after my force blasters were installed. I think I got a bonus that week.

I needed my own threat index. The Gulf Coast Guardians technically had responsibility for this region. They usually stayed in the area between New Orleans and the major cities of Texas. I didn't think I'd have to worry about them for a while. Andydroid was based out of Atlanta and the northern parts of Florida. This was something of a "dead zone" for super powered folks. In fact, the only potential problem I might face would be The Biloxi Bugler.

If Ultraweapon could only beat Imaginary Larry once in a blue moon, the Bugler stood about as much of a chance against Ultraweapon. He had a sonic bugle and a death wish. Best I could tell, he didn't even wear a bulletproof vest! If I was in this to build some kind of reputation, I think I would have picked someplace better, but until I had my own suit, fighting superheroes wasn't something on my agenda.

Still, I needed my own self-assessment after pulling my first job. The police suspected the perpetrators used explosives and linked it to possible gang activity. For the moment, I was in the clear, and I used that time to improve my chances of success.

Things would be much simpler if I had a getaway driver I could count on. Almost half my time was spent getting back into my car. The car was the other problem—it wasn't really suited for a crime spree. I needed something a little bigger and more useful. Like any venture that wants to be successful, I'd have to reinvest a portion of my profits back into my enterprise.

The gold rings I could just melt down. Those places that buy gold with few questions were a blessing. I could mint my own coins, or just give it to them as a bar. The biggest issue with the gold was ensuring that I didn't mix the metal qualities.

The jewelry I'd have to accumulate until there was enough to take to Miami or go straight to Joey's New York connection.

• • •

I traded in the Hyundai right after my first "payday." Replacing it was a used nondescript white van—the kind you see on the highway and don't give a second thought to. Paying cash for a new one was tempting, but somehow I guessed Barton's squad was tracking my finances, so I played it safe.

The getaway driver was a problem, but surprisingly I had trust issues. The answer came in the form of a project I'd been a part of in my second year at UCLA. Our engineering department built a self-driving car. I still had most of the notes. It wasn't as complex as people made it out to be. The idea wouldn't take hold in this country anytime soon. People saw it as taking away their personal freedom. It probably just wasn't marketed correctly. If they sold it as a built-in designated driver, it'd sell like hotcakes, especially around here.

My driver was a blow up sex doll wearing a blonde wig. I named her Tracy, in honor of the dead woman who made this all possible. Beyond that, I used the GPS unit from my cellphone, a laptop, webcam, and some simple control equipment. It would get around this county and obey almost all traffic laws—I did make an exception so it wouldn't pull over for the police.

It seemed prudent. There was also an untested override which I hoped I'd never have to use, where I programmed it to behave like one of those console driver games.

• • •

"Hit it, Tracy!" I said, jumping into the back of the van and closing the doors. Job number seven was actually in Alabama. I didn't want to be exclusive to Mississippi and make the investigators jobs any easier and give them any kind of a pattern to lock in on.

The route I programmed into Tracy took me out of town headed southeast. I was on my way to Florida and figured they'd be looking for my van going back west. Also, getting a bit bolder, I pulled this one at a different hour, because after the job in Jackson, the news started calling me the two a.m. bandits, still assuming that more than one person was involved.

So tonight, Tracy and I were the Midnight Cowboys. I even started singing that *I Wanna Be a Cowboy* song. Sure it wasn't as good as Biz Markie, but few things were.

Halfway through the second verse, I saw the flashing blue lights.

"Shit!" I exclaimed and started pulling on the ski mask back onto my face. I used some stolen plates I'd taken in Jackson. "Tracy, alter our travel path to route three in one minute."

At thirty seconds, I opened the back door and shoved my hand out. I dialed the setting to level three and sent a burst into the patrol car's engine block. Metal crumpled and there was a big dent in his front like he'd just run into a telephone pole.

The pursuit was neutralized, but my worries had just begun. By the time I reached Florida, the dashboard footage of the incident was picked up by the national news. Exposure was something I'd hoped to avoid and now I was on most of the major channels and the 24 Hour Hero channel.

A level four pulse had left the stolen plates an unrecognizable mass at the center of a small crater on a country road off the interstate. I pulled out a stencil and spray painted "General Contracting" on it and used a heat gun to dry it and weather the paint in short order. It would protect my secret identity for now, but the cat was out of the bag.

• • •

My problems only grew when I got to the Sunshine state. Two of my pawn brokers had been burnt down under "suspicious" circumstances. The only good news was that it wasn't Joey. I was halfway to my goal of having enough money to make my own suit, but my middle men were becoming scarce. If Barton's folks caught wind of this, they could easily sick the feds on me. That suit would come in handy when that happened, but I'd need to get the money and drop out of sight.

With that in mind, I came to the only sensible conclusion; I'd have to pull a bank job.

Chapter Three

ManaCALes Versus the Biloxi Bugler

In response to my crime spree, I saw an announcement that The Bugler would be expanding his patrol radius. That gave me an idea. If he was going to be away from Biloxi, that's where I would be. I found a bank with no jewelry stores nearby. The whole broad daylight thing still didn't appeal to me. My plan was contingent on my force blasters being able to penetrate the vault.

Unfortunately, it wouldn't leave much charge for anything else. I'd picked up a couple of A cells, but they'd be useless in the van until I got back to them. For this job, I picked a Friday night with a big cross city high school football game. That would keep most of the police busy elsewhere.

To further complicate things, Tracy drove me by a substation and I sent a class four pulse into one of the big transformers to kill the power for a couple of blocks. That would stretch the city's emergency services pretty thin.

By my reckoning, it might not be the perfect plan, but it was pretty damned close.

The reinforced wall leading to the vault put up more of a fight than I counted on. By the time I was inside and into the metal locker where they kept the cash drawers, there was only enough juice for two full power pulses.

Hoping that wouldn't matter, I stared at the green pastures of Nirvana, and started filling the pair of duffel bags with both fists while wishing that I had made a quick disconnect for the blasters to keep them from getting in the way. Sure, I could be a bit anal retentive at times, with all my planning and such, but I was glad I'd practiced with cut up stacks of newspaper standing in for the greenbacks. All those lockboxes surrounding me looked inviting, like Christmas presents waiting to be opened, but I resisted. The stuff in the boxes belonged to people. This pile of cash belonged to a faceless corporation, insured by the same government that took my invention and gave it to Promethia.

Remorse wasn't in my vocabulary at that particular moment.

I lingered, probably longer than I should have, wanting to make certain that I had enough money to finish making my powersuit. A shadow blocked the light from Tracy in the van and I spun around.

"Surrender evildoer!" A voice boomed, drawling hideously. The bugle was in his hand at the ready.

It probably highlighted the difference between me and this idiot. I would have shot first and then said something stupid. His proclamation gave me enough time to dial the controller setting down two and send a pulse at him. His bloated ass went right back out the hole he came in. I didn't want to ponder how he'd managed to find me, but I knew it was time to go. I looped my right arm through the bags and ran out the gap in the wall with my left arm thrust out like some absurd parody of the Heisman trophy.

The Bugler had hit the front of the van and was slumped on the ground. He staggered to his feet. "A lucky blow villain, but justice plays with an upbeat tempo!"

That was so mind-numbingly stupid that I couldn't let it pass without comment. "Are you brain damaged?"

The next thing I knew I was flat on my back with cash falling all over the place. My ears were ringing. Hardened acoustic energy really hurt!

"Son of a bitch!" I bellowed and shot both blasters at him. The fat pig in a blue and silver unitard moved quicker than I anticipated, and my bolts of energy sailed right by him.

Sometime in the microseconds after that, it occurred to me that my van was behind him. One went into the engine block and the other took out Tracy.

"I just destroyed my damned getaway vehicle! It's not supposed to be like this."

In my slack-jawed stupidity, I was blindsided by another funnel of sonic waves that knocked me into the broken wall. My entire head was ringing and there was blood in my mouth. I tried to use my one working hand to turn the controller up, fully intending to kill the Bugler. After three attempts, I finally got my hand in the right spot only to find that the bits of the broken dial came away in my twitching fingers.

"...your name?" A muffled voice said. My lolling head located the source. The Bugler towered over me. It was hard to think straight. Part of me knew I had a concussion, but that part wasn't really talking to the part of me that was in control of my body.

"Huh?" My reply was very articulate.

"What's your name?"

The question caught me off guard, and I wasn't certain what to say. "ManaCALes."

"Manacles?" He repeated, while pulling my force blasters off and slapping a pair of handcuffs in their place. I put up a token resistance.

There were dozens of reasons for me to be pissed off, but for some reason it was the way he said my name that got to me. "No, you moron! ManaCALes!"

"That's what I said, Manacles."

When I protested again, he wondered whether he'd hit me too hard. I just wanted to go to sleep. I'd been beaten by a guy with a sonic bugle.

"I'll get you for this," I mumbled. It seemed like the appropriate thing to say.

"Of course, you will," he replied and yanking the cuffs to ensure they were tight. "That's what all you supervillains say. C'mon, let's get you to the ambulance where the nice policemen are waiting."

A supervillain? I thought. *I guess I am. I'm a supervillain!*

I just wasn't a very good one.

• • •

Five years. I probably would have gotten more, but the judge was a real bleeding heart who bought some of my lawyer's arguments for leniency. I was a first time offender and all my crimes were committed in a way that I never hurt anyone except that one cop in Alabama. Even my not-so epic battle with The Biloxi Bugler hadn't hurt the loser superhero. The prosecutor wanted to add a count of assault against me for his benefit, but that sanctimonious do-gooder declined.

It was a relief to not face additional time, but it was also embarrassing. I'd gotten a concussion and a dislocated shoulder.

I also didn't try pleading "not guilty," that threw the prosecutors and they didn't have time to properly prepare the case. Plus, they could only pin the bank robbery and the one jewelry heist on me.

Even so, I was going to the SuperMax—the prison for supervillains, where the cells were buried several hundred feet below the North Dakota landscape. To the inmates, it was known as The Pit. The nearest city was fifty miles away, and a pair of satellites sat in geosynchronous orbit watching every square inch of the compound; in both visual spectrum and several of the ones not visible to the naked eye.

There had only ever been one successful mass breakout, and it had been led by the most unlikely of sources: that semi-catatonic Imaginary Larry. After three days, he decided that he didn't want to be there anymore and ripped a way out of that place with his mind. Over two hundred prisoners followed him to freedom. Many were recaptured, but almost as many weren't.

Instead of taking Larry back there, they made a special mental facility for him in western North Carolina. Supposedly, he is living his high school days over and over again. If there were years I had to keep repeating, it would probably be them.

There'd been a number of individual breakouts, but those were attributed to the powers possessed by those people and a lapse in procedures. I had no powers and no hope of getting myself out of this place anytime soon.

Riding along in what amounted to an armored bus, I had my own US Marshal sitting next to me. Two rows up was another prisoner, who looked like he was five or six years younger than me. *He must be more important, because there were three officers surrounding him.* The man was joking with his guards about coming home again.

Without my force blasters, I was just a guy in chains and didn't really pose much of a threat.

"Who is that?" I asked the man sitting beside me.

"E.M. Pulsive," the Marshal answered. "Ultraweapon brought him down in Las Vegas."

"Oh, so that's what he looks like." I recognized the name from the ATAI. He could turn his whole body into electricity. It was a real superpower.

"Have you all figured out how to contain him yet?" Pulsive had some kind of thick collar on that looked similar to the neck braces they put people with spinal injuries in. "I heard he snuck out in someone's cellphone once."

"It's above my pay grade," the suit next to me said. "Even if I did know, I wouldn't be telling you."

I shrugged, and tried to think of a way I would contain a guy like E. M. Pulsive. Keeping him grounded had already been tried in several variations. From the insulation on the brace, my guess was they were going for a way to quickly short him out when he changed.

The armored bus went through four checkpoints on the way in. Each one was a twenty minute inspection. At the third one, a small truck dragged up a small rubber coated platform with two conductive poles. They ushered Pulsive up to the platform and made him discharge his energy. It was actually pretty cool.

"Doesn't that get old?" I asked him when they brought him back onto the bus.

"I'm not worried," he said, ignoring the US Marshals around him. "They'll screw up at some point. They always do. I just have to be patient. I'm Eddie. What are you in for?"

"Cal Stringel," I answered. "Bank robbery."

"First timer, huh?"

"Yeah, what's it like?" I'd seen the documentary the Hero Channel had made about The Pit, but that only told the sanitized version for the public.

"Well, since you don't look like you have any powers, you'll probably end up as someone's bitch."

That didn't sound fun.

He paused to see my reaction before laughing and saying, "Hah, you totally fell for that! It's not so bad. They'll try a bunch of that therapy bullshit on you to see if you can be rehabilitated. Me? I'm still serving my three hundred year sentence, so every time I get caught, they just bring me right on back and we play this little cat and mouse game all over again."

Eddie was an unrepentant criminal, and I just wasn't there yet. He would have no qualms pulling daylight bank robberies or even killing someone who got in his way. Also, he seemed like a colossal ass.

"So, any advice for the newbie?"

"Find someone to teach you the ropes; it's better to make friends inside than it is to make enemies. Most won't do anything when we're being watched twenty-four seven by the man, but they'll remember you when you get on the outside and settle the score then. I hear that no one ever makes parole the first time around, wouldn't know myself, of course, but that's what they say."

I wouldn't be eligible until after two years, so I'd have some time to think about it. "Thanks for the info."

"No problem. Inside, we villains try to stick together. Outside, is a whole 'nother story."

• • •

After passing through the fourth and final checkpoint, I got my first close up look at The Pit. The walls didn't look as high as they did in that documentary, and I'd be willing to bet that they used some clever camera angles and touched up the images using editing software.

As they took me to "In Processing," Eddie went straight to the main building where the sole access to the lower levels resided. Everything else up top had a very mundane appearance—admin buildings and the like. I thought it looked mostly harmless.

Ninety minutes later, after being deloused, subjected to a strip search as well as a cavity probe, I had a new definition for the term mostly harmless.

"Prisoner number eight four seven two six ready for transport below." The ever-present marshal said to the female platform operator.

They ran me through another whole body imager before the operator was satisfied.

"Proceed to the center of the platform, and make no other actions or you will be fired upon."

That was about the time I noticed the gun emplacements ringing the room. It was a hodgepodge of weaponry covering the gamut of the imagination. They had two turrets with fifty caliber machine guns, a pair of twenty millimeter cannons, lasers, masers, plasma cannons, pulse cannons, sonics, gas grenade launchers, and at least three things that I couldn't immediately identify. The engineering nerd in me could have spent hours up here inspecting their defenses. The criminal in me didn't like the way the weapons tracked my every movement.

Guess which one won?

In the center of this giant circle was something that resembled an over-sized port-a-potty. It was the elevator down. The documentary showed they had rooms where they simulated the outdoors, but odds were that I'd seen my last bit of sunlight for the foreseeable future. Two armed guards in Pummeler Exosuits rode down with me. They were militarized Waldos using Promethia's synthetic muscles to enhance their strength. They're presence wasn't as intimidating to me. I'd even used the commercial versions before, at Promethia, but I knew that either of those two 'roid ragers piloting those Pummelers would have no problem ripping my arm from its socket, if he chose to.

Unlike regular elevators, there was no control panel inside, only an indicator of what floor we were on.

I watched with interest as we descended all the way down to level fourteen, only two levels from the very bottom. One of the surprising things about The Pit was that they housed the more threatening prisoners on the higher levels. At first even I couldn't understand it, until I realized that the more powerful villains, like Eddie, wouldn't bother going down to free all the lightweights. Instead, they'd try to head for the surface and not try to start a prison riot. From that perspective, it made plenty of sense.

As the armored door opened, one of the men in the Pummelers addressed me. "Welcome to your new home Eight Four Seven Two Six. There's an orientation film in the room directly ahead of you. Watch it, or don't. It doesn't really matter. Your cell number is contained in your welcome packet. All prisoners are to be in their cells at nine p.m. If you're not, a squad of Pummelers comes down and either gets you to your cell, or the infirmary."

With that, I was shoved out, hard, by one and the other kicked the plastic tub containing my prison uniforms, daily essentials, and processing paperwork at me like a soccer ball. It missed, but just barely and emptied the contents onto the ground. The two shared a laugh while the door slid shut and left me there.

• • •

"You get the top bunk, new meat," the man inside the cell said. He took up most of the cell. The guy was built like an offensive lineman and had long, dirty blond hair and a bushy beard.

"Hey, I'm Cal Stringel," I tried to be nice to "Grizzly Adams."

"Bobby Walton, but everybody calls me Hillbilly Bobby."

I searched my mind for anything ATAI might have mentioned about this guy, but absolutely *nada* was there.

"So, what're you in for?"

"Oh, hell, I don't rightly know," he said. "There was all them bank robberies, the destruction of public property, and a whole bunch of things."

"I'm sort of a bank robber myself," I admitted. "Got caught on my first job, though."

"That sucks."

"Tell me about it."

He asked what I could do, and I answered that I invented stuff. On the other hand, Bobby could lift five or six tons. He ran afoul of the Gulf Coast Guardians when he was working with another villain and I was forced to confess that the Biloxi Bugler took me down.

"I've fought him before," Bobby said. "He don't look like much, but he's real tricky like. Slipperier than a greased pig."

Bobby took me on a tour and showed me where the cafeteria, gym, recreation room, and the automated dispensary were. The prisoners were actually in charge down here. He knew where the library was, but had never gone in. The only time the guards and staff came down was after lights out and lockdown. They refilled the automated dispensers and left before the cells opened again. Our therapy sessions took place via video teleconferencing; there was little or no chance of taking someone hostage.

"What happens if the prisoners break the rules?"

Bobby looked at me and said, "Last time we did that, they didn't refill the dispensers for two days. Things got a little tense down here when the food started running out. They also shut off the shitter pumps and that got everyone's attention real quick-like."

For the first few days, I kept my head down. There were forty-six prisoners on this level. Most had minor powers, but some were just average schmucks like me. Bobby could probably take on three or four of those guys in the Pummeler suits.

On the third day, I was asking Bobby what he thought I could have done differently and he laughed, before saying, "You're a smart guy, Cal, but you're stupid. You didn't have a hideout. They got all the cash and stolen goods back, didn't they?"

"Yeah," I said, not enjoying the feeling of a guy who didn't finish seventh grade tell me what a rube I was.

"Shit! Always, and I mean always, have a hidden stash. You should've hooked up with someone real to be a driver."

"I didn't have any connections!" I protested.

"Well, that's what you need to do while you're here, build up a bunch of contacts. The big boys a few levels up are always hiring us little guys to steal them something or get revenge on someone who did them dirty. A guy like you could make a pretty penny just building stuff for people. Probably a lot less risk and a lot more reward doing that. I'm up for my second parole board in six months, but I'll do my best to get you in the know before I get my sweet ass outta here."

Damned if he didn't have a point. I could learn a lot from a bumpkin like him. My Mr. Miyagi was more likely to swill moonshine than drink hot tea, but it was a start.

• • •

"Mr. Stringel," Doctor Ingalls said on the other side of the screen. "You seem to have considerable unresolved tension with the Promethia Corporation. Before you can make any real progress, you have to confront and overcome this."

"Doc," I said. "You've obviously never had someone both figuratively and literally ruin your life, take your work, and lie about it just so they could make a buck."

The older black man with white hair shook his head and said, "Mr. Stringel, I was just a young child during the Civil Rights movement, but I saw enough of ignorant people trying to ruin my life and my whole family's life, so I'll give you something you probably need to hear. The world does not revolve around you. The sun does not rise and set just for you. You tried to take the easy way out and gave in to your ego. Lazarus Patterson and his employees did not put you in prison; you did that all by yourself. If you don't own your past, you can never hope to own your future."

"I guess we're just going to have to agree to disagree on that one for now," I replied to the sanctimonious prick on the other end.

"This is a journey, Calvin. You're not going to get there in a week, or even a year. I can't change the way you think. I don't have any kind of superpowers, but I can work with you until you are ready to change the way you think. We've got a few minutes left, so let's change the topic; have you written your parents yet, as we discussed in our last session?"

If he didn't have the answer already, he probably wasn't a very good head doctor.

"No, they don't want any contact with me. Dad made that clear when he visited me in jail."

"Once again, your actions have wider ramifications. If you want to heal that breach with your parents, you're the one who's going to have to make the first moves. They may not even respond at first, but that's another thing you've got to work on."

It sounded like good advice, but my parents were capable of holding major league grudges. Shrugging, I knew the prison would be reading everything I wrote or I received. The Semi-transparent man gave me some solid advice, resist for the first six months and then gradually give in to let them think they're breaking you. They can spot someone who is a phony and a suck up.

"Let's finish up with talking about your time at the prison," he said. "What are you keeping yourself busy with?"

Considering my movements were followed around the clock, I wondered why he kept asking questions that he already knew the answer to. "I spend a good deal of time in the library. Kind of odd using so many real books when you're not allowed access to a computer. During the day, I'm working in the prison laundry. It helps to pass the time."

"Have you considered taking any courses?"

"I was already unemployable with a bachelor's in electrical engineering with a minor in mechanical. I don't really see how more education is going to be the answer."

He gave a deep baritone laugh and said, "I'll have to write that one down. Calvin Stringel says more education isn't the answer. That's priceless!"

• • •

Dear Dad,

I'm sorry it's taken me so long to write, but it's one of those things where I'm at a loss for what to say. Sometimes, I look around and it's hard to believe I'm where I'm at today.

Okay, my opening lines gave me the "Little Lost Lamb" theme. I guess I need to show that ownership crapola the Doc is always shoveling.

Still, I know it was my actions that put me here and I'm sorry for how it has affected you and Mom. How is she? I figured I'd write you instead of her, because I'm guessing she'd just ball my letter up and toss it in the trash.

This part is an attempt to show I'm contrite and acknowledge the problems between me and Mom.

So, anyway, four months down. This place isn't so bad. There's a bit of a pecking order, but that's mainly between the folks who have powers. Next week, I start teaching a course in Engineering Fundamentals. I'd wanted to teach a computer language, or some basic Electrical Theory, but we're not allowed to have access to any kind of equipment like that—probably for good reasons.

There was a rumor that Eddie used a computer, even with all the networking gear removed, to escape once. I figured the whole teaching thing would look good at my parole board hearing.

Maybe I can work on getting a teaching certificate, since it's not like I have a whole bunch of other options. One of the Mexican Villains, El Conquistador, teaches Spanish. I thought about taking his class, but after seven years in Los Angeles, I still have no desire to learn another language.

It was true. I hated languages, other than the computer ones, with a passion. I'd tried one year of Italian that almost cost me Valedictorian at my High School. As for Spanish, the few words I knew were profanity, and that's the way I wanted it to stay. Teaching? I had no illusions about ever holding a teaching position, but I needed to sound like I had some goals for when I finally did get out.

How are things at the bowling alley? Is Mom's hip still giving her problems? I understand if you don't want to write back anytime soon, but I hope to hear from you, and wouldn't mind some news from the outside world.

Cal

The last part was me trying to be nice. I was never really good at that. Like the good doctor said, it's not all about me.

Not that I really believed any of that shit; I just wanted to get out of prison.

Chapter Four

Crappy Escape Plans For the Win

"Hey, I heard you don't like Ultraweapon," the squat man pushing the laundry cart said, catching me by surprise. My previous "delivery man" had gotten a marginally better job. I could probably trade up, but I actually liked the laundry room, because, as a general rule, no one messes with the dude taking care of their clothes and that suited me just fine.

The new guy had greasy looking black hair and an oily complexion that made my own skin issues pale in comparison. From the way he casually moved about the place, I suspected he'd been here previously.

"Do I know you?"

"Richard D. Chesterton, the third," he said and extended his hand. I reluctantly took it has he continued, "But everyone just calls me Gunk."

The moment he said that, I wanted nothing more than to release his hand and go find a steel wool pad and go all *Silkwood* on my appendage. Gunk was a superpower cautionary tale. Old Richey here was born into money, but not necessarily brains. He spent his entire trust fund account, in an obsessive fashion that defied both logic and reason, on acquiring an ability.

The fool got his wish in the same kind of way karma came back to bite me in the ass, but on a way bigger scale. His power was some kind of fast metabolizing mucus that sticks to most everything and hardens into the consistency of concrete in only a few seconds, and despite his size, Gunk can produce phlegm by the bucketful.

There is probably any number of more disgusting things on this planet than watching Gunk hack a slime-filled loogie, but you'd be hard pressed to come up with one on the spot.

"Yeah, I hate Patterson," I answered.

He laughed and pulled a little statuette out of the laundry bin. It looked like some kind of presentation show trophy. Sure enough, it was a small Ultraweapon...made of gunk.

"Go on," he said, offering it to me. "Smash it. It always makes me feel better. Damned playboy; flying around and acting like he's better than us!"

Deciding my one hand was already contaminated; I hefted the figurine and broke it across the nearest column. Watching Patterson smash into dozens of pieces actually did bring a smile to my face.

"They still had all the molds I made from the last time I was here," he said. "I have better ones on the outside and even sold some on eBay, but sales never took off like I'd hoped."

Why does this surprise him? I thought, wondering what kind of collector looks online for statues that are made out of someone spit. *I guess there really are people out there who will buy anything.*

"I hear you're from Mississippi, Stringel. It's nice to meet someone else from my neck of the woods." Gunk lived in one of the major Louisiana cities, which sort of made us neighbors, in a sad kind of way.

"Actually," I replied, uncertain of whether I wanted to be known as a Mississippi supervillain. "I was just doing some jobs there when I got caught. I was born in Nebraska."

Gunk scratched the stubble on his chin thoughtfully before saying, "Well I reckon that home is where you're at."

Which would, technically, make me from North Dakota now. As I said, he wasn't known for his brains. "So how did you end up back here?"

"I was framed," he said. "There I was working for a highway contractor in Shreveport, filling potholes and minding my own business when along comes the Gulf Coast Guardians who accuse me of committing a bunch of robberies. I told them I didn't do it and wasn't going to go anywhere with them, and sure enough, we gets to fighting. And the next thing you know, I'm standing in front of the judge with that damned muzzle on my face and she ships me back to this place for violating my parole. Then they tacked on a couple of more years for the robberies—which I did not do."

He seems stuck on that point, so I asked, "Why did they think you did?"

"They found some of my residuals at the scene. My lawyer tried to argue that it could have been someone who done bought some of my statues and set me up to take the fall. If'n you ask me, I think it was that no account jackass Rodentia. Just wait till I get my hands on that rat!"

"That stinks," I said, trying to sound like I cared about the petty squabbles of a pair of lame supervillains. Returning to the task at hand, I began emptying the laundry hamper.

"Tell me about it! I figured I'd give you a nice and friendly warning to steer clear of that loser once you get out. If you partner up with him, that son of a bitch will sell your ass out in a heartbeat."

"Thanks," I said with forced sincerity, trying to think of a reason I would ever need to partner up with a guy who can summon and control a horde of rats. "I'll keep that in mind. To be honest, I don't know if I'll get back into the game when I get out of here."

At the same time, I thought, *And if I was going to partner up with some other villain, I think I'd set my sights a bit higher than Rodentia or even you for that matter.*

"I hear Bobby's getting out soon," he took that moment of silence as a sign that he should start talking again. I wish he hadn't.

"Yeah, he made parole and gets to walk free at the end of the week."

"Too bad they stick me in a solo cell all the time," Gunk said, finally starting to help me unload now that the hamper was almost empty. "We could have been roommates."

"Who knows who I'll get next?" I suppressed the shiver that tried to run through my body at the thought of sharing a cell with this guy. It was bad enough knowing that he will be delivering the laundry to me every day.

• • •

"All right folks, today we're going to go over basic calculations of force and pressure before having a discussion of how this can relate to structural integrity." I said from the head of the table in the therapy room that they allocated for my Fundamentals of Engineering course. Sure, it was only a class of seven, but it's the effort that counts—right?

"Just how the hell does this mean a damned thing out there in the real world?" The outburst came from a red-eyed man with what looked like foam coming from his mouth. Normally, I'd be worried, but twenty seconds after he said that, his eyes turned blue and he seemed to shrink slightly, before saying, "I'm sorry. I spoke out of turn again, didn't I?"

Then again, maybe just showing up counts.

"No problem," I answered The Passive-Aggressive Menace, knowing he wouldn't turn back for another five minutes. "As to your earlier question, let's look at it this way. Use too much force or apply too much pressure to a floor or a wall and it gives out on you. So being able to understand how much force you can hit with is all part of the problem. When you're all angry, you can punch hard enough to smash a brick, right?"

He nodded, meekly.

"Well, say you're fighting say, oh, I don't know, The Biloxi Bugler in a shopping mall and you just pushed him back against a support column. You throw your haymaker, but the slippery bastard dodges and you hit the column. Using the right equations and knowing how much damage the steel core can take, we'll know whether you just bloodied your knuckles or you dropped a chunk of the upper level on your head."

It probably wasn't the usual way these things were taught, but it helps to know your audience. Suddenly everyone was interested in how this fictional encounter would turn out, and I walked them through the basics of the equation to determine how much power The P-A Menace could put into his punch. I then showed them how durable various support columns were. If the construction company skimped and used a thickness of steel that only met the bare minimums of what most codes required, the pillar would either bend or snap completely.

By the time I'd finished my example and asked if there were any questions, Passive-Aggressive had swapped back. He smacked his hands on the table and said, "That's all well and good, but tell me what happens to The Bugler's fat face, if I didn't miss."

The rest of my class seemed to be interested as well, so I crunched the numbers, so to speak, and concluded that P-A would be digging bone chips out of his knuckles. The bloodthirsty buggers even wanted to know how far the blood splatters would travel. Considering what I thought of that Bugle playing fool, I didn't mind the direction the lesson took.

After all, everyone learns differently and this was all for the sake of education.

As the class finished, Bobby came in. "Shoot, if I knew this was gonna be about how hard you have to hit somebody to kill 'em, I woulda signed up."

"Yeah, but you wouldn't have been able to finish. There's still enough time for you to get into a fight and ruin your release, Passive-Aggressive has been getting onery lately."

I wanted to kick myself, or have Bobby do it. I actually used the word *onery* in a sentence. The big slob was rubbing off of on me—even if he was a certifiable idiot.

"All you gotta do is just run from him for a few minutes and then whup his ass when he turns into a Nancy boy. He ain't worth another few months in here. Hell, next week I'll be chasing tail and you all will be stuck here where the nearest girl is two levels up and might as well be a thousand miles away!"

Disregarding the fact that my love life was already in the crapper well before I was brought to justice, I shrugged and said, "So, other than tormenting me with that fact, what brings you out here today?"

"Oh, just making the rounds, seein' the sights, and trying to put all this to memory so I can try real hard not to end back up here again."

"So, you're retiring?" I asked.

"Shit, nah! I just don't intend to get caught."

"Good luck on that," I said and I followed him out into the hallway. Just because the monitor was off didn't mean that the prison staff couldn't be listening. The hallways were considered safer for casual—and not-so casual—discussions involving crime.

"Anyway," he said, clapping me on the back hard enough to send me stumbling forward. "I was thinking that you oughta look me up when you finally get outta this place."

"Doesn't that go against the Outside Code?" I said, referring to how everyone says that anything goes once outside the gates. "You already gave me a few contacts on the outside."

"Exceptions can be made," he said. "Yeah, I gave you a few names, but you're still wet behind the ears. Besides, a smart guy like you could do all kinds of things around my hideout in exchange for some personal introductions."

Okay, I thought. *That makes more sense.* Nodding, I continued, "Sounds like a plan, but odds are I won't be out of here for at least two years. My first board hearing isn't for another eleven months."

"Yeah, there is that. Well, you could always lay low at my place when you break out."

We both shared a laugh at the idea that a guy without any superpowers would be able to bust out of here. "If I could do that, then they need to fire everyone and get some better guards."

Still, it was a genuinely nice offer.

• • •

My new roommate was a guy called The Gardener. The dude wasn't so bad, but there was a definite downside. He had this weird power that made moss grow on the walls, floors, and ceilings, and that he could turn into plant monsters he could control. As a result, my cell was scrubbed clean and decontaminated every couple of days. It would take a month of complaining for me to get them to cut down on the concentration of the cleaning agents. The shit was practically burning my eyebrows off.

As if I didn't have enough problems with my skin to begin with. Gardener's power was odd, but actually pretty cool. Also, he was educated, not a science-type, but a liberal arts major. Even so, it was a huge departure from Bobby, Gunk, and some of the others who associated with me.

"Usually, it takes me a good six weeks to grow a proper horde," Kenneth said in a British accent. He gestured to the small patch of moss growing on the wall behind the toilet. It formed into a green, hairy action figure about six inches tall that landed on the rim of the seat. I watched as he made the tiny construct bow and perform a series of basic martial arts moves. After a minute, he was bored and made it do a bunch of tricks that would normally be associated with a dog. Finally, tiring of his toy, Kenneth made it jump up to the top of the commode and do a forward two and a half somersault dive into the bowl.

"How do you make it do the tricks?" I asked as he stood and sent his little performer into the swirling beyond.

"Oh, they can only do what I'm capable of. I have to learn how to do something before my mossions can do it."

"So you can do that dive?"

"Had dreams of going to the Olympics and representing my country at one point," he replied. "I was hiding my powers, but they came out during competition testing and I was disqualified. I'm also a black belt in Judo. After I was outed, and my good name dragged through the mud, it was either the life of a rogue, or beg my father to let me manage his plumbing shop."

"So, what's the biggest thing you ever made?"

"Made an elephant once. It was a ruddy nightmare to control, and gave me a splitting headache. I usually stick with gorillas when I need pure muscle, dogs when I need numbers and human shapes when I need them to operate anything from an auto to a machine gun. Minions my good chap, or in my case mossions. Why risk your neck when you can get something to do it for you? Sadly, it didn't help me avoid this place. Three years in this hole is going to have me talking like a Yank before I'm out."

"Mossions instead of minions? I would've gone with FunGuys, but that's me. Who got you?" I inquired.

"I was in New York, conducting some business, when I ran afoul of the Guardian team based there. My beasts stood little chance against Bolt Action or that little waif, Wendy. Oh, to be laid low by a teenaged girl! It was a most unfortunate turn of events."

Kenneth was a bit of a drama queen, albeit, one with a decidedly nasty streak. Sure he had a classy air about him, but he was still a thug, who reminded me of the main character in *A Clockwork Orange*.

"I took some Tae Kwon Do, if you wouldn't mind showing me a few things." I left out the part where I took it to impress a girl I was tutoring in high school. Long story short, she wasn't, and I abandoned it soon after.

"I was going to try and teach a class, like you do, but they already turned me down," he said. "Something about not teaching anything violent to the rest of you bloody fools. They offered to let me teach yoga or Pilates."

"You can teach those?" I asked.

"Certainly, but to do it to a class of only men seems a bit odd; but I can show you some of the basics of Judo. That said, it will cost you."

"I can't offer much more than pressing your coveralls."

"You fancy yourself a master of gadgetry, yes?"

"Well, yeah," I replied, wondering where he was going with this.

"When I fought against the Guardians, I found myself at a distinct disadvantage. If my mossions were better equipped, I might have been able to make good my escape."

"That stands to reason," I added.

"Indubitably," he stated. "In return for my assistance now, I would like a future consideration."

We haggled over the price and what he might theoretically want before agreeing that I'd do the work at cost, but he'd have to provide all the materials, and he'd have to give me a couple of contacts on the outside. Future favors were often bandied around as currency, because chances were that they'd never have to be carried out.

When our bargain concluded, he said, "I have the only name a gadgetman such as yourself, needs to know—her name is Victoria Wheymeyer and she can usually be found in Las Vegas."

"What's so special about her?"

"She's a broker. She acquires weapons, people, and whatever else is required for one or perhaps several of the heavy hitters out there. Get on her good side and you'll never want for steady work."

"That sounds like a really good name to know," I said, filing it away in my mental rolodex.

• • •

Time passed. Despite Kenneth's tutoring, I wasn't very good at martial arts. I'd say that I was a lover and not a fighter, but I really wasn't much of a lover either. The meditation was nice though, I'd never done much of that before. I always used to study with loud music on. Growing up, there were dueling garage bands on my block; and in my late teens, I took up the drums and contributed to the noise pollution. Until my studies started taking up too much of my time, I played in a couple of cover bands during college.

Once I joined the real world, I never really had time for it anymore. Now, I had lots of spare time and they had a beat up drum kit in the rec room. It was something to do.

Kenneth listened to me do the drum solo from Golden Earring's *Radar Love*, which always helped me blow off some steam. "You're not half bad, Calvin."

"I'm still shaking off the rust. It might be my only shot at real employment when I get out of here. Most bands would be willing to overlook a felony conviction. Their only real requirement is the ability to play. Of course, most bands treat their drummer like they're part of the road crew. For some, it would probably be a draw—*Our drummer's a supervillain! How wicked is that?*"

"Veritably," he replied, always willing to use a five cent word when a two cent would do.

"You know I could teach you to play. You could make a cover band with your fungus creatures and be a Stones cover band."

He laughed and said, "I suppose I could call it Moss on Rolling Stones."

"See, now you're getting the idea!" If I had his powers, I'd be looking for a way to cash in on them without ending up in prison. It would definitely have gotten me on Letterman's Stupid Superhuman Tricks Segment.

"How long have you been waiting to use that, Calvin?"

"A few days now," I admitted.

"I suspected that much. Still, even though I'd enjoy being a sideshow, novelty act, I'm afraid I have enough hobbies as it is, without taking up another."

Smiling, I started into Bob Seger's *Still the Same*, which lacks something when there isn't a piano playing. The last band I played in had a guy who sounded a bit like the man from Detroit and we covered a whole bunch of his songs. We called ourselves The Silver Blanks instead of his Silver Bullet Band.

Despite my requests, we never did Biz Markie.

As I played, he made a pair of miniature moss soldiers and had them doing some kind of waltz, as I cut into Seger's version of *Little Drummer Boy*, while wondering if The Gardener had to learn the female steps too in order to make his constructs perform.

Kenneth wasn't our only Eurotrash. We had a Frenchman, whom everyone avoided, named Simple Simone. He had this annoying field of mental energy around him that made it difficult to concentrate. When he focused it on someone, they'd turn into a gibbering idiot until he stopped.

As bad as the bleached smell of my prison cell was, I'd still take The Gardener over that guy any day.

"From the amount of energy you're expending, I take it you didn't receive good news from home?"

"Dad finally wrote back to basically tell me to stop writing them."

"I assume that you intend to keep writing them?" he asked.

"Every stinking day now! At least until I get a fan club like yours."

It was true; Kenneth had good looks and an English accent going for him and got a ton of women writing him. I'd never understand it.

"True," he replied. "I had two marriage proposals last month. Things always pick up around the holidays."

"The brunette with the fuzzy dice tattoos looked like a keeper."

He shrugged and made a dismissive gesture while saying, "Doctored, I wager both the picture and the body. She'd sleep with me once like all the rest."

"Why's that?"

"My power makes fungus grow in most any damp and moist place I come in contact with. I am guessing you can imagine the problems that might create."

"Oh," I said. "That's nasty. Well, at least you get to the point where you're sleeping with them. I don't even get that."

He got a good, hearty laugh out of that, disposed of his moss down the water fountain drain and said, "So, I shouldn't expect to see any love letters from Aphrodite anytime soon."

"No, she just shows up for the conjugal visits," I said sarcastically. *Me and Aphrodite, as if that would ever happen.*

• • •

Naturally, I was plotting how I could make my own powersuit through all this. Annoying my parents, the teaching, and even the drums were just a front for the good doctor and whoever else might be watching me. I became even more conscious of this as the months ticked away and the date of my first parole hearing drew closer.

That's me—Cal Stringel, model prisoner.

Unfortunately, I could only picture much of my suit design in my mind. With no access to computers, and anything I put on paper closely scrutinized, I couldn't really make much headway in that department. So, I did my best to commit the main system designs to memory and decided what I couldn't make, I'd just steal from the people who have made it already. The one downside of having a near photographic memory was that it was a near photographic memory and not a completely photographic memory. My plan was one part efficiency and probably two parts laziness.

Then again, Lazarus had entire teams dedicated to each section of his armor. Even if I had The Gardener's powers, I wouldn't have enough manpower to match that. So, I decided to cut corners everywhere I could get away with and focus on my specialty of weaponry. Overcharging the force blasters would mean more downtime for repairs, but a greater ability to deliver damage. The trick was to figure how much I could get away with, and not risk blowing my arm off.

There's a joke in there about being attached to my arm, but I'm not going to bother with it.

Sitting on my bunk, nervously waiting for the summons to the elevators to go to my parole hearing, I reflected on how twenty-six months could pass inside this artificially-lighted hole in the ground and what changes they wrought in me.

Was I a better person?

No. It's made me a better criminal and drummer, I suppose. I know the players who operate on my level and have a few contacts on the outside, but I don't really think I'm a better person for it.

Am I ready to get out of here?

You betcha!

Is it going to happen?

Snowballs in hell have better odds.

"You look like you're ready to bounce off the walls," Kenneth said, I thought he'd been in a deep meditation.

"Sorry, if I'm interrupting," I said. "I just want it to get over with already and hear them say that we'll see you in a year. It's just one big tease."

"Well," he said, standing to stretch. "It's going to be a busy day up there, with your parole hearing and all. If you're open to some advice, just keep a level head and open eyes about the whole experience. You never know what might happen up there today, Old Bean."

I was in the middle of preparing a suitably impressive answer when Mr. Big Voice came over the intercom and requested my presence at Zone A and our cell door rolled back. It was still ten minutes before the rest would open. Some of the jackasses jeered me as I did the early morning perp walk to the elevators

"You ain't goin' nowhere, laundry man!"

"Don't get your hopes up! You'll be back down here soon enough."

I did my best to ignore them and made my way to where the two Pummeler suits waited to take me up. They scanned me and searched me before they would let me board the elevator. When the lift began its upward climb, I'd sensed the movement, and it felt foreign—like I was some two dimensional character who could only move on one axis.

The ride itself was monotonous. The elevator was built to move up slowly and down quickly. I looked at the guy in the nearest Pummeler suit and said, "Did they have to cut out the Muzak?"

"Funny prisoner," the man said and flexed the oversized hands on his powersuit. "How about you just keep your mouth shut? Otherwise, your teeth might decide they should be anywhere other than in your mouth. I'd be the one serving as their travel agent."

I took him up on his kind offer.

• • •

"Mr. Stringel," the woman on the other side of the table addressed me. "We're here today to assess whether you are ready to return to society."

Bobby's words about how no one ever makes parole on their first board weighed heavily on my mind as I regarded the two women and three men on the other side of the table from me. None of the five people introduced themselves, and I figured that was probably so people couldn't come after them when they finally did get out.

It makes sense. I wouldn't want anyone knowing who I was. Besides, who in their right mind would tell a villain their name?

"We'd like to start with your thoughts on the Promethia Corporation," the man at the end began. I wondered which one of these people was in Patterson's pocket. This one had sunken eyes and male pattern baldness.

Since he immediately jumped on that, I pegged him for the person who'd ensure I wouldn't be leaving North Dakota anytime soon. Of course, F. Randall Barton could easily afford more than one stooge.

"Well, I don't like Promethia," I said, trying to channel my best *Shawshank Redemption* style honesty. "I doubt I will ever like Promethia, but I'm willing to walk away from my feelings for that corporation. In all likelihood, I'll never hold another high tech position again, so I think it's time I put all that behind me."

"Do you really believe you can put that behind you?" the man redirected.

"I fought them in court and lost. I tried becoming a criminal and lost. Somehow, I don't think the third time is going to be the charm."

"How can we be certain you're not lying to us now? You could always submit to a telepathic scan."

Almost no one ever does that! "No, I'd prefer not to have someone messing around in my mind."

Fortunately for me and just about every other criminal in here, after numerous abuses, deep telepathic scans were considered illegal search and seizure by the Supreme Court. There were also enough public stigmas attached to them that even using it on known criminals wasn't very popular.

I was certain that they still happened, but just went undocumented.

"So, assuming you were to leave here today, Mr. Stringel," the forewoman took over. The man who'd been questioning me looked annoyed at being cutoff. "How would you get your life back on track?"

"I've been working on getting a teaching certificate. I'm not sure if I'll be able to get a job in that field, but it's worth a shot. Other than that, I've dusted off my skills as a drummer and figure I can make ends meet that way while I figure out my next move."

"Where would you go? Back to Mississippi or perhaps your parents in Nebraska?"

"Neither, I've got a friend in Miami, so maybe there, but most likely Los Angeles, if I want to catch on with a band."

The questioning continued for almost another hour. One thing I noted was that the other woman never asked me a single question. She hadn't said anything since I came in the room and it was rather disconcerting.

What's her deal, I wondered.

"I think we've heard enough, Mr. Stringel," the woman heading the panel said.

She turned to the other female who had been creeping me out and said, "What is your opinion?"

The woman in question was a light skinned black woman or perhaps Latino. It was really hard to tell. Other than her silence, the thing that bothered me the most was her piercing blue eyes that seemed to stare right through me.

"I don't believe the prisoner is telling the truth and I think it would be ill-advised to allow him parole at this time."

"You're reading my mind!" I accused.

"No," she answered. "I am a receiving empath. My gift does not reach into your thoughts, but it does provide me insight to your attitudes and motivations. Better luck next year."

I could tell the rest of the vote was going to be a formality, but that's when the lights went out and the alarms began ringing.

All six of us stared at each other, wondering what to do for about thirty seconds.

The Big Voice activated and said, *"There is an attempted breakout underway in the lower levels. This is not a drill!"*

A guard in a regular uniform opened the door and addressed the parole board members, "Let's get you out of here!"

"Is the situation serious?" The chairperson asked.

She was answered by a low rumbling, which shook the floor, at which point they dropped everything and ran to the door.

"What about me?" I protested, not wanting to die.

The guard gave me a dismissive look and said, "You sit your ass back down and stay here! Someone will come and get you eventually. All right everyone, remain calm, follow me, and I will get you to your transport in the courtyard."

The guard lingered long enough to lock the door before hustling the important people down the corridor. With little else to do, I stood and went to the window amidst the alarms. An eight man squad wearing Pummeler suits equipped with fifty caliber machine guns pounded their way across the concrete below, heading for the elevator staging area.

There was a second explosion that sounded louder this time and I wondered how badly out of control the situation was going to get. I walked over to the table and wondered if I should flip it over to make a barricade...and rifle through all the things the board members left behind.

It's not like I'm already not in prison! Why the hell not?

The empath's purse had her cellphone in it. I thought about calling someone, but didn't know who or if I'd get a signal.

My parents? Nah! They don't even like my letters. Bobby? Maybe, but he'd just laugh at this whole mess, plus he only gave me a postal box address to contact him.

I'd settled on calling Joey, but then saw that she'd password protected her phone and set it aside. There was also a half-full pack of chewing gum, which was nice, and three twenties and two ones. I had no use for them, but I took them anyway. At my current salary of a dollar twenty-five per hour in the laundry room, this was more than I earned in a week.

Walking back to the window, I saw my parole board climbing into a van when a blur shot by them. Blinking rapidly, I tried to follow the shape's progress as it careened around the prison yard. It hopped on the back of one of the Pummeler suits and did a number that reminded me of the Tasmanian Devil from the old cartoons and left a bleeding man in a disabled suit sprawled on the ground.

That must be Maxine Velocity! She's like the fifth fastest person on the planet.

I picked my brain for what I could remember from Ultradipshit's ATAI. She couldn't break the sound barrier and she topped out around six hundred miles per hour, but more importantly, she was the niece of General Devious. Devious was one of the big kahunas of the supervillain world. Someone said Maxine was up on the heavy hitters' level and if she was out, I wondered how many others might be as well.

A flash of lightning struck another Pummeler and sent him into a cybernetic seizure. That caused the fifty cal to sweep right across the van, riddling it with bullets. I cringed and turned away, hoping that some of the people I was just sitting across from might still be alive.

That hope was dashed when the fuel tank exploded.

Sure, they weren't going to set me free, but they didn't deserve that! Why the hell didn't the guards take them to a safe room or something? Idiots!

The energy reformed into E.M. Pulsive, who looked like he'd found a new way to escape today. He waved other villains onward and I started backing away from the window as energy weapons from the towers began firing down on the main yard as everything went pear-shaped down there.

It's a mass breakout. Looks like the highest security level has been breached.

If the bullets and the explosion hadn't killed the occupants of the van, the rain of death punishing the courtyard left no doubt to their fate as a dozen of the most dangerous villains in the world fought for their freedom.

For two or three of them, it was the only taste of freedom they'd get. Eddie and Maxine started taking out the turrets, but the prison exacted its price in blood. One of them was ringed with flames when a plasma bolt slammed into him and he exploded in a brilliant blast that left me rubbing my eyes.

That might have been Fiery Doom, I thought while trying to focus. I tried looking for a body, but there was only a twenty foot diameter crater where the man had once been.

When a plasma bolt hit and dissolved part of the window ten feet away from me, I revisited my "turn the table over and cower like a scared little girl" idea from before. *Like the four inches of wood would really make a difference!*

Even so, it was much better than standing there waiting to be a casualty, and I put myself to work.

Pushing the table over into the corner of the room, I formed a crude little barricade and huddled behind it while Armageddon's warm up band was playing just outside.

It was there, in my pathetic little fortification, that I looked at the paperwork I'd pushed off the table. There before me was my parole paperwork. The chairperson had been passing it to the rest of the board when all hell broke loose. Three of the five had signed it already while I'd been in the pissing match with the empath and then I noticed the most important sentence I'd ever see, right above the signature block.

Parole has or has not been granted for the prisoner at this time. (Circle one and line out the other)

It wasn't filled out! She must have been waiting for everyone to sign it first.

A delightfully evil thought occurred to me, *I'm just a circle, a line, and two forged signatures away from freedom.*

I dug around in the empath's purse and found her driver's license and a pen. After a couple of practice tries on the one dollar bills, I taken earlier, I made my best effort at her name, but that still left me one name short and I had no idea who the last guy was. That's when I began a frantic search of everything on the floor in hopes of finding some clue of the man's name and I completely ignored the ongoing apocalypse that no longer concerned me.

My efforts were rewarded when I stumbled on a sign in sheet. Three government employees can't even talk in the hallway without someone calling it a meeting and producing an attendance sheet.

Saved by procedures! Halle-fricken-lujah!

• • •

It was four hours before someone came and got me and eight more before they had power and a way to get me back to my cell via the damaged main shaft. When the guard said something about rescheduling my hearing, I told them that they were finishing up with me when the breakout occurred. He seemed suspicious, but said he'd take the papers to the acting warden, which didn't sound great if you were the regular warden.

Guess I'll just cross my fingers and wait and see what happens.

"What happened out there, mate?" Kenneth asked when I finally returned to the cell, sweet cell, only to find that it smelled like an outhouse. I recalled that the maintenance crews on the way down said that the plumbing, along with the power, lights and just about everything else on the maximum security level was destroyed. Several of the prisoners in the hallway had been drafted into hazmat suit wearing pooper scoopers, and Gunk was being hailed as the hero *du jour* for plugging up the shitters and stopping all the crap from reaching the lowest point in the prison.

On a related note, we'd need new toilets, amongst many other things.

"It was crazy, man! The max security level broke out like nobody's business. I think a bunch of them made it beyond the gates."

"Bloody hell, did you see any of them get out?"

"The guards were pretty tight-lipped, but I heard a few of them saying that Maxine Velocity, E.M. Pulsive, The Sea Otter, and Captain Caligula got away for sure. Fiery Doom and Whistlin' Dick were both killed and there are at least six more that aren't accounted for."

Kenneth smiled broadly and said, "Good on them, then."

"I wonder if we'll ever hear how they did it." I commented.

"I'm sure we'll never know, mate," he said and I knew something was amiss.

Kenneth didn't have many tells. He was about as straight a shooter as one could find on this floor full of minor league supervillains. That said, when he was nervous about something he had a tendency to call me "mate" instead of Calvin. He'd done it twice since I'd walked back in.

I let it slide and told him about making parole. He was suitably impressed and gave me a calculating look that said he didn't quite believe me either.

That night when, all of us bottom feeders had cleaned up "all the shit we could take," I sat in bed and stared up at the same ceiling I'd looked at every night since I'd arrived, trying to put my finger on what was bothering me. They'd set up port-a-potties in the rec room and a few other spots for us to use. We'd been issued some empty plastic bottles to pee in during the night.

"I wouldn't make any of your little guys until after they get all this fixed," I whispered down to my cellmate.

"Good advice," he replied. "I already have it covered. Night."

"Night," I answered. *I'll miss the way he always makes them dive into the toilets if, they do let me out of here.*

The second that thought crossed my mind, everything fell into place in my own little Keyser Söze moment. In my mind, I heard him say how he was caught fighting solo against the East Coast version of The Guardians and how it takes six weeks of dedicated work to grow a proper horde. Then there was a mental montage of him disposing of the little bits of moss he'd been able to make each day, which finished with him mentioning his father's plumbing business.

Well, I'll be damned! He'd been stockpiling moss in the pipes for a year now. I wonder how much they paid him to spring all these people. He's been hinting that he intends to get out of the game when he makes parole. People only do that if they're beaten down or they hit the jackpot. Damn, they must have paid him a small fortune!

The most badass prison in the world was just punked by a D-List Supervillain and then again by me if the warden buys off on the paperwork. Nice!

Chapter Five

Of Better Guns and High Performance Vibrators

"I was starting to wonder if you were going to show," I said to the hulking frame standing outside my cheap hotel room.

"Cal Stringel," Hillbilly Bobby said. "I didn't think I'd be seeing you for another year or two. Just got back into town and couldn't believe my eyes when I got your letter. So, how you been?"

Shrugging, I replied, "Down to my last thirty bucks. How are things?"

I didn't bother to mention that things were pretty dire. I'd actually looked up the nearest homeless shelters and had spent yesterday in one of those temp places where people waited around to see if anyone needed a person for a crappy minimum wage job. The whole *paroled felon* thing hadn't really been working for me, yet, but perhaps that was about to change.

Things couldn't have gotten much worse than my oh-so brief stopover in Nebraska. Mom refused to see me and Dad gave me five hundred bucks to get the hell out of Dodge. Yeah, I took his money, which was kind of the idea behind stopping there. I wasn't proud of my behavior, but that money helped get me here.

"Well, grab your stuff and let's get you out of this flea trap. Did you check in with the parole office?"

"Some dumbass named Leonard."

"That's one of my cousins, Cal. Second or maybe third, hell, I can never get that shit straight," he said.

"Oh, sorry, man," I said, verbally backpedaling as fast as I could.

"Nah, Lenny's a tool and a kissass to boot. I can't stand the little wuss either, but he's real easy to fool so he's got his uses. For instance, he thinks I was on a charter fishing boat this weekend out in the Gulf."

"I'm guessing you weren't," I said.

"Someone needed a little muscle to convince a guy who owed him money to pay up—easy dough. Guy pissed his pants when I crushed a brick in my hand and he ponied up. I didn't even have to break any bones. It was actually kinda disappointing."

Nodding my head, I started flinging my meager belongings back into my duffel bags and made a mental note to not get on Bobby's bad side—ever. Out in the parking lot, the strongman waited in his full-sized Dodge pickup while I checked out of this fleabag motel.

The truck looked new and I began to wonder how much crime really did pay. Tossing my bags into the bed, I climbed into the passenger seat and said, "So, what does Lenny think you're doing to earn an honest living?"

Bobby laughed and replied, "Of course, I'm on the straight and narrow these days. Five nights a week, I'm a bouncer at Floozies."

"Floozies?"

"Titty bar," he said, as if it explained everything.

Oddly enough, it did.

"I'll put in a word with Chubby and get you on the payroll. You're a little too scrawny for bouncing, but maybe you can DJ, work the bar, or mop up."

"How much does he pay?"

"Nothing," Bobby answered. "I pay him, and he pays me most of the money I gave him right back. C'mon Cal, you worked in a laundry at the prison, only we ain't washin' no clothes anymore. You're on the outside now and it's time to get down to business."

The hulking brute driving gave me his best "you're so smart, but you're so dumb" look that made me feel like an idiot. Bobby used the bar to launder his ill-gotten money. His scheme was practical and simplistic, which made me realize that I still had much to learn about being a supervillain.

"Where are we headed?" I asked after we'd left the city twenty minutes behind us.

"My new hideout. I'm glad you got out when you did. I'm gonna need your help with it."

Driving another fifteen minutes, he turned off the county highway and down a winding dirt road leading to an abandoned farm that looked like it had seen better days—probably four or five decades ago.

"It's definitely out of the way," I said, trying to come up with something nice to say about it. That was the only thing I could think of that didn't start with the phrase, "My God! This is a shithole!"

He didn't notice the look on my face and continued, "Like it? Technically, one of the dancers at the bar owns the land, but it's what's under it that really counts!"

"Interesting," I said, not wanting to commit to a hole in the ground, but compared to what I could see it probably wasn't any worse.

"Yeah, I still have some digging to do. Amydillo did most of the work, before she up and got herself caught tunneling up inside a bank vault, so it's not finished yet."

"When did you meet the 'Dillo?" I asked. Amydillo was one of Doctor Mangler's test subjects who survived. She'd actually been an actress on WhirlWendy's kiddy show and tried to get her own superpowered TV deal. Instead she ended up looking like an armadillo crossed with a pinup—kind of hot and kind of icky all at the same time.

"I called in a few of my markers. Amy owed this guy who owed me. She showed up and started; you shoulda seen her go to town, but she got bored and decided to knock over some banks while she was in town, but on the second one Andydroid came down from Atlanta and got the drop on her."

"How are they going to hold her in North Dakota?"

"They aren't. She's been sent to some island in the Pacific, not Hawaii either. Begins with a G."

"Guam?"

"Yeah, that's the one!"

I nodded. "Can't really dig her way off of that, I guess."

"Yup," he agreed. "But she didn't seem too worried. She said she ends up doing work digging tunnels for the government and they eventually let her go. Word on the street is that Amy dug the Overlord's Omega Base and he mindwiped her afterwards so she couldn't give away the location."

As interesting as Bobby's time with Amydillo was, I wanted to see what I was up against. "So let's see what your base looks like."

I started toward the crumbling farmhouse, but he shook his head and pointed at the old grain silo.

Inside was a hole in the ground with a knotted rope leading down. A pitiful strand of glorified Christmas lights were plugged in to a class A powercell illuminating the way into Hell's bunghole.

Seriously? I should have just stayed in prison for another year! I've just traded one hole in the ground for another and the other one was furnished by Uncle Sam.

Making Bobby show me that the rope was attached to a metal pole driven several feet into the ground, I pushed aside my growing doubts and began my descent. Amy had done some quality work, and the walls of the tunnel were perfectly smooth, but I kept wondering how I could climb out of this place if that rope ever failed. This place was in dire need of an elevator.

After reaching the bottom, I changed my mind. This place was in dire need of everything! Power, water, fresh air, a way to get rid of sewage— Bobby hadn't put much thought into anything beyond the fact that he wanted an underground base and our deal meant I was going to build it for him in exchange for getting me on the ground floor of the supervillain network.

The central chamber was a large circular area about sixty feet wide and twelve feet high. It had a leather couch and coffee table in the middle in front of a massive television. A gaming console and a large plastic trashcan filled with the debris of a takeout lifestyle completed the room.

"I can't get a signal down here, but I reckon you know how to do those kinds of things."

I nodded and said, "We can run an antenna line up the shaft to the silo. Getting free internet out this far might be tricky, but we'll cross that bridge when we get there. We might have to sign up for the Wireless Wizard's underground internet service."

The answer made Bobby happy, even if it did the opposite to me, and he eagerly dragged me down the hallway to where the bedrooms and the main storage area were located. The one bright spot was that his kitchen and pantry area had enough can goods to feed us for two years and several miles of toilet paper. It looked like he'd stolen the contents of an entire Costco truck, but I didn't want to ask. On the other hand, the bathrooms were four stolen port-a-potties and I added plumbing to my growing list of problems.

How much is this powersuit worth to me, anyway? Ah, screw it! What else am I going to do?

Just as I thought my suffering was nearing an end, he led me down a set of steps to the lower level, where I found more storage area and a large circle made out of barbed wire.

"Are you looking to bring some livestock down here?" I asked, almost afraid of the answer.

"No," he replied. "I figure if I ever catch me a hero, I'd toss 'em in there."

Personally, I wasn't certain whether I should be laughing or crying at that moment, so I did neither.

"Unless, it's a pretty lame one, I'd recommend that we build some actual cells."

"Okay," Bobby said. "So where do you want to start?"

Sizing up Bobby, I could tell he could handle all the brawn and heavy lifting, but his fine motor skills were likely to cause more problems than they solved. I was going to need some serious help and I didn't have Kenneth's powers to simply grow some assistants.

"Bobby," I said. "I'm going to need you to steal me a couple of robots."

• • •

"So, how do I use this contraption, again?" The man in the large black outfit said as we skulked around a half-occupied industrial park. My partner in crime looked like the Michelin tire mascot had decided to take up being a ninja.

I, however, was the epitome of stealth and the personification of danger.

I was also prone to exaggerating wildly.

"It's just like a cattle prod," I answered Bobby, who eyed the long metal rod in his hands. "You jam it into one of those robots and it'll drop like a sack of rice. You'll have to wait ten seconds before it has enough juice to knock the second one out."

Bobby nodded and cast a glance at the darkened warehouse with the pair of mechanical watchman ambling around the exterior. "You sure we shouldn't try and steal whatever's inside? If'n they're paying to have robots, the stuff inside must be worth something."

"Oh, I'm sure all that machinery in there is worth a small fortune, but we'd need three semis to haul it out of here, and finding a buyer to sell it to would be a nightmare. They're some natural gas equipment supplier who has too much money, and doesn't want to be bothered to hire real people. I say we go create a few new jobs and help out the economy. Just try not to bust them up too badly."

By "we," I meant Bobby. The big lug would barely be bothered by those taser pistols they carried. I was actually looking forward to getting my hands on them. The two weapons would be a good start to my collection of miscellaneous items. I might even be able to incorporate them into my suit and reserve the force blasters for when I needed to maximize my damage potential.

The nice part of being on Bobby's payroll was that there were at least a dozen witnesses who would vouch for our presence at Floozies. In fact, I was supposedly in the private room right now getting a lap dance from some woman named Jade, Amethyst, or Sapphire. I don't know, some jewel-related stage name, and Bobby was shooting pool with the owner.

Considering my last partner was an inflatable sex doll, I thought I was moving up in the world.

From my time at Promethia, I knew quite a bit about these vintage type A robots. The humanoid frame was in service all across the globe in various uses, ranging from legal to other endeavors that were more of a questionable nature. Patterson would always blow a few of them away whenever he added a new toy to the suit. The Type A's were good for sentry duty or attacking something en masse. Beyond that, they weren't much more sophisticated than any other industrial robot. Even so, there was code all over the internet on how to program one to do various tasks and all it took was a little modification on my part to have a pair of construction workers.

It was one of those cases where I'd have to do the tedious work to prevent me from having to do the hard work. My life was built around that philosophy. Depending on the amount of synthmuscle they had, this brand of robot could carry about a quarter of a ton. Bobby, on the other hand, maxed out at around six tons, but I didn't think I could program him to install a lighting fixture, on my best day.

"They both meet at that point," I said pointing to an area near the parking lot. "We can slip down to that dumpster and use it for cover and I'll toss a couple of flares to attract their attention. That's when you get 'em with the prod. Don't forget to give it time to recharge."

"What's that thing for?" He asked about the box of cobbled together electronics I had in my duffel.

"Static generator. It'll jam their wireless transmissions and prevent them from calling the cops."

"That's what I like about you, Cal. You might not be worth a bent penny in a scrap, but when it comes to planning, you got your shit together."

"Thanks." I think.

We moved up to the dumpster while the two rounded the opposite ends of the building, I lit the pair of roadside flares duct taped together, and heaved them onto the sidewalk.

"Now we wait for them to come to us," I said. Type A's had crude infrared sensors and the flares should attract their attention long enough for Bobby to get the drop on them. There was a slight flutter of nerves in the pit of my stomach at returning to my criminal career by stealing a pair of robots—grand theft mechanical, if you will. I was violating the parole that I hadn't really earned.

I spotted the first one rounding the corner of the near side of the warehouse and steadied myself. Back in prison, I'd plotted out how to be a better criminal, and it was time to see if my studies had made me a better (or is it worse) villain. The robot moved quickly, but I noted a slight gimp in his gait and the engineer in me frowned. It was a sign that they weren't being maintained properly. Nevertheless, I activated my homemade—technically cave made—jammer, and signaled my partner.

Having never seen Bobby in action, I'd expected a lumbering brute, but he was surprisingly agile for such a big man. The robot pivoted and raised the arm carrying the taser pistol and fired at the supervillain.

"Like a bee sting!" Bobby said gleefully and brought the rod down like some maniacal Stone Age hunter taking on his dinner. There was a brief, but brilliant, flash and I smiled, seeing my handiwork in action. The moment was made more delightful by the fact I was not the one risking my comparatively fragile neck.

As I expected, the robot slumped over and toppled to the ground. The humanoid appearing robot weighed in the neighborhood of four hundred pounds, which is why most owners wouldn't consider them a target for a robbery.

The other robot clambered over, firing taser shells from its weapon. There was a blue light flashing inside a clear panel in the robot's chest. Bobby jumped and covered the thirty feet in a single bound and I knew he'd forgotten my warning. The cattle prod hadn't charged and clanged ineffectively off the metal armor with only a crackle.

"Bobby, wait!"

My useless warning was ignored as Bobby's fist separated the robot's head from the body. That meant I was going to fix the robot before I could get any use out of it.

"Oh, sorry 'bout that," he said looking at the mess he made.

Yelling at him would have been like yelling at a puppy—if that puppy was extremely dangerous and could squish my head like a grape—so I did what any sensible person would do in that situation. I pasted a smile on my face and told him not to worry.

• • •

Tweedledee and Tweedledum weren't much to look. Dee had the noticeable limp and Dum's head injury sometimes caused the robot to do the oddest things. After programming it to run some pipes for plumbing, I caught it scratching its ass and taking breaks every twenty minutes, and no, I'm not kidding.

Maybe my programming was a little too "true to life." Regardless, Bobby's secret lair was beginning to take shape, or at least possess the basic services like lighting and ventilation. We still needed a water source that wouldn't flood the base and a more capable power plant than just four Type A powercells daisy-chained together. I used to look down on the Civil Engineering majors at college, but here I was, managing an underground construction project on a scale that would make most of them jealous; aided by a pair of buggy, repurposed guard bots, and Bobby's superhuman strength. Saying that it was a labor of love wasn't quite true, for me it was more like a creepy obsession with completing this job. It didn't help that Bobby was reluctant to start acquiring the things I needed to build my set of armor until he got what he deemed to be a "respectable hideout with all the fixin's"

At the moment, the best super powered criminal I could manage would be something along the lines of the two-gun taser bandit and his odd robots. That seemed like a step backward from my time as ManaCALes.

Bobby would leave town for a job at least once a month and I'd always be concerned. I was still entirely dependent on him. Other than the occasional "shift" I worked at Floozies and my parole meetings with Leonard, my life pretty much revolved around furnishing that damned hole in the ground. My host's assessment of his cousin proved to be spot on. Leonard was about as dim as the lighting in the cave when I first arrived, but other than the night we stole the robots, I'd been too damned busy to actually plot any crimes.

Three cheers for being on the straight and narrow. Hip-hip, whatever!

I was ruminating over these thoughts and only half watching a porno on the big screen, in what I now termed as Central Command, when the motion detectors I'd set up in the silo went off. With Bobby not due back for two days, I became immediately concerned. One hand reached for the taser pistol and the other grabbed a controller box which I could use to set Tweedledee and Tweedledum into guard mode. Before I could even lift the pistol from the table there was a rush of wind and a woman standing right in front of me.

"Stringel?" she said. The woman wore a blue, padded Kevlar polymer outfit, with a large black V emblazoned on her chest. Strapped to each thigh was an empty holster and the two on her belt were empty as well.

Blinking, I recognized Maxine Velocity or Max V as she was known and recalled that the only other time I'd seen her was the day both of us got out of prison. "That's me."

The woman removed her mask revealing short, curly brown hair. Her most distinctive feature was her red, perpetually wind burnt cheeks from when she ran with her face exposed. Maxine had a lean, athletic body, completely devoid of almost any feminine curves and it was tough to tell whether she was actually attractive, because her face was in constant motion. She emptied her backpack on the table and ten plasma pistols fell out.

"You need some kind of elevator or something," she muttered in disgust.

"I agree," I said, disliking the rope ladder arrangement we had upgraded to, at my insistence. Bobby used a chainfall setup to lower anything big that we needed. Unfortunately, the power to run anything like that just wasn't available yet, let alone all the work that would need to be done in the shaft that Amydillo had created.

"So, how can I help you? I'm guessing Bobby is working for you?"

"Something like that. Anyway, Hillbilly Bobby swears up and down that you can fix just about anything and I've about had it up to here with the pricks who've been supplying me," she said almost too fast for me to follow. "These pistols are shit! They stopped working after only twenty shots apiece and half of them are fried. Think you can make something better?"

"Where did you get them?" I asked, letting the useless taser drop from my hand and already picking up one of the pistols. It wasn't a Promethia design, but more like a crude copy, very crude. The emitters were oversized, inefficient, and the whole design was poorly conceived.

"My Aunt's people," she answered and crossed her arms.

"In that case, General Devious should hire some better quality engineers. How many do you want and when do you need 'em?"

"Twenty-Four and as soon as possible," she replied, glancing over her shoulder at the moaning trio of naked women on the screen.

Sheepishly, I hit stop on the remote. *I'm cool like that.*

"You could have left it on," she said. "I might've slept with the brunette a few times, if that's who I think it is."

Her comment caught me off guard, but I recovered quickly. "I'll need materials."

"Make a list. I'll get it either before or after I break the arms on the man who gave me these. How many shots will I get out of yours?" Maxine asked, slowly cracking her knuckles.

"Thirty," I said trying not to let it bother me. I figured I was mostly successful.

"What's your price, gadgetman?"

"Back when I worked for Promethia, there was a rumor that you'd managed to steal the schematics to the Ultraweapon armor."

"It turned out to be an old copy, his first generation, and he'd hidden a worm in it that wiped our mainframe, but I made two copies. Auntie's scientists eventually cleaned it up, but the General didn't want to invest in something that was already dated. Are you saying you're interested, Stringel?"

"Call me Cal," I said. "And yes, I am. The schematics and fifty grand."

With the old drawings, my knowledge of the improvements since, and my own, ideas it would shave months, if not a full year, off my design.

"The schematics and fifteen grand."

"Twenty grand seems more in the neighborhood of what I was thinking; besides you can afford it."

"Wrong neighborhood, Cal," she said and smirked. "Just because I can afford it doesn't mean that I'm willing to pay it. Just for that, I'm lowering my offer to schematics and ten grand."

"Fine!" I said, admitting defeat. "Deal."

"Don't worry, Sweetpea," she said, sounding haughty. "I deal with your type all the time."

"All right, give me a couple of minutes to put a list together." I didn't like my nose being rubbed in it.

"Where's the bathroom?"

I pointed down the hallway. "First opening on the right, Bobby's got the port-a-potties there."

"You're kidding me!"

"I wish I was," I said. "The base is a work in progress, very slow progress. We're still a month away from running water. If you make sure Bobby gets a nice bonus, your future visits will include more amenities."

"Wonderful," she deadpanned and raced off in search of bladder relief as I pondered how having the runs would cause problems for someone moving at superhuman speeds. The engineer in me wondered how fast her shit would move.

Sighing, I scooped up a pad of paper and a pen, and began to scribble whatever I thought I might need in order to prevent my own set of broken bones. Naturally, I threw in some of the things I *needed,* which had nothing to do with her equipment. She was lowballing me after all and I had to make up the margin one way or another.

We're both criminals after all.

• • •

"Nice work, Cal," Maxine said as I watched her quick draw with four of the pistols. I'd made a favorable impression on her when I took the time to measure her hand to make certain the grips were sized for her.

It had taken me a week longer than I'd initially promised, but the design was pretty slick.

"Pulse action, dual energy emitters," I said watching her toast a pair of targets. "It cuts down on your range, and you'll lose most of your punch over twenty-five yards, but they'll give you a greater rate of fire, and I'm guessing you're no stranger to hit and run tactics. Much better than the tinkertoys you were using. The microcells in them are warrantied for fifty recharges, but I'd recommend replacing them before then."

"Considering you're the supplier, I'm guessing you would," she said with a smirk. "Good stuff though; too bad you're so damned slow."

"I don't have your powers," I said, once again trying to hide my jealousy. If I did, Bobby's base and my suit would be done already—except I probably couldn't use a suit then—but I wasn't about to rain on my own little parade.

"It's not all fun and games," she said, putting the pistols on the charging stations so quickly that I couldn't even follow.

"Careful when you do that, sensitive electronics! So, what's the downside to your powers?"

"Ever been in the line at the grocery store and the person in front of you separates their cart into the part their going to pay with food stamps, the part that's going on their credit card, and the part they're paying with a check."

"And there's a price check on at least two of the items?" I added for effect.

She nodded. "That's every single conversation I have, except when I'm around another speedster or a telepath like Auntie. You might think you're quick with your wit, but to me there're seconds in between every single word you say. Everyone else is in slow motion and I'm the only one moving at normal speed. Drives me apeshit, sometimes! Remember the girl from your movie? I had her and five of her friends because that's how many I have to have to even have a chance at getting off. You slowpokes just can't move fast enough for me."

"That's way, way, way too much information," I protested.

"Well, I figured the sooner I told you that, the sooner it would shut you up. But since you do such good work, maybe I'll have you tune up my vibrator. I want to add another five thousand rpms, but I don't want the damned thing to explode. Whatdayathink?"

She probably enjoyed the cringe on my face, but I shrugged and said, "If the price is right."

Pinching my cheeks like an overzealous relative, Maxine laughed, "Spoken like a true business man! You're a funny guy, Cal Stringel. Maybe if this business arrangement works out, I'll let you work on my private toys, but for now, just stick to building pistols. Here are the keys and the address to a storage locker in Huntsville where there's a duplicate of your order, except for the extra crap you snuck in there last time, and twenty grand. Better get started on the next batch there, Snailman, because I'll be back for them at some point. Consider yourself on retainer."

"Fair enough, Ms. Velocity. Nice doing business with you."

Maxine zipped out of the room and up the exit shaft.

"Too bad she's a lesbo, Cal," Bobby said coming out of the hallway from the private rooms. "Otherwise, I think she'd rock your world."

"How long were you there?"

"Long enough to hear that you have your first steady client, not too shabby. It also means you can start chipping in for our salaries at Floozies and for the things you keep saying we need around the base. But that's why I steered her in your direction in the first place."

There went half that money. Bobby wasn't nearly as stupid as everyone, including myself, made him out to be.

"How'd you know it was going to work?" I asked.

"Wasn't certain," he said. "Still, you pick up a whole bunch being the hired muscle. Most times you just stand there and keep your trap shut, probably something you'll have to learn. I can see you having problems with that."

I started to take offense, but realized he was probably right.

Enjoying the look on my face, Bobby continued, "The heavy hitters are so used to having bodyguards and extra muscle around that they stop noticing us after a while. It's like fishing. You can get a few interesting nibbles, if you're willing to wait around long enough."

"Do you have any other nuggets of criminal wisdom for me today, Master," I said laughing.

"Seeing how good those guns are got me to thinking that I need to get you to make me some weapons too."

"Are you a decent shot?"

"Nah, I like hittin' things too much. I don't need nothing fancy, just a pair of clubs that won't snap like twigs when I take a swing."

"What about an ax or a sledgehammer instead? I could put a shield generator on something like that."

"Nah, clubs," he said, adamant. "I like the feel of a piece of wood in my hands."

"If that's what you want," I said, realizing this wasn't going to go anywhere. Just when I was starting to give Bobby some credit for not being such a yokel, he goes and asks me for a pair of over engineered baseball bats.

Sighing, I knew Maxine's vibrator would have been more of a challenge.

Chapter Six

My Mouth Tends to Get Me in Trouble

Life, such as it was, progressed; just not at the speed I would have liked. Maxine turned out to be very *protective* of her employment of me. When I asked her to drop my name to any of her friends, colleagues, or what have you, she actually concentrated so that she could reply slowly.

"You work for me, Cal. You only work for me. If I catch you working for anyone other than me, not only will I terminate our retainer arrangement, but I'll terminate more than that. You can barely keep up with my needs and outfit this shithole at the same time, but you think I'll be your little brokering agent. Think again."

"That's not it!" I protested—even though it was.

"Sure, it isn't," came her mocking reply, laced with rapid-fire laughter. "Besides, in lieu of this month's payment, there're three spools of synthmuscle in the storage locker."

"Really?" I asked, not bothering to hide my greedy look. It was enough to do the entire lower torso and more than my usual retainer would cover. "Where'd you get it?"

"I was raiding one of Patterson's warehouses and it was just lying there looking for an owner. I could've probably given it to my Aunt's people, but they make their own, even if it isn't as good as Promethia's. I figured, given your history, you'd appreciate it more."

"Synthmuscle, and you stole it from Lazarus Patterson? I could kiss you right now."

She scrunched her nose and said, "No, thanks, I'll pass. A quick peck for you is a tedious experience for me. Now if you were a really hot chick, I'd consider it. Speaking of which, if I move now, I'll be on the beaches of Florida in forty-five minutes, where I can round up tonight's entertainment. See you around, Snailman."

I understood. We both dug hot chicks. Unlike me, she could actually get them, even if it required kidnapping. The best I could manage was a date from the occasional skank at Floozies. Technically, I was living with one, which meant I paid half her rent in exchange for Sparkle collecting my mail and helping me fool Leonard, which really wasn't that hard. Sparkle, real name Leslie, and I had slept with each other twice. The first was a drunken mistake and the second was done sober to make certain it was a bad idea.

New Coke and the Hindenburg were better ideas than that train wreck.

Walking to my cluttered workshop area, I looked at the five tables and the mess on them vanished, in my mind. On each, I could see a major section of my soon-to-be-built masterwork. It would be a combination of black and gunmetal gray. The arms would end in my force blasters. I had a workable design for an armored jetpack, which would be housed on the unit's back. Synthmuscle, the only thing that prick Patterson ever came up with on his own, would fill the chassis and allow me to lift up to three tons when standing on the ground. The jetpack's thrust would limit me to about a half a ton extra in flight. Sure, it wasn't quite in Bobby's league, but I could fly circles around him and zap him with my blasters without him ever laying a mitt on me.

It's all coming together! I thought, while wringing my hands and sparing a glance at the printed sheets duct taped to the cave wall. I'd printed out Ultraweapon's schematics and upgraded them with my own ideas. It wouldn't be anywhere nearly as elegant and streamlined as the one I saw him in, posing for pictures with the Olympians on the cover of an old issue of Superhero Weekly. The title, *Olympians and Ultraweapon Thwart Rigellian Menace*, mocked me.

If Patterson was any closer to Aphrodite, she'd be inside the suit with him!

It didn't matter. I'd have my revenge on him, F. Randall Barton, his entire corporation!

• • •

"So, Calvin," Leonard said, tossing a little stress ball back and forth in his hands. "You want to go to Miami for the week and need a travel pass? Tell me why I should allow this?"

There are few things more humiliating than dealing with your parole officer. Leonard, here, had delusions of grandeur and liked the power and control that came with his position—a real legend in his own mind.

"I'm due for a vacation, Leonard. Some sun and sand would do me good."

"Is this a solo vacation, or is Ms. Leslie accompanying you?" he asked, perhaps a little too interested in my fake girlfriend. I stashed that tidbit of info away as something that might be useful down the line.

Leonard Dozier was a tall and lean kind of guy, wearing an off-the-shelf suit that he should really take to the tailor and a pair of tinted, prescription glasses. I was of the opinion he was trying too hard to look official and reeked of middle management. Maybe he just reeked; I couldn't be sure.

"No," I lied. "She's got something planned with one of her friends—chick stuff."

He nodded sagely and said, "Yes, it's best to give a woman space every now and then, if you want it to last. So, how's my cousin doing?"

"We hang out at work, bowl every once in a while and go fishing," I said. He was sniffing around to see if he could catch us in a lie.

"Catch anything decent lately?"

"Nothing but a cold," I said joking. "Have to keep an eye on Bobby when we're at the lanes, more than three beers and he's liable to chuck his bowling ball so hard it strips the finish off the wood."

"You know," he said, pivoting in his chair and looking both wistful and every bit as jealous of his relative's super strength as I often was. "I almost skipped school and went with him to that pond. It could have been me in that water with him and my little sis when that bolt of lightning came out of nowhere on a clear day and zapped 'em both."

"Is that how it happened?" I'd never bothered asking Bobby how he'd gotten his powers and had thought he'd had them from birth.

"Yeah, but I had a ball game that day and there was a scout there. Still, I got to play two years of Double A before I trashed my ankle sliding into third."

Oh, so, he's a frustrated former baseball player and a guy who missed out on getting superpowers. His alter ego must either be Captain Regret or The Blown Opportunist!

Knowing the second one could have equally applied to me; I shrugged and said, "I dunno, Leonard, I ran into lots of guys who got jacked over by their powers. For every person getting super strength, speed, and what not, there're guys like Gunk or Mud Dauber. Trust me; I had to do their laundry and I wouldn't wish that on my worst enemy."

Actually, I'd get a kick out of seeing F. Randall Barton and Lazarus checking out Gunk's "tighty whities" with his latest Streak of the Week. His mouth and nose weren't the only orifices that shit came out of!

Truth be told, I usually just tossed them in the incinerate pile along with Mud Daubers clothes. It was much easier that way.

"How did that audition go for that one band you told me about?"

"They got another guy," I answered. "My travel restrictions made them a bit wary. I've been checking out the local scene to see if anyone's looking for drummers. I might be able to pick up a few gigs along the way, to keep me from losing my edge, but if I do get one, I would be in here all the time asking for travel passes, like I am now."

I really liked drumming, and had a kit at my apartment with Sparkle and another down in Bobby's hideout. It was a good way to blow off some steam, but I was beginning to believe that I'd never get very far pursuing that direction. It was either that or the fact that I was getting close to building my very own set of powered armor and my former college roommate had scored me some high grade material for the shell of my suit.

"Well, you haven't been giving me any problems," he said, making a show of taking his pen out of the holder and closely inspecting my form. "Everything looks to be in order, so I'm going to approve your trip to Miami. I hope you have a good time."

Me too, I thought and waited patiently for my parole officer to sign the document.

• • •

"Dunno if this was included in our arrangement," Bobby said, wiping the sweat from his brow. He wasn't a very good blacksmith. That much was certain, but my old college roomie had come up with some very fine metals, courtesy of a turf war between an Eastern European gang financed by a Russian construction corporation and a Latino gang backed by South American *interests*—that was as good a description for them as any.

Lacking the equipment to properly forge the metal into the shape I needed it to be, I had to rely on my new roomie's power to beat the material into submission. Our two worker robots ambled around the open space. Dee was welding the steel plating onto the prison cells while Dum held it in place. There was no way I would trust Dum with anything combustible—not after the last time. In fact, until there is a prisoner, Tweedledum would be spending his downtime in one of those cells.

"Just think of how profitable your jobs will be when I get this suit finished," I said, trying to spin this into a positive.

Bobby wasn't necessarily buying what I was selling. He watched as I spoke into the microphone in front of me, recording commands and then verifying that the commands called up the correct subroutine on my laptop and there was a whirring noise on the bench where the half-finished arm assembly, mounted in a pair of vices, began charging the one finished force blaster. From the waist down I was covered in synthmuscle and servos and I did my best side kick and felt the artificial sinew respond and amplify my kick. Still, the kick was a little too high and I could feel my leg muscles protesting both the angle and the force used. I'd pay for not properly stretching.

"So, you're just going to tell the suit what to do?" he asked as I gingerly lowered the leg.

"That's the fact, Jack!" I quipped in reply, and tried to ignore the pain in my thigh. "Voice control, it's the only way to go. Patterson keeps sinking money into some kind of neural interface, but I doubt he'll ever get it off the ground or make it small enough to fit inside his armor."

As much as I didn't want to admit my personal shortcomings, it looked like the suit would be limited by the jackass inside of it. I'd have to adjust the programming to not exceed my own capabilities. No wonder Patterson was always with his physical trainer—aside from the fact that he was also diddling her, but nobody was supposed to know that. Even though everyone did.

"Seems complicated," he said and took a swig of his beer. I pondered whether alcohol and metalworking were a good combination.

"That's why I'm going to practice until wearing this suit is like second nature. Fire force blaster!"

Nothing happened. I paused and glared at the arm assembly and then at the laptop screen, as if a dirty look from me would correct the problem. In the background I heard Bobby stifle a guffaw.

Sighing loudly, I corrected myself and said, "Fire left force blaster."

The embedded weapon responded and a burst of concussive energy splashed against the opposite wall. The discharge left a watermelon sized divot in the stone comprising our cave's lower level.

"Guess you do need to practice," my *compadre* observed.

"I forgot that I changed the command this morning," I said trying to explain away my stupidity. "I'm going to have to take the suit outside to do anything more than test fire the jet pack."

A loud chirp acknowledged my words and the jet pack rumbled to life. Panicked, I jumped out of the way screaming, "Cancel last command! Cancel last command!"

Unfortunately, my servo assisted leap carried me into the wall where I collapsed in a painful mess that made the earlier pain in my leg a forgotten memory.

The worst part of all that was it took Bobby five solid minutes to stop laughing at me. It was going to be one of *those* days.

• • •

"Are you sleeping at the apartment tonight?" the barely dressed bottle blonde asked me.

"Hot date?" I asked from the DJ stand as the music blared. In the middle of her routine, Afrodite, a tall, well-built black woman, tossed a discarded knock-off of the Olympian's costume on the stage. The woman was a traveling headliner who worked the clubs all over the southeast and was responsible for the large crowd here tonight. Without the contributions of Bobbie and me, this rat hole could never afford top tier talent like her. Even to my jaded eyes, the woman had some serious skills.

"Actually, yes," Leslie answered. "What happened to your wrist?"

I looked at the cast on my hand and replied, "Masturbation injury. I have to switch to my off hand now."

She laughed and I was thankful for the loud music. Leslie's laugh was so annoying that I'd considered weaponizing it for the armor. The Bugler had nothing on her audible jackhammer! The actual truth behind my injury was that two days ago, a faulty relay had shut down my jetpack after thirty minutes of flight, and I took a four story fall in my first day of flying practice, but she didn't need to know that.

Until I could make two more shield emitters and repair the one I'd fried during my *soft* landing, I wouldn't be flying higher than twenty feet off the ground. A badly sprained wrist and the bruises on my right leg were painful, but I'd gotten off easy compared to what could have happened. I used to think Joe Ducie was lucky to be the only other guy allowed to pilot the Ultraweapon armor, but now I realized that my former supervisor was really Lazarus Patterson's well-compensated crash test dummy.

My injuries were a painful reminder that I needed to pay more attention to quality control or start building my mechanized assault wheelchair.

Actually, that has possibilities; I thought and returned my attention to my fake girlfriend. "I can make myself scarce. Though, I guess I should be mad that you're cheating on me. Should I be jealous? It's not Leonard is it? I think he's got a thing for you."

"Oh, please!" Sparkle said and rolled her eyes at me, before regarding the gyrating Nubian amazon onstage. "Maybe I should do a superhero routine? If I got a brunette wig with pigtails maybe I could be WhirlingWendy or WendyWantsToWhirl."

Groaning, I shrugged and said, "You could probably make it work. Give 'em the old naughty super schoolgirl routine. Maybe you could have them set up a couple of heavy duty fans to fake her powers. It probably wouldn't be too hard. Of course, every mark would be asking you for a blow job after that."

Scrunching her nose, she nodded and said, "Like they don't anyway. Even so, it might be worth looking into, anyway. You could probably do that thing with the fans, right?"

I nodded, realizing I'd walked into that one, and she said, "Cal, you're the best!"

We both knew that wasn't true, but she was in the business of selling fantasies and falsehoods to men, so I let it slide. As she left, I noticed a few of the locals were causing a disturbance because of all the extra people in here tonight. Afrodite had a biker gang that followed her around and our regular crowd wasn't really appreciating all the extra bodies nearly as much as the cash registers were, and it appeared that things would get ugly at some point.

If I was being completely honest, I might even go so far as to say that the locals didn't exactly appreciate the skin color of the entertainer's groupies. They also knew that this was Bobby's turf and were probably instigating something just so they could see the big lug crack some out-of-towners' skulls. It was probably just as entertaining as what that extremely limber woman was doing at the time.

I caught one of the other employee's attention and gave her a hand signal that indicated trouble. She excused herself from the gent she was chatting up and bounced her curves over to the bar. I saw her lean over and whisper into Bobby's ear. The strongman grinned and smacked his beer mug down on the countertop. Standing, he unfurled his limbs like a cat getting ready to go on the prowl and turned. A couple of the other bouncers flanked him as he waded into the area where the pushing and shouts threatened to overcome the music.

Bobby pushed his way into the center and snatched up two of the bikers like they were rag dolls.

"Knock this shit off!" he roared. I killed the music, since only a few were still paying attention to Afrodite.

One of the idiots he was holding busted his beer bottle across Bobby's scalp. The big man shook his head for a moment and gave his attacker a dirty look. "Seriously? I'd throw your ass through that window right now, but that would be a waste of some perfectly good glass."

"Put them down!" one of the others shouted. He was clearly their leader and looked pretty formidable for a normal human. The man was somewhere around six feet four, with a shaved head. He wore expensive clothes instead of the biker jackets and jeans the rest had. I'd originally pegged him as Afrodite's manager or bodyguard.

"And if I don't feel like it?" Bobby said with a sneer.

"Well, I suppose then I'll have to kick your bumpkin ass all over this place."

"If you think you can, you're welcome to try," Bobby said and tossed the pair in his hands away. "I'll even give you the first punch."

Bobby hammed it up as all the locals shouted obscenities. The man made a show of taking off his sport coat. "No need to get your blood all over my nice threads."

"Keep on dreaming," Bobby said and spread his arms wide open. "Show me whatcha got, little man."

Bobby's opponent looked like he knew how to throw a punch. Like all the regulars, I expected Bobby to absorb the blow and laugh while the other man howled in pain. Hitting Hillbilly Bobby was like punching a concrete wall.

Instead, it was Bobby who let out a woof and crumpled forward. The black man wasted no time and tossed my friend out the very window Bobby had threatened the others with.

Who the hell is that? I thought.

Bobby had landed on someone's truck and left a broken windshield and a large dent in the hood. He rolled off and stood on his feet looking pissed.

"Didn't figure you for a super," Bobby said and spit on the ground. "Step on out here and let me have my turn!"

"If you insist, Hillbilly Bumpkin! The Wall can take more than you got."

The Wall? The Wall? Who the f...aw crap Seawall!

I tried to push my way through the crowd heading out the side door and warn Bobby. Seawall wasn't as strong as my buddy, but he was damned near invulnerable. Bobby could drop a truck on D'wan Walter and it wouldn't so much as wipe the smile from Seawall's face.

By the time I got out there Bobby was already taking his free swing. I literally felt the impact as the force was reflected away from Seawall. The people who were unfortunate enough to be close to the duo were thrown backward, howling in pain, as I noticed that none of the biker gang had been part of the crowd.

Sure enough Seawall just stood there and smiled at Bobby. "Any time you're ready."

Bobby threw two quick jabs and a haymaker that would've dented a tractor trailer, but Seawall just stood there laughing as people scrambled away and car windshields cracked. From what little I knew from Patterson's threat index team, Seawall had been a worker on an oil rig in the Gulf and not a very popular one at that. When a hurricane blew into the area and everyone else evacuated, he'd been "overlooked" by the rest of his crew and left behind to fend for himself. Something squirrely happened during that storm and the Coast Guard found D'wan clinging to the wreckage three days later. He was naked, but untouched, and invulnerable.

Growing bored, Seawall hit Bobby a second time and sent the redneck 'roid rager backward.

"Oh, I know all about you Hillbumpkin Bobby," D'wan said. "You've been coming down and taking jobs from me these past couple of months, and I don't really care for that, so I figured I'd come up here and tell you that in person."

Seeing red, Bobby threw a kick at the man's leg. Once more the force was turned away and scattered in all directions. Seawall mocked him and punched my friend two more times.

Think, Cal! Think! He has a weakness, otherwise he wouldn't be so low on the threat index. What was his Achilles' heel? Concentration! That's it! He has to be focused on being invulnerable. Break his concentration and his protective field starts to fall.

As I recalled that nugget of information, it dawned on me that Bobby was well and truly screwed. Bobby's strategy relied solely on hitting something until it fell. I needed something to rattle Seawall for a moment. There was a water spigot, but no hose attached, so dousing him in water was out, unless I ran back in and grabbed a bucket.

Bad idea, I thought. *That'd put me real close to a guy who could cave my skull in.*

At that point a light bulb went off in my head, literally. Running back inside, I ran to the booth where Glenn usually sat and ran the lightshow. Pulling out a twelve-volt halogen portable spotlight, I figured it would serve as a decent distraction and give me a minimum safe distance. For a bonus, I grabbed an air horn.

In the forty-five seconds it had taken me to get the gear, Bobby's predicament had taken a turn for the worse. His face was puffy and swollen, blood drizzled down the side of his mouth, and one eye was almost completely shut. He was down on one knee and keeping his guard up, unused to being on the defensive.

"That's right! That's right!" Seawall circled Bobby and chanted, sounding like one of those fake wrestlers on television. "You think you can come down to *my state, my city,* and take money outta *my pocket!*"

I cranked up the spotlight and shined it at the side of Seawall's face and blew the air horn. The man turned away, but Bobby looked at me confused.

"Hit him now!" I screamed.

Bobby followed my order and this time Seawall went flying and landed with a thump. Several of his gang ran to his side while a few of the others started walking toward me. Fortunately, the locals, who were licking their wounds as a result of all this, got in their way. In this case, the rednecks had accepted me as one of their own and if it kept me from getting my ass kicked by a bunch of bikers, I was actually fine with that.

Before a few more altercations could break out, the shining lights of Johnny Law could be seen coming down the highway, so everyone decided to calm down. The Sheriff and his deputies took a good look at Bobby and Seawall and started asking some questions. The owner of the bar jumped in and sold them a lie that the two of them were settling a bet about being super strong and it spiraled out of control. The Sheriff nodded and I knew there'd be a payoff involved, but I had firsthand knowledge of how money could get a person out of a tight squeeze.

"I told you to not start any shit until I was done! Since I didn't finish my set, I only get half my check, D'wan!"

The outburst drew my attention to Afrodite who'd just been told to get her ass and her entourage off the premise. I wasn't surprised that the owner had stuck to their contract. He's a tight-ass with Bobby's and my money.

Afrodite, upset at missing out on several thousand dollars, brought the cringing Seawall his jacket, and was beating him with it. It was safe to say his concentration was so jacked up right now that I probably could have sucker punched him and caused some real pain. Still, this wasn't the end of things. While trying to talk his woman down, he was giving Bobby and, surprisingly, me, a death glare. My guess was he had a couple of bruised ribs, maybe even fractures. D'wan's ride home wouldn't exactly be domestic bliss, either.

It was tempting to have a good laugh over it, but I wanted to wait until Bobby wouldn't punch me out of reflex or something. *Self-preservation is my middle name. Well, technically, it's Matthew.*

Leslie handed me a first aid kit and I went to work cleaning Bobby's bruises as the bikers and the silver Mercedes sped from the parking lot.

With a captive audience, I explained Seawall's power to my friend and gave him some advice.

"Carry a plastic bag of flour, or sneezing powder with you. Get him off his game and he's as vulnerable as you. Come to think of it, he wears goggles and a mask with his costume, so something like pepper spray would probably work too."

Wincing at the peroxide, Bobby said, "Thanks, Cal. When you get your suit ready, I think we should go down to the bayou and pay our respects to Seawall; don't you think?"

Truthfully, Seawall was pretty far down on my list of people whose asses needed kicking, but I could see how upset Hillbilly Bobby was over this and threw him a bone.

"Yeah, I reckon we should."

Chapter Seven

She Who Hesitates

My hope of completing my powersuit in a few weeks stretched into four additional months of calibrations, rework, bruises, and interruptions. Surprisingly enough, Maxine wasn't too keen on her weapons designer sidelining as a supervillain. Her orders and demands were coming in at a rate that I could barely keep up.

"It worked! Itworked! Itworked! Itworked!Iwrkd! Itwd! Id! ! I!" I could barely make it out as she cackled with a buzzing laughter and became a blur standing next to me. In truth, I'd never seen her so excited.

"Slow down, Maxine!"

"Ohsorry! Youshould'veseen the lookonHermes' face whenIhitherwithyourlight!" she exclaimed. It was better, but still barely comprehendible. I keyed the digital recorder I carried in my pocket, so I could slow down the audio later and ensure I didn't miss something important. She'd already played the "I told you that" card on several occasions and had gotten tired of my "I must've missed that" defense.

Maxine's new kick was designing weapons specifically for use against other super-fast people. My best design, inspired by my encounter with Seawall, was a handheld stroboscope connected to a backpack that held the powercells. To a normal person it looked like a very powerful solid light, but to someone moving as fast as my temperamental patron, it was actually a chain of multicolored pulsing lights. It only gave her a three second window, but to a speedster, that was a very, very long time. Maxine had put that to good use.

My other designs had been somewhat less effective and the test phases had left Max V angry and covered in goop from my "gummy bomb" or me with a painful day at the eyewash station, coughing out the contents of my lungs and washing off the airborne irritant blown back into my face by her arms creating a gust of wind.

Mental note—Never forget your safety glasses and mask when testing out a new weapon.

Sometimes Maxine's behavior made me think she was more temper than mental, but on other days she was definitely more mental than temper.

Today was the latter. She'd intercepted Hermes, who'd been protecting a valuable collection of gems being transported between New York and Washington. The "Stringel Bedazzler"—trademark pending—had blinded the fastest woman in the world and allowed the relatively slower villain to get a little revenge and a lot of shiny rocks.

"Even my aunt is impressed," Maxine said. "She asked me if she should offer you a position."

I would be lying if I said that an offer to work for General Devious full time didn't intrigue me. However, considering what happens to the engineers in her employment when there were "less than satisfactory" results soured me on that idea. The life of a freelancer appealed to me and probably added to my life expectancy, because for every brilliant *hit* I had, there were usually several spectacular *misses*.

Also, several of the people who shared that prison block with me had at one time or another believed what General Devious had said to them, only to find out later that it wasn't true. There was a reason they called her Devious, after all.

Even so, I needed to look grateful, lest I piss off the woman in front of me. "I'll keep it in mind, but I'd rather finish my suit first. From my perspective, I'd be worth more money with the suit. Speaking of which, does this mean I finally get my hands on a C class powercell?"

My question was important. I had two B cells running the suit at the moment, but it was too underpowered. I needed at least one C for the main systems. Two would be nicer and ultimately three would work best—because I'm greedy like that.

She frowned, or at least I think it was a frown, tough to tell with her. "Why does everything with you revolve around your suit? We're talking about me here and my perfect day! But no! I have to hear you whining like a little baby! 'When do I get my powercell? Why can't you get me this? When can I have that?' Is that all you ever think about?"

Crossing my arms, I looked at her for several seconds before saying anything, just to annoy her. "Pretty much, yes. That's what I'm always thinking about. Do you have any other obvious questions you'd like to ask?"

"Fine!" she muttered, sounding annoyed. "But for such a valuable commodity like a class C cell, I'm going to want something special in return."

"Such as?" I asked, wondering if the mercurial speedster was about to ask if I would reengineer her sex toys.

Max Velocity shot me a wicked grin and said, "I want you to build something that will take down Ultraweapon."

What! That was not what I'd been thinking. "Excuse me?"

"C'mon, Cal," the woman said. "Anytime someone gets him in a bad situation, Ultraweapon flies away or holds on long enough for his teammates to bail his ass out. Give me something that will knock out his flight system and keep him stuck on *terra firma.*"

She's going to try and steal my chance to be the one to humiliate and destroy Lazarus Patterson! I can't let her do that.

"So," I said, looking for the words to stall her and try to drive this foolish notion out of my patron's mind. "What would you do with him if I could prevent his suit from flying?"

The woman paused and stood rigid for almost 30 seconds. For her, that time must have seemed like an eternity. Finally, she spoke, "Well, I think I could toss a two hundred pound C4 poncho over his neck, back off a few hundred feet, and then push the detonator. Boom! No more Ultraweapon. My aunt has never been able to do it. Hell, even The Overlord has never taken him. I would be a legend!"

Her plan actually sounded workable. That fact bothered me. "Maybe you oughta think this one through."

Maxine did not appear to be deterred. "You know his suit better than he does! If anyone can do this, it's you."

Now she is just trying to flatter me, even if it is true. Could she actually do it? Why am I even standing in her way?

"Yeah, I do," I admitted. During my resignation and subsequent blacklisting, I had never interacted with Lazarus Patterson. It had always been Barton one of his bootlickers causing me no end of trouble in Promethia's name.

That said, Lazarus was Promethia and Promethia was Lazarus.

"Give me some time to think about it," I said. "You're asking a lot from me."

Placing her hands on her hips and tilting her head, Maxine said, "Do you honestly believe that you're the only one who's ever been screwed over by Promethia? They created me and my aunt!"

"Say what?" I certainly never heard that before.

"My mom and Aunt Elaine were twin sisters, both Air Force pilots who had volunteered for Promethia's version of the enhanced human project that Patterson's pappy lost out to Doctor Ivan Manglev."

I considered myself a fairly well-informed jackass, but this was all news to me, and I told her that. Doctor Mangler, as he came to be called after the name change, supposedly never had any real competition for his flawed process. This must have been some kind of behind the technological curtain deal that most people never heard about.

"I'm not surprised," she said. "As soon as Aunt Elaine began manifesting her psychic bursts, they couldn't figure out why my mother wasn't demonstrating any powers, but it turned out that she was less than a week pregnant with me and I got the powers instead of her. They didn't figure out that she was knocked up until she fell into a coma. Mom's body started to shut down, but they kept her alive so I could be born after only one month. Old man Patterson lied to my aunt and said that neither of us survived, but when her telepathy emerged, she found out the truth. The rest was history. The General never did find out who my father was for certain, but let's just say that there's a decent chance I might be Ultraweapon's half-sister. So if you think you're the only one who has an ax to grind with them, then maybe you're not as bright as I give you credit for being."

That explained why General Devious, or Elaine Davros as she'd been known before, eventually murdered Lazarus Patterson's father. In retribution, Lazarus had shattered her spine with his prototype powersuit. They had created Maxine just as they created me. In a strange and twisted way, that sort of made us kin, at least in spirit. She appeared to genuinely believe the story she just told me, but, having been raised by one of the most notorious liars in recent, or perhaps all of history, I took it with a healthy dose of skepticism.

Think about this too long, Cal, and it will give you a headache!

I didn't need any further convincing. "Okay, I'm in. I'll start working on it right away, but I want the C cell up front."

Maxine agreed and said she'd have it delivered to the storage locker in three days. I sat down and thought, after she left, and didn't even work on the suit. The more I considered it, the more I didn't mind Maxine killing off Lazarus with my assistance. Sure, I'd like to put the pompous ass out of everyone's misery, but if I did that, I'd be a marked man. Every hero in North America and others around the globe would be out for my blood. Even this hole probably wouldn't be deep enough for me to hide in forever. Max V, on the other hand, was a top tier villain and had her aunt's organization at her disposal. She'd have a better shot of weathering that shit-storm.

Besides, there was always F. Randall Barton. He'd make an acceptable consolation prize and wouldn't be nearly as dangerous.

Getting others to do your dirty work should be a villain's motto, I thought and concluded that I would be better off letting Ms. Fast and Homicidal do the heavy lifting.

Spreading out the original blueprints, I began following the paths around the flight system. The flight system was considered sacred during all of the design meetings I'd been forced to attend. It was one of the few things besides the synthmuscle that Lazarus had actually done himself. One of the first things Joe Ducie had told me was to, "never mess with the flight system." Chances were that the one in his current suit wasn't that different from what I was looking at right now.

Familiarity breeds contempt, or that's how the saying goes.

When it came to Promethia, I had lots of contempt built up.

• • •

There was a nervous, jittery feeling as I triggered the mechanism and slid the larger and more capable powercell into the cradle. A whine came from the connectors as they screwed down onto the ends. The shielded plate on my stomach retracted and locked into place and the meter surged from the red level up into the green.

Yeah, boy! It's on now! I thought.

For the first time since I calibrated the power systems, NOMINAL flashed on the bottom right corner of my heads up display and I resisted the urge to break out into that one Muppet song that sounded like that word.

Aloud, I said, "It's really a powersuit and not a really slow jet pack with a forty-two minute flight range!"

Sure, it didn't move with the grace and speed of Patterson's and there was still plenty for me to do to it, but I wasn't just Cal Stringel anymore. I was much more than just ManaCALes. I'd given plenty of thought to what I should be called when I'm wearing it.

I am Mechani-CAL!

Bobby rounded the corner into my workshop and bedroom, "Cal! You gotta come see this."

"What's up?" I asked, enjoying the digitized sound of my voice coming from behind the helmet. It was a little too loud; I'd have to adjust that later.

"It's Maxine," he said. "They've got her on the TV."

I ambled after him to the big screen in Central Command. A pair of talking heads was at the studio desk, with an inset of a chopper circling over a cluster of buildings and three more with other idiot know-it-alls in them.

"...still following the action. So far what we can tell you is that the high speed supervillain Maxine Velocity has taken several Promethia employees hostage inside the industrial park and is demanding only one thing, that Ultraweapon come and face her."

The anchor at the news desk nodded and tried to sound grim. "Do we have any word about the condition of the hostages, Lori?"

"No, Dan, we don't," the traffic lady answered the obvious question. It's not like Max V would contact the helicopter.

"Thank you, Lori. Let's bring in Doctor Yun Lee, our superhuman expert. Dr. Lee, thank you for joining us on such short notice. What do you make of the situation?"

The Asian doctor, known for his encyclopedic knowledge of heroes and villains steepled his hands before saying, "Without demands for money or anything other than facing Lazarus Patterson in combat, we can only surmise that today is about humiliation or perhaps even misdirection. She did not stipulate that he appear without his armor, so she must clearly want a fight."

"But is it a trap?" the female co-anchor asked and I wondered where they got these people.

"It depends on how much thought Maxine Velocity has put in to her plan. She has shown time and again to be rash and impulsive, so this may be a spur of the moment attack or a carefully laid trap."

"Way to hedge your bets there, Doctor," I said, scoffing at the image on the screen.

"They sure do repeat themselves a lot," Bobby added, while they turned to their next expert, an associate editor at *Superhero Weekly*.

"Of course the last time someone tried to trick Lazarus Patterson into coming without his armor, it turned out to be Ultraweapon's teammate Rakashsi, the shape changing Buddhist monk, so Maxine would probably anticipate such tactics."

"How can her super speed be used against Lazarus Patterson?"

"I'm not entirely sure, but one possibility Doctor Lee just mentioned is that she's fast enough to get away. She may be working with someone else, and luring Ultraweapon into a confrontation guarantees that they know where he will be. This whole thing could be just to get Ultraweapon away from their real target."

They continued to debate back and forth for several minutes, and I was about to tell Bobby to come get me when the action started, when the windbag in the anchor chair, said, "I'm getting word that Ultraweapon is approaching the hostage situation."

The inset with the traffic copter's view expanded. In the distance, I could see the tiny streak of something flying through the air— Ultraweapon. Naturally, he was heading directly for the chopper to ensure he got his promo shot.

"Kelly, you've been close to Ultraweapon in the past, what must be going through his mind right now?"

Considering the co-anchor was blonde and attractive, I had little doubt as to what she might have been doing in such close proximity to my former boss. Odds were that her interviews were conducted when she was flat on her back.

She seemed a bit startled by the question, but hid her blush well. Clearing her throat she said, "Lazarus is a phenomenal multitasker. He is probably evaluating three different ways to take her on, as he approaches."

I knew those attack plans were being generated by the ATAI database and he wasn't nearly as great as she made him out to be. Still, even I had to admit that he could think on the fly.

He's a world class douchebag, but he does actually have to run the suit. Given all my minor mishaps, I had a new appreciation for just how much work went into that.

Ultraweapon sent a series of bolts from his force blasters, which was really just gauging Maxine's ability to compensate and react.

"C'mon, Max!" I shouted. "He's calibrating his targeting system for your speed."

Maxine burned through two of my pulse pistols sending a barrage of energy against his flaring shields.

"I'm concerned about that object on Max V's belt," Doctor Lee spoke over the action. "Can we get a close up of it?"

The producers of the show struggled to comply and they focused on the item strapped securely to her belt. My latest invention was on national TV. It was black, about the size of a cantaloupe that had been cut in half, and I said a quick prayer for my ass if it didn't work, because I knew Maxine would have my sorry behind.

I tried to tune out the commentators and focus on the action. Ultraweapon scattered his fire, allowing his targeting system the opportunity to predict where she might be next. So far, Maxine continued to give as good as she got; hitting him repeatedly with the pistols I built for her. At some point, Patterson would have to land to take the strain off his systems. Running flight, shooting weapons, and absorbing damage with his force field generators took a toll on his personal power grid. My guestimate, based on what I knew of his armor, was five minutes for his old suit. How long he let this go on would tell me how much more efficient his platform had become, and give me something to measure my suit against.

Sadly, I knew my suit could go "all out" for a whopping two minutes and thirty seconds under the hoops Max V was making him jump through, and I was still nowhere near as comfortable flying in the suit. The bastard made it look easy!

To be certain, I was pulling for Maxine Velocity to take him out, but I had that sinking feeling in my gut that it wouldn't happen. Lazarus was a sneaky piece of work. I told her if she gets him and thinks he is dead, to go a little overboard to make damned sure he wasn't just faking it.

It's what I would do, given half a chance. Too many times his opponents had thought they'd finished him, only to be proven wrong.

Maxine disappeared behind a series of shipping containers and came out on the other side with a shoulder launched Stinger missile and fired it right at him. Clearly, she'd brought along some heavy artillery.

Ultraweapon's energy pulse detonated it, but the shockwave bounced both of them around a bit and he dropped from the sky. Immediately, he fired his weapons into the asphalt surrounding them, sending chunks of pavement flying in her direction. It also made her path to him more rugged and difficult to cross. It was a good strategy to slow Maxine down.

Not one to be deterred, Maxine circled and sent a steady stream of beam energy from what must have been her ninth and tenth pistols. From the satchel strapped across her back, she produced a series of grenades and tossed them at the besieged buffoon. They exploded in a sea of blinding light and thunder—a dozen flash bangs mixed with several standard fragmentations lit up the battlefield.

Patterson tried pulling a runner right there, and fly away, but Maxine was ready for him. She stopped right behind him, yanked my device off her belt, and slammed the flat side of the hemisphere just above his attached jetpack, where the control circuitry for his flight system should still be.

It was a moment of truth as the Stringel "Chilly Pimple" (patent pending) sent a burst of liquid nitrogen fueled cold in a six-inch wide circle. Realistically, Ultraweapon's fuel lines were too insulated for my weapon to freeze the lines, but the temperature monitoring system wasn't protected nearly as well. The device didn't have to cause a blockage; instead it needed only to trick the failsafe mechanism into thinking the lines were clogged. Automatically, the flight system would go offline for no less than ninety seconds while the pumps recirculated his fuel to clear something that wasn't actually there.

Good old Lazarus had his takeoff aborted and he dropped back onto the rubble in a rather undignified heap. I smacked my gauntlets together and gave myself a mental pat on the back for the success of the Chilly Pimple. *Way to stick it to the man, Cal!*

While I was making my internal victory lap, Max V wasted no time and emptied two more pistols before diving back into the alley separating two of the buildings, and returning with the first two of her Boomrings—made from a circular detonator wrapped in a layer of C4 explosive. Like some psychotic carnival gamer, Maxine played the most deadly game of ring toss ever imagined. Her first attempt missed and she detonated it next to Patterson, tossing the so-called hero into the side of the shipping container. Her next attempt was snatched out of the air, but before Ultraweapon could hurl it away, she blew it up as well.

C'mon, Maxine, finish him!

With the symbol of everything wrong in my life dashed to the ground and struggling to rise, the blue streak of the woman who may or may not be Patterson's half-sister darted to where she'd staged more Boomrings. This time she had four and was a bit sluggish, for her, getting back. She paused about thirty feet away from him and it felt like my heart wanted to stop.

No! No! Don't stop to rub his nose in it. Just end it!

Every second she wasted caused the gnawing pit in my stomach to grow. Just as Maxine Vivian Davros started to move, there was an explosion that was followed by several more in the surrounding buildings, including the one where the Promethia employees she kidnapped were held hostage.

Disbelief flooded my soul as the scene unfolded and I tried to comprehend what had just happened. Two of the surrounding buildings were heavily damaged and another had partially collapsed. A police chopper closed in and blew the dust cloud away as I swallowed, suddenly concerned for the fate of the fifth fastest person in the world. Maybe she'd been able to get clear if she realized quickly enough what was happening. The optimist in me hoped, but the engineer in me doubted, that she could get far enough away from ground zero to save her psychotic ass.

As I feared, Ultraweapon was still moving, but he was obviously in bad shape and I wished that Maxine had brought some backup. If I was there, I could've finished him right then! *Dammit to hell!* But I wasn't, and neither was anyone else.

She'd failed. Her failure felt like my failure and I looked over at Bobby, who shook his head and cracked open another beer.

"Damned shame," he said. "She was okay, in my book."

• • •

It took me a couple of hours to figure out what had happened. The rings Maxine used were detonated by a radio signal from her controller. Beaten, Ultraweapon broadcast on every frequency and triggered the explosives she held and the ones in the surrounding buildings. Now, I was watching a hastily called press conference where Patterson's spin machine was trying to put the chaotic mess in a positive light. His latest PR doll was a "retired" model and though I couldn't say for certain that he was doing her, if he wasn't then I had even less respect for Lazarus—if that was even possible.

"First, Mr. Patterson, and the company as a whole, extends our thoughts and prayers to the families and friends of those who lost their lives on this terrible day. Even while being treated for his injuries, he wanted to let the world know that Promethia looks out for their own. Today, and the ones that follow, are a time of mourning for our extended family."

I had my own opinions of how that company really looked out for their employees, but the words I could use probably wouldn't be aired.

"Is it true that Ultraweapon triggered the detonation to save himself?" One obviously angry reporter interrupted. I recognized the woman who'd been *involved* with the serial womanizer a long time ago and hadn't particularly taken the breakup very well. Still, this was pretty brazen even for Ms. Bostic. Someone had reached the same conclusion that I did and sent it to a woman who had an emotional ax to grind.

It occurred to me that I needed to get her contact information at some point.

The spokespuppet cleared her throat before saying, "At this time, the authorities have not finished their investigation and it would be unfair, and even hurtful, to those who have lost loved ones to engage in dangerous speculation at this time. Rest assured as the facts become available they will be released to the public."

Ms. Bostic looked anything but assured and tried to ask another question, but the speaker had moved on to a friendlier question about Mr. Patterson's injuries. I smelled a plant.

"All I am permitted to say is that his injuries are significant, but not life threatening and he is being treated at an undisclosed location."

"How long will he be out of action? Is First Aid attending to him?" The same man followed up over Ms. Bostic's question concerning whether Lazarus would be prepared to shoulder the responsibility for even more blood on his hands. Security was already moving to escort her out of the room. She went willingly, cognizant that being dragged out while frothing at the mouth would undercut her credibility.

Despite the fact that she was clearly out of my league, I now wanted to proclaim my eternal devotion to her.

"I am not at liberty to discuss Ultraweapon's treatment and whether or not his teammate is with him at this time. Speaking on my own personal behalf I, and probably all of you watching, am wishing Lazarus a swift recovery and look forward to seeing the armored titan patrolling our skies once more. Thank you for coming this morning."

It was theater, pure and simple. There was a dash of caring mixed with compassion, wrapped in the drama of an implied catfight between two women who'd never give me the time of day. Hell, I even expected that the angry journalist had been allowed to attend in the hopes that her verbal barbs could be spun for sympathy. First Aid was a metahuman who could absorb other people's injuries and regenerate fairly quickly. Other than his ridiculous pain threshold, he wasn't worth a piss in a fight, but there was an undeniable reason Lazarus kept him on the West Coast Guardian's payroll.

The hosts of the Superhero News Channel came back on and did a quick recap of the presser before moving on to the implications of Maxine's death and how General Devious might respond. For my part, I was still somewhat numb over her loss. Luckily, I'd been too busy constructing the Chilly Pimple and servicing her pistols to make her Boomrings. Whatever unfortunate soul was behind those, he or she probably suffered a great deal before being killed. I was moderately concerned that someone would try and finger me as the reason for her failure and subsequent demise, but I would handle that if and when it became a problem.

Self-preservation—it should be first and foremost when dealing with the big leaguers! Hopefully, I'll never forget that.

With the death of Maxine, I was now free to pursue other clients. The feeling of freedom from the deceased speedster's possessiveness was all too bittersweet, but I couldn't let that get me down. Villains don't always get away to fight another day. If things were different, the two of us would still be in the bowels of North Dakota. They weren't and now the industrial park where she died would be another stop on the Battles of Los Angeles tour. There'd be a memorial and a cheesy gift shop.

If I'm the one to finish off Lazarus Patterson, I'd stop by there afterward and pay my respects to Maxine Velocity. She'd come about as close as anyone could get to doing it.

"C'mon, Bobby," I said, putting my feelings aside, deciding my next move and putting the events in perspective.

"Where're we going?"

"Her guy should've filled the storage unit in Huntsville two days ago. I reckon we should go clear it out before someone else beats us to it."

The big man scratched his chin. "Now you're learning, Cal. If you wanna take a trip down to Miami, I might know the address to her penthouse."

Chapter Eight

The Kansas City Caper

One of the problems I discovered with Maxine's death was that it was still difficult getting development work. Even though the items I designed performed as advertised, there was still something of a stigma attached to the fact that the speedster perished.

Put simply, her death wasn't doing my business a lot of good. Feelings aside, being a supervillain was a tough business and your situation could change at a moment's notice.

It was yet another item to blame on Ultraweapon.

Still, my remaining stock of pulse pistols was selling nicely and I was now free to price them at what I felt they were truly worth, without the fear of Maxine deciding that I didn't really need all ten fingers. Jetpacks were a commodity, even though they required considerable practice, which allowed me to sell jetpack lessons as an extra source of income.

With my gadget-making career somewhat at a standstill, I had little choice other than putting my powersuit to use.

"Bout damned time you up and decided to start pulling some jobs in that thing!" Bobby exclaimed as he racked up the balls for another game of pool.

It was my turn to break, and I was counting on my brilliant mind and mastery of the principles of engineering to crush my opponent. Also, I was counting on the fact that Bobby had already downed a six pack.

"I'd still rather wait for two additional shield generators so I can use a quadrant-based protection scheme instead of the hemisphere arrangement I currently have," I said and swiftly realized that I was wasting my time.

Bobby shook his head at either my words or my pathetic opening shot and asked, "Well, are you planning on fighting someone?"

"Uh, no," I eloquently responded.

"Then let me tell you something—the secret to staying out of prison is simple—try not to get in fights with superheroes. Yeah, sure, every now and then you have to throw down with one, but generally speaking, it's not a great idea."

"You're right," I conceded and twisted the cap off another beer. *If I can't beat him, I guess I'll join him!*

"'Course, I am," he replied and laughed.

"I guess I'm just nervous. The only other bank job I ever attempted wound up with me being a rather sad looking notch on the Biloxi Bugler's belt. That's one experience I don't plan on repeating."

"That's why you gotta man up and start with one! You know; get that monkey off your back first, before you start thinking about revenge on the Bugler, Ultraweapon, and that lawyer fella you're always going on about."

Whenever Bobby started making too much sense it was a sure sign that I was already drinking too much and needed to slow down.

Back to the task at hand, I offered, "Maybe I should just start small and rip an ATM right out of the wall."

With the strength the armor provided it would be a cinch; my own version of the grab and go.

My partner in crime barely gave my compromise any consideration. "Chump change," he declared and broke his pool stick. "If that's all you're after why even waste your time building your fancy suit? You crack open the ATM if you still have a free hand on your way out! Otherwise, you're just pissing in the wind."

Shrugging, I quelled my lingering doubts and knew that I should quit while I was ahead, or at least before he started to call me a wussy boy. Instead of my force blasters, I'd built a plasma breeching charge out of some of the miscellaneous parts left over from my weapon building. It was crude, but wouldn't make the world immediately think that there was someone running around using the same weapons as Lazarus Patterson did. There was no sense in revealing my suit until it was necessary. Bobby asked me if there was a way we could pin it on Seawall, but that sounded a little too complex for my taste, and I told him as much.

I don't even know what I'm getting all worked up over, I thought. It's not like my target is even in a city. I'm just going to hit a small branch bank in a sleepy little town on the Florida Panhandle about twenty-five minutes away from Pensacola. I've even done my homework and made damned sure the chances of me running into a superhero are about as low as possible. Andydroid is in Washington DC playing bodyguard to his creator and most of the Gulf Coast Guardians will be at the Superdome as special guests of the football team there. The only two superheroes in a one hundred and fifty mile radius that I know of are the Bugler or a Manglermal who calls himself The Pelican. The first I wouldn't mind seeing and the second never really goes after supervillains. He's more of a DEA agent with wings and a funky helmet that has a taser ray in it. Besides, Pelican never travels farther north than Tampa.

Whether Bobby was right remained to be seen, but I was going to do another bank job.

• • •

Descending, I used my armored foot to kick the camera covering the back of the bank from the wall and landed right at the employee entrance. The breeching charge made me look oddly like a kid carrying a trombone case on his way to band practice—except that my instrument was designed to burn through a steel locking mechanism in less than a minute.

Using one of those ridiculous force clubs I'd made for Bobby, I smashed the door until it gave way under the third blow.

This thing would look so much better on a sledgehammer or a maul, I thought while ripping the door from the remaining hinge and tossing it aside like it was made of cardboard.

The pressure sprayer mounted on my left arm came to life as I smothered the inside camera with a layer of glossy black, limiting the footage they'd be able to recover of Mechani-CAL in action. Stopping only to knock the warbling alarm out of the wall with the club, I trudged straight to the vault and jammed the flat face of my breeching charge against the area where the locking mechanism went into the frame. When I activated it, hot flames and smoke billowed from the back which would take care of any other cameras trying to see me and also set off the fire alarms.

"Switch to enhanced night vision," I said and watched my field of vision turn green, loving the voice activated commands. The glow from my breeching charge provided a strange cascade of colors washing over my heads up display as I counted the seconds.

Like clockwork, I was through in one minute. I set the charge down and used both hands to yank the vault open. One of the things that still took some getting used to was, the strength amplification of the suit. It didn't matter in this instance, but just doing things around our base had caused considerable havoc and kept both Dee and Dum repairing chairs, countertops, and many, many other items as I was still learning how to deal with my newfound strength.

The locker where the stacks of cash were located offered less resistance than your average kitchen pantry door and I began shoving everything inside a flame proof bag. Triggering my sensor array, I looked for any type of transmitters hidden within the loot. Banks, in general, aren't stupid. They know supervillains are out there and that their vaults aren't impregnable. To counter us, they rely on technology, although there were rumors that some of the banks on the west coast have a deal with the Grand Vizier and Mystigal to use magical tracking spells on their money, but I was certain that kind of protection didn't come cheap and a little "Podunk" branch wouldn't have something like that.

A magnetic field generator, I thought and located the device on the inside of the cash locker. *That means a transmitter will be active when I pull it out— probably on a timer. No worries, I'll run it through an industrial magnet in the back of my van while Bobby drives.*

Bobby was an upgrade over Tracy, the inflatable getaway driver, and he'd even offered to come to the bank, but I impressed him and insisted that I conquer my fears alone. One might think that was some epic moment where two men came to a powerful and deep understanding...not really.

The truth was, Bobby said, "You want me to tag along in case something goes wrong?"

My reply, "Nah, I got this! Probably better if you stayed with the van parked about twenty miles away."

"Okay," he replied and the profound moment was over. We were guys and not even particularly complex ones at that. My partner was a good old boy with more strength than sense and I...well, I guess I'd be classified as a disgruntled genius with a chip on my shoulder about the size of Ultraweapon.

But I now had a full bag of cash that would fill the coffers quite nicely, a bigger haul than one of Bobby's muscle jobs. Sealing the flap of the bag, I pushed my way out into the burning lobby and scooped up my plasma cutter. A check of the timer showed I was at the four minute mark and needed to hurry. I lumbered back down the hallway and back out the way I came. The moment I reached the back of the building, I triggered my jetpack and got airborne. I'd faced my inner demon and come out of it not a better man, but a wealthier one.

• • •

The arson, combined with the lack of useable video footage, didn't give the authorities much to go on. I was labeled a mystery criminal who is strong and probably able to fly. I was okay with that. The less seen of me, the better. In fact, I was already trying to work on a better way to take out security cameras. The paint sprayer was good, but when I got back to our base—it was a base now, because hideouts were for chumps—I thought it over and realized that the paint could have easily caught fire from the plasma cutter. Quite frankly, I'd already made the countdown on the *Annual Dumbest Criminals Captured* for my time as ManaCALes, and didn't want to be remembered as the guy running down the street in a burning power armor suit; with people captioning pictures of me with phrases like

EPIC FAIL, STOP, DROP, and TROLL, or WONDER IF MY WIENER IS ROASTING.

Yeah, not interested in that. Let's move along shall we.

"How much did we get?" Bobby asked. I pretended not to notice his use of *we*, unable to recall a time when he was pulling a job that *we* got any credit for.

"A little over two hundred grand in roughly five minutes," I said. "Not too shabby."

He agreed and asked what *we* should spend it on.

"I'll need more synthmuscle and a better autowinder. The good stuff Maxine stole from Promethia went into my legs and torso. As much as I hate saying it, the brand name stuff is much more durable than the cheap shit I put into my arms. I've got a bunch of microrips in the bundles up there from manhandling the vault door. Those will need to be replaced before too long. Other than that, I think we can finally afford to put a real power system in here. Whatever's left we can toss in the recreational fund."

Bobby seemed to be satisfied by my last sentence. He liked to have his fun. I was a little more reserved. By contrast, even on my most hedonistic day, I was a prude compared to him!

"I heard it through the grapevine that someone is looking around for muscle, and I was thinking of tossing my hat into the ring," he said, changing the topic. "You interested?"

"Any idea who? What's the pay?" Those both seemed like important questions. I was legit now, sort of, and didn't want to jump at any old job.

"Nah," Bobby said. "I just got word through one of my contacts. With you having no rep, you probably would only get twenty-five. I'm asking for fifty minus my guy's ten percent. He gave me the impression that someone had a score they wanted to settle."

The numbers would have sounded impressive if I wasn't sitting on much more than that right now. One of the things that had been drilled into my head by my experiences thus far was that being a supervillain was a dog eat dog world. That probably made me some kind of mongrel that the "adopt a pet" campaigns flash on screen for just a moment to guilt people into donating, but this mongrel had just eaten a full meal. Plus, fighting meant dishing out and taking damage. My armor still had that new armor smell and I was reluctant to throw it—and me for that matter— into someone's petty vendetta.

"I'll pass on this one and pull a few more bank jobs," I said. "If I go out into the open, I'll tip my hand about my suit and what it can do. Right now, I'd rather remain a mystery and build up enough money to fix the suit. If it gets too badly damaged, I'm back at square one."

"Suit yourself, wussy," Bobby said, acknowledging my decision and asserting his manhood at the same time.

I gave Bobby my *shopping list* to give to his arranger. I'd never met the dude, but Bobby was using him to sell my pistols through and buy the stuff for the base. Adjusting for the markup, my haul probably wouldn't go as far as I needed it to.

That meant I'd need to make another withdrawal, or perhaps several, from the banking industry soon. With my suit complete, it was high time I finished furnishing this place and do it right.

• • •

By my fourth bank heist in as many weeks, my luck had run out and I didn't count on the bank I'd robbed being cagey enough, or so paranoid, that they'd paid the surrounding businesses to have security systems in them as well as a camera in the vault itself.

Becoming a known quantity was the price of netting my first million dollars. Sadly, when I stopped to think about it, that million wasn't going very far. The power plant for the base, even stolen...I mean secondhand...ate up four hundred grand. The equipment for an actual elevator system chewed away another two hundred, and that was with me, Dee, and Dum doing all the installation, but at least we could now descend in style with two tons of goodies at a time.

Admittedly, I could easily become obsessed in a project and neglect everything else. That trait had served me well over the years, but not without an occasional mishap. Case in point was the three day old email from Leslie I was just now looking at. I was celebrating connecting the base up to the network Wireless Wizard runs for criminals to access the internet. It cost five grand a month, but pretty much guaranteed anonymity, and had porn channels from one hundred and sixteen countries. Or as Bobby liked to say, "Kenya? Hell, yeah!"

Cal,

Where the hell are you? Leonard came by and was looking for you. He said you missed your check in with him and if he doesn't hear from you by tomorrow, he's going to tell the judge that you're a parole violator! You'd better not screw this up for me!

"Shit! Shit! Shit!"

"What's the matter?"

"I missed my parole officer appointment," I answered Bobby. "There's probably a bench warrant out for me already."

"Well, you haven't left this place in probably two weeks," he observed. "Except to rob that bank in Georgia."

I looked at the calendar, a pinup of Aphrodite that Bobby had given me, that was hanging above my workbench and tried to figure out where I'd lost track of the time.

Deciding I didn't have the ability to travel through time, I turned back to Bobby and said, "What am I going to do? Should I try and cut a deal with Lenny?"

"Nah, he lives for this shit. Makes him feel like he's a big man."

It was true. There was no denying that Bobby's cousin was a tool. I considered seeing if Leslie would go out with him, but decided it wasn't worth hearing her bitch.

Taking a deep breath and trying not to think about how I just screwed myself, I said, "Well, no use in crying over it. I'm a wanted man."

"Well, you don't really go out much. I can see if my guy can set you up with a new identity and whatnot, but..."

"It's gonna cost me. I know," I finished for him. Everything seemed to cost me these days. I began to miss the good old days when my biggest problem consisted of trying to get running water in our hideout. Clicking on the terminal, I started searching and cross referencing my name.

"Yeah, but it's not like you're really trying to fit in anymore. You stopped pulling shifts at Floozies. I don't really see what the big deal is."

Bobby was right. I was either working on the base, working on my suit, planning a crime, or committing said crime. In truth, I hadn't showered in three days or slept in thirty-six hours. My internet searches kicked out some results and I found a "Be on the Lookout for" notice on the police blotters for the surrounding three counties with my name.

Damn! Leonard got them to send out a BOLO.

It took only a moment to reach my decision. *Screw parole! Screw Leonard!* "Is your guy still looking for extra muscle?"

"Not for the one you're thinking. That turned out to be Rodentia and as soon as word got out, no one wanted to work that job. That worthless shit never pays up! However, EM Pulsive's looking for some guys. I was gonna sit that one out, but if you're in, I'm game."

Recalling the one time I'd spoken with Edward Michael Pulsive, I knew he was farther up the supervillain ladder and might be able to get me access to people who wouldn't give somebody like Bobby a second thought.

Being a villain—it's not about who you know, but who knows you.

"Yeah, I'm in if the price is right. Any idea what he's planning?"

I held my breath and hoped it was something on the west coast. Since my parole was a bust, it didn't really matter anymore and I could pay Mr. Barton a long overdue visit.

"Nope, not a clue."

"Then I guess we should hear what the man has to say."

• • •

"Mechanical, huh?" EM Pulsive said looking me over in his glowing form. His voice had an odd buzzing sound to it. He circled me, inspecting my suit. We were gathered in an abandoned warehouse in St. Louis auditioning for the job. Bobby was a known quantity, but the villain leading this was hiring his crew and definitely interested in little old me.

"Mechani-CAL, actually," I corrected, trying not to sound irritated.

"How fast can your suit fly?"

"I can hit one eighty unloaded. If I'm carrying up to five hundred pounds I can still hit one hundred. I can't get off the ground at nine hundred pounds."

"What's your range?"

"A little over forty minutes," I answered.

"Are those force blasters? How'd you get ahold of Promethia's designs?"

"I made the originals for Ultraweapon. He has *my* designs."

The man in lightning bolt form nodded. "Fair enough. How much can your shields take?"

"I've emptied two pulse pistols into it and took it down to eighty percent."

"Pulse pistols are toys," he said and I wanted to be offended. "Think you can stop me?"

"Why would I want to fight you?"

"It won't be a fight, but you're asking for top dollar, with only a couple of bank robberies under your belt. Tell you what, stand over there and shield one of my blasts. If you can take it, you get your hundred grand. If you can't, well then maybe you're not ready to run with the big dogs just yet. What do you say there, Mechani-CAL?"

At least he got my name right. My nerves fluttered, but the engineer in me was confident that I could withstand his best. "All right," I said and started walking. Whispering under my breath to my voice activated controls, I said, "Divert weapon power and flight systems to shields."

The bar on my HUD grew as I watched Eddie summon a crackling ball of energy that swelled to the size of a basketball. Dormant lights in the rafters above him flickered, picking up some of what he was giving off, and I started to worry that my calculations might be wrong.

That's probably gonna hurt.

As he tossed it at me, I resisted the urge to dodge or run away. A proximity alarm alerted me to the blatantly obvious and a crude electronic voice said, "Power surge detected."

No shit Sherlock! I thought as I instinctively threw my arms in front of my face. My whole suit vibrated as the electrical storm impacted and washed over me. Even with the shielding, the backlash that bled through and my suit had what could only be termed as a mild seizure.

The sheer power of it knocked me backward about ten or so feet, but I recovered and let out the breath I'd been holding.

"Well, how'd you do?" Eddie's crackling voice laughed.

I checked the display on the inside of my visor and said, "Sixty percent left." I wasn't sure whether to be proud or concerned. My mind began to race and wonder if there was somewhere I could cram another shield generator that I hadn't already thought of and discarded.

"So, that was after you pulled your power away from all your other systems. Not bad, but still kind of weak. Just remember there Tin Soldier, that means you can block two shots from me, but number three gets through and you're a dead man."

"That's why I'm on your side," I replied. "Satisfied?"

"Yeah, I suppose, but don't freeze on me, noob. So, do those blasters actually work?"

He gestured and I obliged, unleashing them on a stack of discarded wooden pallets that had done nothing to me.

"So, do you think I'd stand a chance if I threw down with Ultraweapon?" Since he'd fought against Patterson several times, I figured that he would be in the position to know.

"In that mobile deathtrap? Not a chance in hell!" he exclaimed and started laughing before stopping and saying, "Oh, you were serious? That makes it even funnier."

I thought, *Way to rain on my parade...asshole!*

For a moment, I considered telling him where he could stick his hundred grand, and just leave, when one of the large wooden doors slid aside and Seawall and another person entered.

"Seawall and Rodentia?" Bobby said and spit. "You want us to work with these two losers?"

"Wanna go right now Deliverance Boy?" Seawall answered. "I'm ready for a rematch."

"Shut up! Both of you!" Eddie commanded. "Either of you can walk right now. Since I called this little get together, if you stay you're gonna play nice together, or I'll fry both you miserable jokers." He paused and looked at the waif of a man and said, "S'up rat? I don't recall inviting you."

"Mr. Pulsive," the simpering man said. "I was hoping I could be of use."

"Story of your life," EM Pulsive deadpanned. "But you're here anyway, so how about twenty-five? I could use an extra distraction."

Rodentia was a pathetic specimen. Other than his psionic ability to command rats, he was about as normal as you could get. At five foot three and a hundred fifteen pounds soaking wet a thirty mile per hour gust of wind would be a worthy opponent for him. Gunk's words of warning from back in prison immediately came to mind. On a job, he wore this rubber rat mask. Without it, he didn't even really have any rat-like features.

"I was hoping for a little more," he said.

"Hope in one hand, shit in the other, and see which fills up first," Eddie answered. "That's my only offer."

That made me feel slightly better. Sight unseen, he was willing to give me fifty and I talked him up to a hundred.

At least he's taking me seriously, or at least more seriously than Rodentia.

"Fair enough, twenty-five gets you a top-notch rat horde."

Gunk had a small obsession with Rodentia and unfortunately had to tell me all about him. The rat man worked as a janitor at this one lab where a group of scientists were attempting to reverse engineer Doc Mangler's process. Their first lab rat mutated uncontrollably and went berserk, killing everyone except for the guy who was thin enough to crawl out of a storeroom window with a chunk of flesh missing from his calf before the place went boom. Rodentia's lame assed power developed while he healed.

Now if he'd been bitten by a dog or a bear that would have been useful. Instead, he's a modern day Pied Piper.

"Are you going to need some to help carry away the loot? I've got dozens trained especially for that."

"No," Eddie said, while I wagered that half of the specially trained rodents would deliver their money to their master as opposed to our employer. "There's not going to be anything to carry."

"No loot," Seawall said. "What kind of bank job is this?"

EM Pulsive laughed and switched into his human form. "Only the biggest kind, boys! The Federal Reserve in Kansas City is meeting on the same day that the Fed in New York meets. Everyone says that they're going to lower interest rates. That means everyone is buying stocks and driving the prices higher. We're going to take the fat cats in KC hostage for a few hours and create a little ruckus."

I did the math. Whoever was giving orders to Eddie probably had a legion of short sellers lined up to take advantage of any sudden market volatility.

"I don't get it," Bobby said.

"Don't worry, Bobby," I said while Pulsive rolled his eyes. "There's a bunch of people betting on the stock market to go down on the day when the Fed meets. They'll make money when it drops and we're going to make certain it does."

"That's right! Listen to the man in the metal suit. Why rip off one bank when you can rip off dozens at the same time."

"I still don't get it, but as long as your money is good, I don't really care." Bobby's summation was everything I'd expected it to be.

"So, who's cutting your check?" Seawall asked.

"That's for me to know and you to never find out," he answered. "Let's just say that if any of you screw this up, you'll have a hard time finding work on either side of the Mississippi. Got it?"

I'd already lived that life on the other side of the law, so I got it. The other three nodded even if they didn't.

Satisfied, Eddie continued, "All right. Now all we have to do is hold onto these fat cats for five or six hours and make a few over the top demands and threaten to send a body out every hour or so and then we skedaddle. Can't have any of those fat cats getting hurt, we want the market to come back. It's that buy low and sell high crap."

"That's it?" Seawall said. "How're we supposed to get out? They'll have the place surrounded."

"Rodentia can be a couple of miles away, so he doesn't even need to be in the building. I'm going out through the power grid. As for the rest of you," he paused and pointed at me. "Mechoman there can fly and carry up to nine hundred pounds. I suggest you catch a ride with him."

• • •

"Here's what we know, three hours ago, a group of supervillains, apparently led by Seawall seized the Federal Reserve Building in downtown Kansas City. The Board was in session and in a conference with the New York Federal Reserve when they were taken hostage. Most of the building has been evacuated, but the board members remain

on the upper floors as prisoners. We've had reports of hundreds of rats terrorizing the people fleeing the structure. That indicates the presence of the villain, Rodentia. A third villain, who goes by the name Big Ripper is also inside. Big Ripper is widely believed to be an alias of Hillbilly Bobby. Also, the mysterious armored criminal who has been involved in a number of bank robberies in the southeast is rumored to be inside. We don't have a name for him yet, though his identity is believed to be Calvin Stringel, who formerly went by Manacles. At this point their list of demands includes one million dollars for each of the board members, a mint or at least very good condition Honus Wagner baseball card, a lime green Ferrari Testarossa, and, most baffling of all, that Milli Vanilli's Best New Artist Grammy be reinstated."

Listening to the news report, I smiled. The last one was my idea. It was the most outrageous demand I could come up with. EM Pulsive had snuck inside and was staying out of sight. He was letting Seawall do all the talking. Part of me was worried that he was setting us up.

I found him hovering by an internet terminal, "How's the DOW?"

"Off by two hundred points, it's working, but we need about fifty more points. I think it's time we wired them up. At two thirty the New Yorkers are supposed to announce the interest rates. Right before that is when we toss the dummy out of the window."

Modeling clay, food coloring, and baling wire make for some pretty convincing looking C4, if you don't transmit a high resolution picture. I'd just as soon use the real stuff, but Eddie was adamant about not harming any of these bigwigs. That, naturally, led me to wonder if one or more of them were actually in collusion with the man I was speaking with.

Bankers as villains? Who'd have ever thought?

"Do you know Victoria Wheymeyer?"

Eddie looked up from his screen and nodded. "If you're somebody, then Vicky knows who you are, why're you asking, Mechani-CAL?"

"I heard if you get in good with her, you'll never want for steady work," I said quoting what the Gardener had told me. "I like steady work."

"Well, if this is successful and you keep trending upward, I'm sure she might get in touch with you at some point. Word to the wise though, don't go looking for her, wait until she sends for you. Now, get back in there and keep an eye on Bobby and make sure Seawall is getting the dummy ready."

I acknowledged his instructions, went back to the hostages, and looked for the person who appeared to be the least worried, just to satisfy my own curiosity, and to make certain I knew who to grab as a hostage if this deal went south. Bobby took the opportunity to take a bathroom break. Staring at the collection of cell phones and other assorted gadgetry, I picked the nearest one up and jacked into it initiating a copy program and watched their faces while I did it.

"I wonder how many of you have lists of your passwords inside of these. I bet at least one of you does. If I'm lucky, there might even be some juicy text messages or maybe a picture or two that should never see the light of day. Seriously? You have one click access to your bank account enabled. Sounds to me like someone is about to make a substantial charitable donation! I'll give you all a chance to vote on the recipient of this magnanimous gift. It'll give us something to do while we wait."

The board members couldn't see which device I was holding and I could see the concern on their faces while I listed off my nominations and called for a vote. The top vote getter immediately received a fifty thousand dollar donation courtesy of someone who didn't even bother to password protect their phone.

I was feeling generous, so the charity in second place scored twenty-five large while we all took a "pause for the cause."

The second device was also unlocked and had access to online auction websites. I enjoyed using the instant buying features on this one immensely. In addition to sex toys, porn videos and a crate full of three hundred pairs of red galoshes, the biggest ticket item I could come across was a fan group selling their replica of the *Ghostbusters* Ecto-One vehicle. It had relatively low mileage and, even though it was against my better judgment, it would make a sweet ride to work for the lucky winner, and immediately deleted the confirmation emails so someone would be in for a surprise.

After all, these fine folks enjoy abusing other people's money; it's high time someone abused theirs.

By the time Bobby came back, with a swagger in his step that made me wonder if he bothered to flush, I had a virtual treasure trove of information that I could mine later for useful data. Since this was a fixed price job, anything I could get extra would be my own little bonus. *Fortune favors the brave and all that carpe diem shit.*

Over in the next office, Seawall was prepping the dummy. It looked pretty realistic and would leave a fairly convincing blood smear on the pavement.

"Is it ready yet? Eddie wants it ready to go just before two thirty."

"Almost, you all could've had the bumpkin doing this while I was downstairs."

"Nah, Bobby isn't good with this kind of thing. I could, but I'd have to get out of my suit and Eddie's signing our checks."

"You outta drop that loser you're running with," he said. "That suit would give you some pull down in New Orleans and Texas. The Gulf Coasters aren't as good as they think they are, and there are a lot of opportunities down there."

"I'm still working out the kinks," I replied, ignoring the slight to my friend and trying to hold my tongue. "Besides, it's easier to keep my suit running when I'm not looking for fights."

"So, what you're saying is you're a chickenshit! Guess I was wrong about you."

That was all my tongue needed to get the better of me. "Seriously? How is it you've managed to stay out of jail so long when you're such a clueless moron?"

His invulnerability would probably protect him if I tossed him out the window instead of the dummy. It was...tempting.

"Because I'm not a loser like you, Stringel. That's your name, isn't it? Forget I mentioned New Orleans, small time, you ain't ready for it."

"Instead of insulting me, you should be thinking about how much ass kissing you'll need to do when we leave. Unless you've got some other way out of here, that is."

• • •

Our requisite *financial correction* happened shortly after the dummy splattered and the markets had been sufficiently manipulated for one day, so we decided to get the hell out of Dodge...or Kansas City, in this case.

We set of a series of smoke bombs and Rodentia directed his rat horde to charge the mass of police and national guardsmen at the barricades. That was our cue to blow out a window and take to the air, with Bobby and D'wan clinging to me, and head due north toward the Missouri River.

"Get me to the boat I have under the bridge," Seawall shouted. Members of his biker gang had a fishing boat waiting for him under the I-29 Bridge.

We had a decent head start on those choppers flying over the scene with all the commotion, but loaded down with these two I had no chance of outrunning them, so I'd need to lighten the load a little. Two hundred and seventy-five pounds of jackass was about right.

Zipping under the bridge I hovered for a moment and nodded to Seawall. As he started to let go, I swung my arm slightly and instead of landing on the deck, he went into the drink. He came up sputtering and pissed, which suited me just fine as his men scrambled to help him in.

"That's for calling me small time, Seawall!"

It was probably petty of me, but, if we're being honest, Rodentia bugs me less than Seawall and that says a lot.

We flew down the length of the boat and away from Seawall's thugs before they were tempted to start shooting at us. I made certain Bobby had the breathing mask on and jacked the line into my environmental system. My escape plan also involved the Missouri River and a bit of high speed snorkeling. From high up the only thing visible would be our wake and that would end as soon as we caught up to a barge we could clamp on for a short period of time.

Boat-hiking west, the two of us stayed out of sight for a little over thirty minutes, and broke away at the coordinates where we'd stashed our van with Michigan plates. Sneaking up to some rich dude's private dock, Bobby led me to where the van was waiting for us. I clambered in and sat down while he grabbed a towel and dried off before getting into the driver's seat.

"Sure you want to go to California?" Bobby asked.

"When they lost track of us, they'll probably assume you and I are headed back to Alabama. We'll head west and then circle back later. Besides, I want to pay a visit to my good friend F. Randall Barton."

Chapter Nine

Stops on the Cal Stringel Revenge Tour

The houses overlooking the Pacific Ocean were a testament to the excesses in life. The communities, dominated by the rich and famous, mocked those who were beneath them. F. Randall Barton had reached that pinnacle of existence and climbed pretty far up the summit of Mount Success.

Part of his journey had included deliberately going out of his way to destroy my life. Between his machinations and my own shitty decisions, I'd been kicked into a hole which I'd only recently climbed out from. Nietzsche said, "That which does not kill us makes us stronger." I knew I wasn't strong enough to go after Ultraweapon just yet, if ever, but that didn't mean I couldn't topple the man who'd engineered my downfall with Lazarus Patterson's approval, tacit or otherwise.

On the way out west, I'd been pleased to see that I was a trending topic on the Internet. There was rampant speculation that I had planned the attack and had used the money I'd stolen as investment capital. That was different; people were overestimating me for a change. It made me admire Eddy's decision to stay out of the limelight and pull the strings. The suspicious side of me that had been nurtured in prison led me to believe that Eddy was out there encouraging the idea that I'd been behind it all.

If the roles were reversed, it's what I would do.

While on the topic of prison, I considered sending a letter to my therapist and seeing if he would approve of my personal growth decisions. Before moving forward with my life, I was going to confront the problems of my past head on. Well, it was more like taking my inner demons out for a night on the town. Something told me that this wasn't exactly what he'd had in mind, but the world was an imperfect place. Still, being on east coast time, I sat around and waited for Barton's son to drive off to high school in his expensive "look what pappy bought for me" mustang. Thermals showed one male and one female still in the house. Considering what they doing and that he was a divorced man, I figured this must be the much younger, much prettier girlfriend.

Taking to the sky, I landed on his balcony and felt it creak under the weight of the suit. The naked, redheaded woman, not much older than the man's son, screamed, jumped off, and clutched at the sheets to cover her body.

Barton has good taste, I thought as the man dragged on a pair of boxers and walked toward me. *He must think I'm Patterson! That's a laugh.*

"Mr. Patterson," he began. "Is that one of your older suits? I haven't seen that one before. Taking it out for a spin, I see. Is there something urgent at the office, or is this a social visit?"

"Social," I said, deciding to play along. "How are things?"

"Fine, fine," he said.

"Grab on," I commanded. "This discussion needs to be held in private."

"You don't have to worry about Miranda. She's harmless and knows better."

"Just grab on," I said, and tried to sound annoyed. Come to think of it, it wasn't such an act on my part.

"Okay," he replied slowly, and I took off. There was a beach far below and I saw a rocky outcropping jutting out maybe two hundred and fifty yards offshore. We landed over there and I set him down and looked at the water splashing up against the rocks of this tiny little spit of land.

"May I ask what this is about, sir?"

"Do you remember Cal Stringel?"

Part of me was actually worried that I was such an insignificant gnat that he wouldn't. At a minimum, I always strove to be a memorable gnat.

"Yes," Barton replied. "Last I'd heard, he'd been effectively marginalized and was working at some titty bar in Alabama, but as you know, I've been out of contact with the office. Why do you bring it up? Is there a problem?"

"Do you consider that project to be a success?"

I could see the man making calculations. "Only two people have left your team since we implemented that strategy, and one was understandable, so yes I would consider it a success."

He's proud of it, at least. Wonder what happened to the one who was allowed to leave.

"Do you ever think the tactic might lead to problems down the road?"

"I doubt it, sir. At least as far as Stringel is concerned. He poses no threat to our organization, unless there is something you know that I don't."

Actually, there are several things I know that you don't.

"Maybe not to the organization, but to you, personally," I said, wanting to gauge his reaction.

He drew himself up and stood as proudly as a slightly out of shape, middle-aged man in boxers could and said, "Don't worry about me, Lazarus. I eat chumps like Stringel for breakfast, but if you feel like he is a credible threat and see fit to supply security, I won't make a fuss."

"Actually, I think you need to be worried," I said and popped the mirrored metal mask on my helmet. "I think you need to be very worried."

"Stringel!"

He did suddenly look very concerned and that made me very happy. "What are you doing here?"

"I wanted to come by in person and thank you, Mr. Barton. Without your interference, I never would have made my own armor. I probably would have just invented things for Ubertex until I felt I could move on to my next payday. Did you know that in the past month I've made over a million dollars and I owe it all to you."

"I apologize, but I've been on vacation recently, so I haven't had a chance to keep up with your comings and goings. Rest assured that anything you do to me will be returned on you threefold by Ultraweapon."

Didn't realize that I'd invoked some kind of Shakespearean curse. "Yes, I can see the good time you've been having," I said. "I'm here to pay you back, personally, for all the growth you've helped me with. Stay right here and don't move, if you want to live to see the sunset. Or move, and that will just make my day a whole lot easier."

Closing my visor, I flew back to his house. Miranda had pulled on some clothes, which was a shame. I was waffling between actress or model, but either one seemed to fit her.

"Where's Randall?"

"He's safe, but you need to leave," I said. "There's a good chance that a supervillain could attack this house at any minute."

An extremely good one, I thought. *Almost a certainty at this point.*

To twist the knife a little more, I said, "In fact, there may even be a price on his head, so you may not want to be seen with him for some time to come."

"Is he still going to introduce me to his director friends?"

"Miss, I hate to be the one to break this to you, but he doesn't have any director friends."

"That sonnuvabitch! Now I hope someone does destroy his house!" She stalked away and a minute later I heard the slamming of the door.

Your wish is my command.

• • •

Not wanting to waste much time trashing his house, I took his laptop, identity card, and desktop, ripped his safe out of the wall and set all that at the end of the driveway along with a couple of items from Barton's garage. His Porsche roadster went over the cliff first and then I flew around and cranked up the force blasters to maximum. There were probably plenty of other things I could have pilfered from the place, but this wasn't a money making trip.

It took more effort than I thought and half my available power, but I carved a trench in the side of the cliff. A slow rumbling built as first his endless pool emptied itself onto the beach below and then the whole structure began to slip over the side.

"Looks like the land value here has plummeted recently," I observed, returning to the man, holding a life jacket from his kayak and his Harley-Davidson FX Super Glide. The motorcycle looked to be a well maintained, highly collectible 1971 version. It was a sweet ride and what I was about to do, to me at least, was more criminal than destroying the man's house.

"You can have one," I said. "Choose wisely."

The look on his face told me I'd struck a nerve. "This thing's a little heavy, so I can't stay here all day."

"I'll take the vest," the words squeezed out of his mouth painfully.

I dropped the bike into the water and tossed him the vest. "Smart man. It's a pretty long swim back and the water temp isn't doing you any favors. Maybe you can just wait here and see if you can flag down someone walking along the private beach. Might be a long wait, though, but I'll be pulling for you. Now, I'm sure if you make it out of this, you'll go crying to Ultraweapon. Make sure to tell him that I'll get to him one of these days, but if he comes looking, then I might have to make a habit of hitting his business interests. That's the problem with being all over the place, so many things to protect."

"You'll get yours in the end, Stringel," he said, making an empty threat.

"It's Mechani-CAL to you, Francis. Plus, you can count on me coming around every now and again to kick over whatever anthill you call home. I'm guessing after the first couple of times, you'll have a hard time getting any kind of insurance and the nice thing is, I can show up any old time and drop in on you. You made a game out of destroying my life, now I'm going to make a game out of doing it to you. See you around Francis. Enjoy your swim."

Flying away, I stopped to pick up the goods I'd taken. The contents of his safe might be interesting as well as the things he keeps on his computer. Twenty miles inland, Bobby was waiting for me and gorging on In and Out burgers. I wouldn't mind a bite to eat either; my appetite for revenge had been sated for the moment, but I'd be hungry again by my next stop in Biloxi. Ultraweapon might come looking for me but, more likely, he'd waste assets protecting his branch offices and his turd of a vice president.

Bobby warned me that I shouldn't go looking to fight any superheroes and I'd done my level best to stick to his advice, but for the Biloxi Bugler I'd make an exception.

• • •

The armor itself was a little uncomfortable to sleep in, but I managed. Bobby would drive several hours and then stop at whatever hotel caught his eye and pull in to get some rest. I'd just wait in the van.

"Cal, are you going to take the armor off eventually? It's been a couple of days now."

"Not until we're back at our base," I said. "And not when I'm so close to taking my revenge!"

"Don't you think that's a little...odd?"

"Don't judge me! Besides I'm making sure I'm ready to fight The Bugler."

"You need a lot of planning for that? He's kind of a has-been."

"Bobby, he beat me once," I said. "I don't want that to happen again."

"I could probably knock him around a bit, if you want. We fought a long time ago. I took him then; I could take him now, especially since he looks more like the Biloxi Blob. The guy has really let himself go to shit, but hey, don't let me get in the way of your vendetta."

Maybe it was a touch of megalomania, or that I was feeling good about getting back at Barton; either way I didn't really care. Today was "Biloxi Appreciates Our Bugler day" and I wanted it to be one he wouldn't forget.

Ignoring Bobby's jibes, I tuned into the local coverage. Naturally, there was a parade and people lining the streets of the city waving plastic bugles.

There he was, sitting on a float with his uniform on and a big sash that said Grand Marshal on it.

"All right, Bobby, I'm going to go and get him," I said.

"Have fun, I guess," he said, clearly not approving. It was tempting to throw his grudge against Seawall in his face, and call him a hypocrite, but I wasn't sure he'd understand the word.

I took to the air and started flying. Today was about exorcising demons. Bobby couldn't get it. Streaking over the parade route, I saw people pointing up in the sky at me. They were cheering and thought it was some kind of special surprise, which in a way, it was.

Pulling ahead of the main float, of course it was a bugle, I turned and hovered. Beauregard Carr, also known as The Biloxi Bugler looked at me sideways and held his bugle at the ready. He moved next to his motorcycle, painted to look like the state flag of Mississippi. Carr had taken enough flak over the years for his cape looking like the Confederate flag, and had changed it out in favor of a simple gray one, but he never budged on the motorcycle. It was somewhat commendable.

I pointed at him and kicked on my loudspeakers, "I'm Mechani-Cal and I'm here for my revenge on you, Bugler."

What Bobby said was true; time hadn't done Mr. Carr any favors. Several cops on motorcycles pulled up and the parade drew to a halt.

"If that's really you, Calvin Stringel, then, I guess there's no talkin' you out of this," the man answered in his southern drawl, seemingly not nervous. "I'll fight you, but let's not do it here—too many innocent people around. I don't mind endangering myself, but no sense in anyone else getting hurt."

"Fine by me," I replied.

He mounted his crotch rocket, which sagged under his girth, and said, "Follow me."

The crowd cheered him as he started the bike and a few even chucked stuff at me as I trailed behind him. It got me wondering if my bright idea to humiliate him on "his day" was such a great idea. It wasn't playing out nearly how I thought it would.

He pulled into the parking lot at an abandoned factory and hopped off the bike. As I touched down, the first blast of concentrated sonic waves smacked against my shields.

Fatman isn't so slow on the draw, I thought as another burst hit me. My shields were holding nicely, but I had to admit he was good and didn't use any kind of targeting system that I could see.

"My turn," I said, giving him a shot of low intensity force blasters that sent him spinning sideways. I thought the bugle would go flying, but he seemed to have some kind of tether on it that kept it close.

He jerked it back to his hands and fired twice more and I noted that his best efforts had so far knocked only eight percent off of my shields.

The Bugler dodged my next blast and I was impressed that he could still move that well for his size.

Instead of trading energy blasts with him, I started walking toward him and right through his bursts. He tried to back away, but I was too quick and grabbed his arm. He screamed and I realized that I'd put a little too much effort into it and had broken his arm. He fought through the pain and managed to flip his bugle into his off hand and let me have it point blank. Even my shields and ear protection couldn't stop that from getting through and ringing my bell.

Somewhere in that, I let go of him and he staggered from me trying to keep up his sonic assault. I threw my hand out and dialed up a higher level force blast that hit him like a sledgehammer. *Maybe too much,* I thought and stumbled over to him.

He was still alive and clutching his chest. The Bugler tried to raise his instrument, but didn't have enough breath to blow it.

Sputtering some blood from the corner of his mouth, he looked at me and wheezed, "You can break me, but you can never truly defeat me."

"You look pretty defeated to me," I said. "The ribs? Are they broken?"

He nodded and I continued, "Since I can't put you in prison, I'll settle for putting you in the hospital."

"Does that make you happy? Do you feel like a bigger man?"

"No, I suppose not. I had it all in my head where I beat you and snap your bugle in two."

He looked at his invention and said, "I'm in no position to stop you. Can't even take a deep breath right now."

Looking down at his weapon, I appreciated the craftsmanship he'd put into it. "Nah, you'll need it for the next time we tussle."

I doubted there'd be a next time. This was a bad idea from the start. I was just a little too obsessed to see it.

He managed a painful smile and said, "I'm a little old to be picking up an archenemy, Mr. Stringel. Then again, I might come up with a better version that'll crack your armor open like a can of tuna."

The emergency sirens were getting close and I lingered just long enough to see the first of them pulling into the parking lot before I turned back to Beau Carr and said, "I'll stay out of Biloxi as long as you're out of commission. Plenty of other places around here."

"Evil never truly prospers, Calvin Stringel. It might seem like it does for a short time, but it never wins."

His pithy expression had no real effect on me; I shrugged and activated my jetpack. The Bugler had humiliated me years ago and I'd returned the favor today. This wasn't like Barton, who'd kept after me. As far as I was concerned, the scales were balanced.

Revenge might be a dish best served cold, but sometimes cold revenge leaves a bad aftertaste in the mouth.

• • •

The fallout from my *Bugler Beatdown* had the Gulf Coasters putting me on their most wanted list—at number seven. Then again, considering half their payroll was coming from Lazarus Patterson, it might be due to Promethia's influence.

I was relaxing in Central Command and considering what kind of surface defenses our base needed when I received an email, courtesy of the Wireless Wizard's bootleg internet. Sadly, even a supervillain isn't immune from getting spam...or sending it, in the case of my weapons designing career.

Mr. Stringel,

A mutual friend of ours, who tells the most shocking jokes, said you'd be interested in meeting me. I will be in Branson this week and would like to meet with you to discuss a potential business opportunity. Please respond at the below location if you are interested.

V

The reference to EM Pulsive was obvious. Suspicion was almost second nature now, but I followed the link anyway. It was to a book discussion forum started by someone who went by the moniker *Heinlein_FanGurl.* The poster would have a little discussion on which book of Heinlein's she was reading at the time along with other tidbits like vacation plans, places to eat, and so forth. I studied the posts and tried to determine if this was the elusive Victoria Wheymeyer. If so, then the others must be various criminals she was arranging meetings with. I'd ponder it later. For now, I went to the last post.

Can't wait for my trip to Branson next week. I'm thinking of bringing along either The Moon is a Harsh Mistress, or Starship Troopers (cuz you know how much I loves me some powered armor). Which do you think I should take?

It was open for guest posting, so I replied.

Speaking as a fellow Roughneck enthusiast, I say go with Starship Troopers. Powered Armor beats moon rebels every time. I've been thinking of visiting that city as well and seeing the sights. I hope your trip is everything you hope for.

Thirty minutes later the reply arrived via my email.

Mr. Stringel,

Thank you for taking me up on my offer. The address below is the estate where I will be. It is in a rather remote area and your best approach is from the south. Please do bring your suit. I would like to see it for myself. Also, bring suitable attire for dining.

Looking forward to meeting you,

V

"Almost sounds like a date," Bobby said when I told him about it.

"Damn!" I exclaimed. "I left the two nice jackets I owned at Leslie's. Think I should knock over a men's clothing store? Nah, stupid question. Guess I need to go clothes shopping anyway."

Somehow, I didn't think my collection of jeans, sweatpants, and the like would really impress her.

• • •

The first thing I noticed, approaching the estate, was the massive pool. It was the kind that you could invite fifty of your friends to and have a rousing game of Marco Polo in. Instead of the slides, they might as well just put a dock in it. The main building was a three story affair with the garage looking like an additional house had been slapped onto the slide. Slightly to the east was a stable and riding trails, according to the satellite maps I'd studied. Still, it was one thing to see the place on a screen and another to see it sprawling out in front of you.

My hole in the ground seemed somewhat inadequate by comparison.

I spotted the two security guards first. The woman in the large hot tub didn't immediately register, but she saw me, set down the book she was reading, and climbed out. Considering that she wasn't startled by a man in powered armor landing a short distance away, I figured I'd found Ms. Wheymeyer. She was a brunette, five eight-ish and in a blue bathing suit. Vicky wasn't ugly, but she wasn't exactly smoking hot either. *Somewhere in the middle,* I supposed.

"Isn't it a little early for the hot tub?" I asked.

Victoria scrunched her nose and shook her head. "It's never too early for a hot tub, Mr. Stringel. I like to catch the sunrise in it. So, this is your armor. Let me see it."

I set my bag down containing my clothes and allowed her to circle around me.

"Very nice," she concluded after a minute. "You wouldn't believe how many people set out to build their own set of armor and quit when they figure out how difficult it is. It's refreshing to see a person willing to put in the necessary work."

"Do you like it?" I asked. "Are you really a powersuit fangirl?"

"You bet your ass I am! I can see a lot of early Ultraweapon in your design. Not surprising since you once worked for him. Did you steal the specs yourself?"

"No, I got them from Max V. Did the rest from memory."

"You must have a good memory," she said.

"It's not photographic, but it's pretty close," I replied.

"Well, let's go inside and have some breakfast. There's a changing room over there where you can leave your armor," she said and walked back to retrieve the novel she'd been reading. I figured it would be Heinlein's classic, but was surprised to see a grocery store romance novel.

"I thought you'd be reading *Starship Troopers*," I said. My guesstimate said that she was in her mid-thirties, which put her a couple of years older than me.

"I have that pretty much memorized by now. This just passes the time," she said.

As Victoria turned, I saw a pair of dice tattooed on her right shoulder, with a four and a three facing out, and it struck a chord in my memory. Combined with the way she leaned over to grab the book, it suddenly clicked. "Wait a minute! I've seen you before."

"Really? Where?"

"It was a picture, sent to my cellmate. I'm guessing you know The Gardener. I remember the dice, but you had several more tattoos."

She also had considerably less clothes on, but that was another matter altogether.

"Oh, that," she said and laughed, somewhat nervously. "Body painting, but I've had my lucky dice for years now. Your memory is very impressive to remember a picture from roughly eighteen months ago."

"It was a nice picture," I blurted out and felt immediately embarrassed, thankful she couldn't see my face.

The lady actually blushed. "You're too kind."

My mind tried to picture her and Kenneth as a couple and it wasn't working. That's when the other shoe fell. She was either the evil genius behind the mass escape or worked for the evil genius behind the mass escape.

"Something wrong, dear?"

"Just putting puzzle pieces together in my mind. Say, didn't that prison break happen shortly after Kenneth received that picture?"

She smiled and wagged a finger to me, "Now, now, we're not here to discuss old news. Go change and let's talk about what you can do for me."

Victoria had a brash confidence to her; and that had me getting out of my suit as quickly as possible, which still took about ten minutes—something I'd have to improve on in the next version.

• • •

"Cleaned up, I see," she said while nibbling on a strawberry. "Please, sit. Do you like blueberries in your pancakes?"

"They're okay," I replied, taking the chair across from her and spearing a pair of flapjacks with a fork. "I'm really more of a chocolate chip kinda guy. So, if you don't mind me being blunt, what exactly do you do and who do you do it for?"

"I guess the closest thing to a job description I have is I'm one part personal shopper and another part event planner. Big events, usually. As to the person I work for, let's not get into that right now."

It probably meant either General Devious or the Evil Overlord. Since Maxine was freed during that breakout, I was leaning toward the former.

She drank a glass of milk and reached for a bag. My appetite disappeared when she pulled out a pulse pistol. Fortunately, she set it on the table and it was safe to continue eating. "Do you recognize this?"

I picked it up. It was one of a set of three that I sold two months ago and not one of the ones that Max V had been using. "Of course, I built it."

"Yes, you did. Of the three I bought, one was broken down by our group of engineers, the other was given to the head of development, and the third is in your hand. The engineering group was suitably impressed by your design."

I smiled and thought, *As well they should be*. "What did your head of development say?"

"He said it was crude, uninspired, but functional."

When I frowned, she said, "Coming from him, that's actually a compliment."

Oh, really! "What do you think?"

She held her hand out and I returned it to her. "I think I like it. This one I'm keeping."

"The grip's a little oversized," I said. "I'll measure your hand before I leave and get you a custom one for it."

"Well, aren't you the sweetest thing?"

"That's usually not something people say to me," I confessed.

"You should hang out with better people then, Calvin."

"Maybe. So, you have an engineering team, and a head of development. Why do you need me?"

115

"Our head is a very busy man and he keeps getting redirected to various tasks. Since he and our engineers are, shall we say, occupied at the moment, I've been authorized to do some outsourcing to complete several initiatives that have fallen by the wayside."

"Such as?"

"This," Victoria said and reached into her bag handing me some schematics.

I unfurled them and studied the design. It was for a next generation pulse cannon, too heavy for a regular human to use. That meant either a synthmuscle suit mount or robot platform. Still, there were several problems that jumped out at me.

"It's nice, but it won't work," I said after a minute.

"We already know that. We need you to make one that does work. Actually, we need you to make about two hundred that work."

"Two hundred?" I'm sure my eyes were bulging. *Holy Shit!*

"Well, that's our pilot program. We can negotiate more down the line. It's a refit program for some of our older Type A robots, to bring them up to the cutting edge, or at least this decade. Promethia is sticking with their plasma weapons and stunners for now, but after seeing your work, our head of development dusted off this half-finished design and is giving it to you to work. He believes you might actually have the wherewithal to complete it and deliver a functional weapon."

I caught the reference to *some* in her words. If they have more than two hundred robots, they basically have an army. Now, I was leaning more toward the Overlord instead of Devious. He had more robots.

"How many times does it need to fire?" I asked, trying to gauge their requirements.

"As many as possible, but no less than eight," she answered.

Concentrating, I knew the expense of outfitting each one with a B powercell would be cost prohibitive, so that was out. However, if I used two of my power compressors daisy-chained together with one or two A cells there to keep them from losing charge, it might work. Sure, they'd have to be charged externally, but if expense is a problem, there has to be some give and take.

"Look at you!" Victoria said, pointing at me with her fork. "Already working on the problem. You're such a geek!"

"Funny," I deadpanned. "When do you need it?"

"How soon can you make the prototype?"

"Twelve weeks," I replied.

My hostess smiled and said, "I'll give you ten."

"Rush jobs mean a twenty percent markup," I countered.

"Oh, if I'm paying for a rush job, you'll be done in eight and I'm only paying that ridiculous markup on the prototype. I won't pay any more than a ten percent markup on the production run."

This wasn't like haggling with Maxine, where my life was being threatened. Victoria was smiling and having a grand old time. So I said, "You know you can pay fifteen."

"Just like you know you can accept ten."

"But that cuts into my bank robbing time," I explained. "That's easy money."

"Until the feds sic a super team on your ass, then that well is going to dry up pretty quickly and this offer may not be around then. From what I've heard, the Gulf Coasters are already rooting around like pigs looking for truffles. How about we meet in the middle at twelve?"

I scratched my chin, enjoying the mental image of the Gulf Coast Porkers, and said, "The middle would be twelve and a half, but I'll take it if I can call you Vicky."

She almost choked on her pancake from laughing too hard before struggling to say, "I only let my friends call me that, but you drive a hard bargain. Twelve, you get to call me Vicky and I get to call you Cal...plus, you have to let me try out your armor."

What? She's going there! "Seriously? You want to test drive my armor?"

"But we're friends now, Cal," Victoria whined. "Besides, I know you'll rig it with a kill switch. C'mon, what do you say?"

"I wouldn't let my family into my armor, Vicky. I'm going to have to say no."

She shook her head and offered, "Say 'maybe' instead, and we'll negotiate it at a later time."

"Fine, maybe," I said.

"Then, it's settled. Now, would you like to catch a show with me this evening? I always try to take in the sights when I'm out this way. It's not Vegas, but it has a certain charm just the same."

"Maybe," I said with a grin. "I do have this hot project I should start on and the new boss is a real..."

"Careful, Cal, I have a rolodex full of hit men and assassins at my disposal."

"...nice lady that I hope to impress." I finished.

"Well played," Vicky said and raised her glass of milk to me.

It was the start of one of the nicest days I've had since before I decided to quit Promethia.

Chapter Ten

A Familiar, Yet Unfamiliar Face

"I could be doing something else, you know?" I said, firing a burst from my force blasters.

The woman known as Eyelash dived behind the protection of the Dynamic Discus. His energy discs blocked most of attack, but some was absorbed, and the lanky man expertly hurled the two psionic constructs filled with my own power right back at me. One missed and the postal box behind me exploded. The other smacked into my shields. He created another set and jammed them onto studs on his wide belt. Smoke filled one and flame the other.

The old, where there's smoke there's fire, routine, I thought and dodged the flames. The smoke impacted the ground between us and hid me from the pair of superhumans for the briefest moment.

Twin whips created by some form of telekinesis cleaved through the smoky barricade snapping out from the woman taking shelter behind "Double D." Instead of just trying to beat on my shields, the cowboy-hat-wearing Gulf Coaster tried to ensnare me this time. Considering my mass and relative strength, it was a bad idea on her part. She was probably just trying to hold me long enough for her boyfriend there to hit me with some of his more potent discs. Then again, Eyelash wasn't necessarily the brightest mind on that team.

One thing is certain; I wasn't going to get the silly string filled ones that he uses when he visits kids at the hospital!

I let her plan happen and immediately triggered a three second burst from my jetpack, essentially jumping backward. My tactic caught her unprepared and dragged her right into the back of the man shielding her. I let out a small chuckle as the two went down in a heap, and sent a heavy taser pulse to keep them down for a couple of minutes.

Turning my attention away from the fallen pair of heroes, I saw She-Dozer and Spirit Staff were giving Bobby a fit, while above, EM Pulsive was duking it out with K-otica in a swirling mass of energy that my sensors told me would be a very bad idea to interrupt.

Eddie knows what he's doing, I thought. *This is his idea anyway. Better help Bobby!*

Spirit Staff was an Oriental monk with some kind of magic, unbreakable staff. He turned aside Bobby's force clubs with an ease that bordered on contempt. The legend around the man's weapon was that it channeled the fighting talents of every warrior who had ever owned it. Though short, and with a slight build, he rained a veritable whirlwind of blows down on my buddy. It wasn't hurting Bobby nearly as much as it was distracting him from his real problem—She-Dozer.

The woman matched his strength and looked like she trained extensively in Mixed Martial Arts. Bobby's training regimen usually involved a case of beer and trying to burp the alphabet. Spirit Staff frustrated Bobby while the Amazon was really taking it to my partner in crime.

She-Dozer was about as invulnerable as my *compadre* and I put aside any reservations about fighting a woman and sent a burst at her. It knocked her about twenty feet away and gave Bobby a breather. The Staff repositioned himself to defend against both of us. I had hopes that my technology would be more than a match for his staff, but my next burst was deflected.

"Power levels at sixty-five percent," the mechanical voice announced. "Shields at seventy-seven percent. Estimated flight time is twenty-six minutes and eight seconds."

I ran through the numbers as Bobby recovered. The police had cordoned off the area, and that was the point. Seawall's gang was launching a crime spree and we'd be clogging up the works and limiting the emergency response. Eddie's plan was simple. The Guardians wanted both him and me and we were happy to oblige, knowing just how the police and the do-gooders would respond. Naturally, we knocked over a bank in the middle of the city. I wouldn't have even come along, but Eddie called in his favor that he'd earned by introducing me to Vicky.

Give Eddie some credit; he likes to rob many places at the same time. Sure he's a bit of a show off and a complete and utter tool, but he dreams big.

The only thing that hadn't gone our way so far was K-otica's unpredictable power level. She could be the most useless enemy you'd ever meet; about as effective as the almost-normal groundskeeper they employed who could make five copies of himself. Other days, you needed to run away from her as fast as humanly possible. Today, we were getting something close to the latter and K was giving EM Pulsive all he could handle and then some. Otherwise, we'd have already steamrolled these clowns. At her weakest, she throws around pretty colored lights like some kind of small scale special effects show. Today, her lights were concussive beams of pure power and she was able to use them to fly.

Truth be told, I was a little worried that she'd beat Eddie or he'd do a runner and I'd be left fighting her. Lining up a shot, I gave Eddie an assist. My full power burst chipped away at my remaining energy, but distracted her long enough for EM Pulsive to give her a full barrage and the Latina with rainbow colored hair plummeted to the ground, but got up just as quickly, looking angry.

Eddie was looking noticeably dimmer and that wasn't a good sign.

I couldn't offer any additional assistance. She-Dozer was back on her feet and charging me. I jumped to the left and fired both my blasters at her. The one that hit spun her around and sent her sprawling to the ground. I was smiling until she leapt up with a manhole cover in her hand and threw the thing at me like a damn Frisbee.

The heavy object broke through my shields and hit so hard that it shattered my chest mounted light and left a big dent in my front armor plating. The warbling Master Alarm activated.

Damn me for underestimating her! She's stronger than my suit and can take as much punishment as she can give.

Bobby continued taking continued abuse from Spirit Staff and we needed to buy at least another five or ten minutes.

"Surrender Stringel and I won't have to rip that armor off of you piece by piece!" Dozer threatened.

"Kiss my boil ridden ass, Dozer!" Technically, I do get an occasional bout of skin irritation when I stay inside the armor too long—another item I'd need to correct in the next design. Perhaps I was sharing too much.

The Gulf Coaster was a much better hand to hand fighter than I would ever be, so I boosted skyward just before she got close to me and sent a burst down on her.

It was slightly stronger than that kiss I'd offered her moments before. Swooping down, I grabbed one of those small metal dumpsters from an alley and lifted it up. I tossed it at Spirit Staff and mentally challenged him to block that.

He dodged instead, but Bobby staggered around and ripped the lid off the dumpster and caught Spirit Staff flatfooted as a result. The next owner of the staff might pick up something useful from that experience, but the present owner would need a few minutes and maybe some medical care to sort things out.

Unfortunately for us, Bobby's attack and the subsequent injury to her bed warmer, sent K-otica over the edge and she took issue with all three of us villains and most anyone still upright on that city block.

"Shields under heavy assault! Sixty three perc...forty-nine percent."

Bobby took a bad hit and the outburst had even winged She-Dozer. I wasn't faring that well either. K-otica, all amped up on power, had a tendency to let that go to her head. In her place, it would probably piss me off too, knowing that you have that much energy inside of you, but only ever get to tap into it when fate smiles favorably in your direction. It would almost be worse than having no superpower at all.

I'd still trade; I thought and tried to get to the unconscious Bobby. Eddie had vanished and I couldn't see him anywhere. *Time to grab and go!*

Another barrage sent me off course and into someone's apartment. I crashed through the bedroom and out into the kitchen on the other side of the wall and found my shields at a measly twenty-one percent.

Not good! Not good!

I stumbled back toward the opening, but saw K-otica now standing on Bobby's limp and bloody form looking back up at me with a half-crazed look on her face. She-Dozer was next to her, trying to calm her down. When the overpowered lunatic caught sight of me, she raised her hands and Dozer had to knock the other woman's arms skyward. The burst of energy went to the heavens and I counted myself lucky for the interference. Maybe Dozer wasn't so bad after all. I froze for a second while the two women struggled. Eyelash was already on her feet and so was Discus. Four against one was shitty odds and I didn't see a way out of it that didn't involve Bobby in custody.

"No!" She-Dozer shouted. "Calm down, Karina! You can't destroy a building. Taiki will be okay!"

As much as it pained me to do it, I turned and ran through the apartment, into the hallway and out the other side of the window, triggering my jetpack. With Eddie gone, and my shields about down to tissue paper, there was no way I could get Bobby. Flying away, I tried to justify it that Bobby was injured and they'd be obligated to take him to a doctor, but I still felt like a failure.

• • •

"I've seen the available news footage, Cal," Vicky said. "It doesn't look like you could've done much more than you did. EM Pulsive was in charge, and left both you and Bobby hanging out to dry."

"Yeah," I agreed with her. I could count the number of people I considered friends on one hand and one of them was in a hospital under armed guard and awaiting transport to the SuperMax.

"Besides, it's like you said, he's still in a coma and it's not like there's a supervillain hospital out there. Most tend to use a private doctor service. I could've gotten you in contact with one, but not on such short notice."

After collecting my slightly larger than expected share of the multiple heists from an apologetic Eddie and telling him my rates would be double on his next job, I made it back to Alabama and stuffed the prototype I was working on and my other important gear in the van and drove to Vicky's estate near Branson, Missouri.

Before leaving I gave two pulse pistols to Tweedledee and put him in guard mode. I started to give Dum one of Bobby's spare forceclubs, but shut him down instead. There was no telling what that deranged robot would do if left alone.

"Thanks for putting me up these past couple of days," I said. She came out for the weekend, but left me all alone there during the week. My armor was repaired and the prototype was nearing completion, right on time.

"I like your level of paranoia, even if it's unwarranted," she answered.

"Just because it's illegal to use telepathic scans on a criminal to learn where his base is, doesn't mean they wouldn't do it on the side and just say that Bobby confessed."

"True," Vicky conceded and passed me a can of cola. "But, Bobby's mind is impenetrable. Whatever gave him his powers, keeps out mind probes."

I was suitably shocked. "You're shitting me! Bobby never told me that!"

"He might not even know," she answered. "Why do you think he gets so many bodyguard gigs? Bobby is strong, but he's not really that powerful when it comes down to it. General Devious checked him herself and she couldn't get in."

"So you're finally admitting you work for her! I knew it!"

Vicky rolled her eye at my dig. "Assuming your pulse cannon prototype works as advertised, you'll get the answer. Until then, keep guessing."

Instead of pressing her on that and not getting an answer—again—I went back to something that bothered me, "So why didn't you tell me that when I contacted you? I could've stayed back at my hideout."

"I figured you needed a place to decompress, plus I'd get a chance to watch the magic happen in person."

"You're just trying to get into my armor," I said, playing one of the only cards I had against her.

"Also true, but it is working. I can tell you're close to caving on that front. It's only a matter of time."

It was my turn to give her an "oh please" look.

"How close are you to finishing?"

My best guess was a week, so I lied. "Ten days."

She grinned and said, "In that case I'll set up the big demo for eight days from now, right after I get out of the hot tub."

• • •

I'd hoped that her employers would have come out east, but instead I rode on a private jet to Nevada and then in a delivery van a hundred miles into the desert. At least I had my armor to keep me occupied.

Using my GPS, I found that the only structures in the area belonged to a ghost town that was abandoned around the start of World War I. To pass the time, I watched imported porn that I'd downloaded and tried to figure out whether I'd correctly guessed which villain bankrolled Vicky. It was a shame that she went ahead instead of hanging out with me. Then again, she probably wouldn't have approved of my viewing choices.

Wow, those girls really put the lay in Malaysia!

The delivery van came to a stop and the back door rolled up revealing armed men in coveralls and several Type A robots, along with three Type B's. I hadn't seen any of the gyroscopic balls in quite some time. None of them had any insignias, which was either a security precaution or Vicky screwing with me—or possibly both.

Definitely the Overlord! No doubt in my mind.

"This way please," one of the men with a plasma rifle strapped across his back said.

I picked up my prototype and hopped out the back of the van. *It might be a dry heat outside, but the air conditioning worked plenty fine in here. Scanner is picking up a live power source straight ahead. I guess that old barn isn't nearly as dilapidated on the inside.*

The guard led me in and there were numerous lab-coat-wearing flunkies running around the well-lit, modern interior. Over at the main table, I spotted Vicky speaking with several of them and enjoying being the center of attention. She was wearing a tight skirt and a blouse that flattered her. *The woman has some really nice legs.*

One of the lab coats directed me to another table with a metal cradle on top. I did as the douchebag instructed and set my prototype down to let the man hook up their instruments to it.

Amateurs! Like I haven't already done all of this.

"Cal, get your butt over here," Vicky yelled. "There's someone I want you to meet."

Since I was in direction following mode, I complied and made my way over to the perky power broker.

The man next to her turned around and I damn near shit myself.

"Joe? Joe Ducie! What the hell? Is this some kind of Promethia trap? Activate shields! Power to weapons!"

I wasn't going out without a fight! I started scanning for Ultraweapon. *Where is he? Where is he?*

I caught the look on Vicky's face; she'd looked like the cat who'd caught the canary a second ago, now she looked horrified.

"Cal! Wait! It's not what you think."

"Shit! I can't believe I fell for your act," I boomed through my speakers and turned my attention to Joe. "You and I go back a ways, Joe, but don't think I won't grease your ass the moment Patterson shows his face."

Joe looked angry and turned to look at Vicky. "You were supposed to brief him!"

There was no hint of an Australian accent in his voice.

Vicky was stammering out an apology and looking suddenly afraid, "I'm sorry, sir. I didn't realize..."

"No, clearly you didn't. I'll deal with you later. Now, Mr. Stringel, be assured there will be no appearance by Ultraweapon today. Please power down your offensive systems. Keep your shields up, if you must while I explain what Ms. Wheymeyer neglected."

"Place weapons on standby," I said loud enough for him hear. "Increase shielding to maximum and bring flight systems online. All right, old buddy, let's talk."

"I'm the clone of Joe Ducie. You may call me Joseph or by my moniker, The Merchant of Death."

The MoD? He's The Overlord's right hand man! Joe? Seriously...Joe? Clone Joe? They Cloned Joe Ducie...sounds like a bad science fiction movie. Weird. Guess I should say something.

The first thing that came to mind was, "Two Joe Ducies running around the world; I'm guessing there's a shortage of scotch somewhere. Shouldn't you have a goatee or something?"

The man cracked a slight grin. "Indeed. We did actually meet once, but I doubt you'd remember."

"We did?" I asked.

"You were just promoted to the weapons team. I dropped by pretending to be the other version of myself and we talked and drank well into the night while you regaled me with the details of Project Force Blaster. Your drink was laced with a short term memory suppression drug."

"You date raped me?"

He laughed. "Mentally, I suppose. Was it good for you? Patterson's team all fell for that one time and time again. Sadly, they finally caught on a couple of months ago when one of the new members had left his web camera on, of all things. Promethia hasn't revealed my existence to the world at large yet, but I'll have to come up with some new tricks at some point."

Thinking back, I remembered the morning after my promotion and the nastiest hangover I'd ever had. It was one of the reasons I never touched scotch again.

"So your boss decided the easiest way to steal Patterson's tech was to copy the man who makes his tech work. That's pretty..."

"Evil?" Joseph said. "It's in his title."

"Nah, I was going to say hardcore. I guess that explains why you figured I could finish your design."

He smiled, "You have some talents. I acquired your force blasters from after your unfortunate capture and was impressed by what you'd built."

That really caught me by surprise. "I thought those were destroyed."

"My people got there first. I see you've utilized two of your compressors in this design to hold the charge rather than relying on powercells."

"Keeps the weight and the price down. For defense, you can just use your power plant to keep them juiced up. I'm averaging nine point seven shots per charge. That's more offense than you spec'd."

"Let's see the damage potential, then."

Joseph went over to the cannon and activated it, checking the output on the weapon. A sheepish looking Vicky walked up next to me and said, "I guess my little joke didn't go over so well. Sorry."

"I'm usually the one with the dick move," I said. "So, I should let it slide. You want me to say something to Joseph?"

"He'll calm down in a bit—especially if your cannon makes a good impression. So, are we good, Cal?" she asked and gave me the sad eyes treatment.

"I guess so," I said.

Glancing up at me, she smiled once more, and said, "Good. Care to explain what you meant by falling for my act?"

I was glad she couldn't see my face behind my visor.

"Not right now," I said, wondering how I could talk my way out of this...without letting her try on my armor.

• • •

"I'm going to need a bigger base," I said to Vicky on the flight back. For the return trip, I was out of the armor and celebrating the windfall on my horizon, almost giddy. The Merchant of Death was suitably impressed by my capacitive pulse cannon and gave the initial production run the green light.

And by green light, I mean the Cal's going to make a ridiculous amount of money light.

"From the sound of it, you do need some place a little more accessible." I had a suspicion that Vicky knew exactly where Bobby's hole in the ground was, but was afraid of her answer.

"Yeah," I agreed. "There's not enough space for storage, assembly and testing."

Vicky refilled her champagne glass and sat down next to me on the couch. Private charter definitely was the way to go.

Grabbing her tablet, she quizzed me on my requirements and asked how much money I had available. All that money wouldn't go very far when it came to outfitting another base.

After she finished peppering me with questions, I had to ask why she was doing this. "Not that I don't appreciate the help, but what's with the sudden interest in my accommodations?"

"Well, I suppose I need to make some kind of gesture to balance out my feeble humor," Vicky offered. "How about I help you track down a good base and the equipment you'll need to set up your production line?"

"What's the catch?" I asked, casting a suspicious glance over at my empty suit of armor. "You really want to play around with my armor don't you?"

"Not today," she said and shifted on the couch. With that being her only warning, she turned and crawled onto my lap, straddling me. She pressed her palms down on my shoulders and looked me straight in the eyes.

"What are you doing?" I asked, throat suddenly dry even though I'd been drinking a beer just a second ago.

"I figured I'd skip past the phase where we kind of tiptoe around each other and keep flirting. Don't get me wrong, flirting with you is a lot of fun, but you wouldn't believe how hectic my week gets, and I want to just skip ahead to some of the other things that're fun too. Don't you Cal?"

"Uh, huh," I babbled. More intelligent conversation had kind of deserted me at the moment. Leslie had been better looking, but Vicky was way more attractive and had the confidence that went deeper than skin deep. She dug me and my armor. Vicky had a wicked sense of humor and brains.

Leaning forward, she kissed me. Her arms moved up to around my head and she worked her fingers through my hair. Though not a virgin by any stretch, I wasn't exactly Mr. Smooth Moves and Casanova; this kind of thing usually didn't happen to me.

Breaking away and smiling somewhat devilishly, she undid her blouse, letting it fall to the side and while I'd seen her show more of her chest in a swimsuit, this blew that image away from my mind. "Don't get me wrong, Cal. I'm still going to get into your armor, but right now, I'm only interested in getting into your pants."

Chapter Eleven

Love and Other Clever Ambushes

A lot can change in six months, especially when there's someone who matters in your life. That was something that hadn't really happened to me before and it was worth savoring.

I stared out at the poorly maintained road leading to my new base and pondered just how much my life had changed and how much that had to do with Vicky. For starters, I wouldn't have even known this place existed. She found this shuttered junkyard and provided me with the fake identity that I needed to buy the place without putting it in someone else's name. My cover identity was the name of one of Heinlein's heroes; her idea as well. My shell company also bought the land Bobby's base was on from that one dancer. I'd come a long way from when I was scraping up rent money for a doublewide the last time I'd lived in Mississippi.

The junkyard was perfect. No one would care if there were vehicles taking stuff to or from a junkyard. No one would be concerned if there was work being performed at all hours of the night. There was raw material everywhere I looked.

It was my version of heaven.

Sure, there were permits to be filed and inspectors to be bribed, even with keeping it shuttered. My often delayed Grand Opening was never going to actually happen. Instead, the basement under the main office had been expanded significantly. The left half of that new area was dominated by the assembly line; a long metal bench. For the operating system of the assembly line and the base, I repurposed Tweedledee and hooked him into a larger computer.

Tweedledum? It was tempting to leave him in the Alabama base, but that was just a recipe for disaster. I'd probably come back to check up on the place and discover a deathtrap waiting for me. Instead, I gave him digging tools and had him start making my escape tunnel for this place. One of the pitfalls to the Alabama lair was only one way in or out. Besides, Dee would keep an eye on him and let me know if he started digging south again. I didn't empty my piggy bank to buy this place only to flood it if he has another of his glitching.

"What're you thinking about?" Vicky asked coming up next to me and sipping on a cup of coffee. She threw an arm across my back and leaned her head against my shoulder.

"I was thinking that I should look for more Type A robots to steal and put them on base construction duty."

"If you really need them, I can get some broken out of storage and have them here next weekend."

"But if I'm just borrowing them, it takes all the fun out of it," I complained.

"It also takes the possibility of a deranged one damaging your base. I saw Tweedledum doing what might have been line dancing downstairs. Besides, you've still got to increase your production if you're going to make your quota. Besides, I like to pull strings and make things happen. It's probably the closest thing to having a superpower a gal can get."

"Slave driver," I accused. "I just don't want to get too used to you snapping your pretty fingers and solving all my problems."

"You know it! Maybe I'll make you start calling me Mistress Victoria."

I cocked an eyebrow at her. "Really? Don't worry; I only work ten hour days when you're around. When you're not here I do sixteens. You'll get your run of pulse cannons."

"So, I only rate six hours of your time," she said, mocking me. "I'm surprised you're not spending more time with your armor. Before we started dating, I had you pegged for one of those *My Precious* types."

"After getting beat, well getting run off, by the Gulf Coasters, I've been assessing the weaknesses of my suit."

"Sounds like someone is thinking about upgrades," she said in a singsong voice.

"No, more along the lines of a complete redesign. I've squeezed about as much performance as I can out of this suit, but I was working with Patterson's earliest specs. My jetpack can't even out run a helicopter if I'm carrying any load."

"Mechani-CAL revision B? Or are you going to call it the Mark II? Can I call dibs on your old armor?"

"Mark II sounds better. After the initial production run of your cannons, I'll begin working on it. Of course, that depends on how long you have to wait for funding for Phase Two of your robo-refit."

"I like Rev B. It just sounds more 'boss'. Some things have come up; it might be a few months. Unfortunately, an evil empire ends up being run like a Fortune 500 business; except the staff meetings can get downright nasty. Let's just say that someone's gigantic screw up has eaten into the budget and he was summarily audited out of this existence," she said. Vicky didn't discuss her work and I didn't press her on it. I figured that if she needs to get something off her chest, Vicky would tell me.

"I suppose I could take a break after the cannons are finished and installed, pull a few last jobs in this suit, and then get started on a new build. I turned down the last job Eddie offered because I'm too busy right now. Refusing too many would be rude."

"True," Vicky commented and gave me a playful look. "Plus, Pulsive has a vindictive streak in him; you'll want to watch out for that in the future. My plane flies out at three, what do you want to do today?"

"Well, I guess if you're calling dibs on my old armor, I should teach you how to pilot it." I'd broken down a month after she and I started dating and let her try on the suit. She was surprisingly clumsy in it, but determined—very determined.

"Really? You're going to actually let me do more than walk around the room in it? Don't tease me, Cal."

"There's an old school bus in the back part of the yard that is so rusted out, it isn't even worth the scrap metal. I was going to tear it to pieces after you left, but if you want to..."

"Can I fire the force blasters?"

I smiled at her eagerness. "If you must."

"Oh, I'm pretty sure I must."

• • •

I usually wore a t-shirt and boxer shorts inside the suit. Vicky's choice of a sports bra and panties seemed better, but I didn't have the figure to pull off the bra.

Thankfully, I'd cleaned out the inside before she came down this weekend. It gets a little funky in there after a few hours. I also removed the...ahem...sanitary attachments that allowed me to take a wiz and a dump in there. She probably wouldn't appreciate the technological equivalent of how the sausage gets made.

"How am I doing?" her digitized voice emanated from the speakers. She was still wobbly and I fought the urge to cringe with every step she took.

"The sensors are still calibrated for me. You're body just isn't shaped like mine; something I'm extremely grateful for."

My comment was probably good for a smile from her behind the visor. Then again, if I had boobs, I probably wouldn't need a girlfriend.

"So you're saying I should slouch more when I walk and maybe scratch my ass every couple of minutes? Will that help?"

"I'll hit the kill switch and put you in time out," I threatened.

"Need I remind you of my rolodex of hitmen and assassins?"

"Won't help you here," I said. "Okay, despite my misgivings, I'm arming the weapons system. Just point your hands at the engine block and say, fire force blasters level two burst."

"Fire force blasters level four burst!"

I jumped aside as twin eighty percent blasts slammed into the front of the rusted bus and sent chunks of metal flying through the air. It wasn't the debris I worried about, sure enough Vicky's balance wasn't good enough to handle the reactionary forces, and she fell over cackling with laughter.

"Did you see that? That was awesome!"

"I should be mad at you," I said standing over her and looking down.

"But you're not," she said and popped open the visor.

I wasn't. She was like a big kid in the suit, with a maniacal grin on her face. With the nearest neighbors a good distance away, they'd probably think I was just shooting a gun or something. If any bothered to come by, I'd tell them an old gas cylinder still had something in it and exploded. The idiots wouldn't know the difference.

"Well, you're getting lots of practice standing up."

"Killjoy," she accused. "I'm not this bad in a Pummeler suit. I'm actually pretty decent. We've got a few around for base defense, but they're too limited for anything else."

"Aw, that's sweet," I replied. "You can ride a tricycle, but can't figure out why you're having problems operating a motorcycle."

She flipped over onto her elbows and knees and said, "My, aren't we full of ourselves today, Mr. Stringel."

"It'll work better when I get all the sensors calibrated to you. When I get my new suit built, you'll be so good that we'll do a powered armor waltz together."

"Do you know how to do a waltz, Cal?"

"I can program it."

"If you're going that route, I want to do a tango instead."

"As Mistress Victoria commands."

"And don't you forget it. Now, go find me more stuff to blow up!"

She ended up catching the late flight back to Vegas and I added the hours on to my work day that I spent having fun with her.

• • •

Stringel,

Don't know if you'd heard, but Seawall finally got his dumb ass caught by the Gulf Coasties last week. I'm low on good help and could really use you on this job. Don't leave me hanging, bro!

Eddie

I looked at the email and wondered if I could slip it in my spam folder and say I never saw it. Unfortunately, I'd heard that the Wireless Wizard ran a tight mail service and would be able to tell Eddie that his email was read.

Eddie,

I'm almost done with my project for that lady I asked you about. If you can push it back a week, I can do it. Otherwise, I'd be taking a chance on pissing off someone higher up on the food chain, if you catch my drift.

Cal

Outside, there was driving rain as a hurricane moved into the area. It had foiled Vicky's plans to come out and hang with her "boy toy," as she so aptly referred to me. Powering down my secret base as a precaution, I didn't much feel like sitting in the dark and assembling another set of pulse cannons. Instead, I was slapping an extra fuel tank onto the armor to extend my range. The oil companies had evacuated the humans manning the rigs out in the path of the storm. That meant it was time for me to go shopping. I figured it was cool because it's okay to hate Big Oil. There was some nice tech out there and nothing except a few guard bots watching them, if that.

Some politician somewhere said to never let a good crisis go to waste. Being short on liquid assets, I decided to cut out someone else's markup when buying stolen equipment and just go get the damn things myself.

Powercells and anything that caught my eye were on my shopping list as I started out into the darkness of the predawn hours. Two of Vicky's loaner bots were lashing down anything that might be a missile hazard to my base. They had their work cut out for them.

I kept just high enough over the waves to not get wet and hopefully not show up on anyone's radar.

The first rig was secured, nice and tight. I bypassed it for the sake of not robbing the one closest to me. In fact, I was going three or four rigs down the proverbial road.

I've been accused of being stupid before, but I'm not that stupid.

The one I picked was a little farther out and I burned some fuel getting there, but it was more modern and, from my perspective, had a better chance of having the nicer goods onboard. The headwinds buffeted my suit and much of my extra fuel was eaten up flying into the strong gusts. The bonus would be a tailwind at my back when I was on the return leg with my ill-gotten booty.

Fortunately for me, some yahoo had gone and made a video about his life out on this rig and I happily used it along with a few other sources to create an interactive map.

"Approaching coordinates," my suit's GPS announced. I decided I was going to get Vicky to read off the commands so she could replace the voice in the armor.

I came in low and up into the area where the supply ships came in. The helipad was exposed and if there were any cameras active they'd probably be looking there.

With only emergency lighting on, the place looked like a cool spot to film a horror movie.

C'mon Cal, time to get moving, I thought, and punched up the map I'd created and started toward the parts storage. With this rig only a few years old, some of the equipment might still be in their original packaging.

Of course, looking at an oil rig online and being there were two very separate things. One fun fact I discovered was that there was almost no wasted space, which made it difficult for a schmuck humping around in a powersuit to get down the hallways and through the doors. There was a loud crash behind me, causing an involuntary jump on my part. The cargo net I had attached to my back had caught on a fire extinguisher and ripped it free of the mount on the wall.

Definitely a little on the edge there, Calvin. Should've used the storm to do a bank job instead.

Disgusted with my feelings of apprehension, I made my way to the first storage locker and broke the chain and padlock. Inside wasn't the gold mine I'd hoped for, but a pair of never used B powercells along with some other useful equipment that struck my fancy.

Of course, I already realized my problem; the net was good for carrying the loot across the water, but dragging it from one storage locker to the next wasn't going to get it done.

By my map, I was closer to the top level exit rather than doubling back to the area where the ships pull in, so I took the items out of my net and made my way topside feeling the ladder shuddering under my suit's weight.

Another five minutes was wasted squeezing out the doorway and laying out the net on the ground. The only thing that kept my amusement level up was trying to picture how well my girlfriend would fare if she was trying to do the same thing.

The little numbers in the corner of my heads up display, monitoring wind speed and barometric pressure, abruptly changed—for the better. The eye of the storm wasn't anywhere near here. It was puzzling to say the least and that naturally started my worrying again.

A flash of something darted overhead and my superhindsight powers kicked in and reminded me that Mom used to warn me not to go out and play in storms.

Sucking it up, I decided to try and see what I was dealing with. Edging my way around the place where they mix the mud that gets pumped down to the ocean floor, I got a look at the helipad. It was still well-lit and in the middle of it, with arms thrust outward, was a smallish looking person in blue tights and a cape. I increased magnification, but already had a good idea who I was looking at.

Shit! WhirlWendy!

For a moment, I wondered what she was doing down south when she normally partied with the New York crowd, but it made sense. Even a few years out, folks along the Gulf were still a little snake bitten from Katrina. The supers converged on New Orleans when the levees gave way, but everyone else in these parts pretty much got the short end of the stick and the federal money. I actually felt bad for WhirlWendy. She'd been in Europe trying to promote her movie and people were screaming at her because she wasn't there when everyone and their brother had downplayed the threat. Her presence in the area was something I should have considered.

People are ingrates, I thought. *I keep my expectations pretty low and most of the time they don't even make it up to the bar that I've set.*

She was jabbering into her communicator, so I tried scanning the frequency, but found it was encrypted. Settling, I turned up auditory sensors to maximum and eavesdropped on her side of the conversation.

The little brunette's accent was about as New York as one could get and still be understandable. "That's what I'm saying, Bolt. I'm just pissing in the wind here. The storm's too big! I can calm down localized parts, but realistically I can only shave off maybe five miles per hour on the whole thing before it makes landfall."

There was a pause while she listened to what the other person was saying. Whatever it was did not sit well with the young woman I looked at.

"Okay, I get it. Public relations! I'm all for doing my part to maintain our image, but this is ridiculous! I'll be sure to remind you of this shit the next time you're moaning about your charity appearances. I'm out here soaked to the bone. If I was actually doing some good it might be worth it!"

It was easy to see that Wendy LaGuardia was a headstrong teenager. Whatever her mentor, Bolt Action, was saying to her must have really been ticking her off. The pressure was falling again and the wind gust were picking up. It made me wonder if she was strong enough to slow down this juggernaut by a fraction, what would happen if she threw her power behind the hurricane.

Probably a good thing she wasn't a villain, I thought. *Still, she's probably better adjusted to her powers than someone like Maxine.*

"Besides, I know you're just sending me down here to keep me and Mike apart! I don't care about the age differences, I like him, and I won't let you come between us."

"What?" she demanded, responding to something Bolt Action said. "You don't think I can tell whether it's real or not! Why don't you pucker up and kiss my ass!"

My little bit of voyeurism had crossed the line into being awkward now. On the other hand, it was nice to see an unedited moment of how the other side lives and find out that it wasn't all sunshine and daisies. *Who would've thought?*

"Yes, sir, Mister team leader, sir!" She was yelling now, I no longer had to boost my reception to hear her. "Your orders are loud and clear and, for the record, bite me! Wendy, out!"

WhirlWendy ranked amongst the top tier of superheroes. She packed a mean punch. When it came to raw destructive ability, it was best to avoid anyone who could bring an F5 tornado to the party. The people on Patterson's threat index team often speculated who would win if Wendy and Imaginary Larry threw down without restraint. The only thing they could agree on was that the real loser would be whatever city they were fighting in.

I'd seen enough of her tantrum and backed away. Maybe she heard me, had some really great intuition, or had just been at the super game too long, but her head whipped around.

"Is someone there?" she yelled and peered into the darkness while I stood stock still. There were no lights around me.

Pausing, she scanned the area before muttering, "Of course there's no one else around. Only idiots would be out here right now!"

She's probably right about that!

Seconds later, winds swept her skyward and the Tiny Tornado went off in search of something useful to do. She probably would have enjoyed the distraction of fighting someone like me at the time, but I wasn't looking to get my ass kicked six ways from Sunday and having the other villains mock me for getting whipped by a teenaged girl.

I went back to gathering my loot and was grateful that she hadn't spotted me. I'd been planning on making at least three runs today while the storm was coming ashore. Some might say that I was being chickenshit, but I decided not to press my luck more than I'd already done today.

• • •

E.M. Pulsive regarded me while I held the plasma breeching charge to the vault. I had just finished relating the encounter with WhirlWendy as I cut through the locking mechanism on the vault.

"If it was me, Stringel, I'd have sizzled her, dropped her bitch ass into the water, and fed the fishes."

"Dude? We weren't fighting. I don't have an ax to grind with the girl." Robbing banks with Eddie was surprisingly easy. He could block the activation of the alarm. We might as well have been the cleaning crew.

No wonder he thinks robbing a single bank is just too easy. Guess that's why Seawall was always happy to ride his coattails.

"Dude yourself!" Eddie spat. "You wanna come up to the big leagues; you're going to have to get some blood on your hands. You'd have mad cred on the streets if you waxed that little guidette."

"She's like America's sweetheart, Eddie. Suppose I did kill her, and then was stupid enough to brag about it. Everybody and their brother would be after me, or don't you remember what happened to the Photon Crew when they killed Thunder Claws?"

"The Photons were chumps," Eddie said, as if it explained everything.

"Yeah, they were," I agreed. "If they weren't dead, how would I do in a fight against them?"

God! I hate being a realist.

"You're probably right, Stringel," Eddie conceded as the cutter finished.

Setting the device down, I pulled the vault open as Eddie prepared to fry anything inside. The lights inside in the vault had been on an internal circuit and Eddie couldn't get in via his normal methods.

Inside was nothing to be worried about.

"Yeah, I popped this one vault in St. Louis and the damn Cybernetic Sisterhood was waiting, armed with high tech super soakers. That's how I ended up in the joint last time. I hate those robot bitches! One of these days I'm going to find that Albright guy and give him the electric chair treatment."

Unlike Patterson's killing machines for sale to the "legitimate" governments of the world, Doctor Albright's creations were programmed not to kill. That probably pissed an amoral bastard like Eddie off more than anything else.

I appreciated fine robot workmanship that didn't blindly maim. *Hell, I didn't even kill Barton. Probably should've.*

"Gotta admit, though," Eddie continued as I began removing the collapsible bags so we could fill them. "You're better company than Seawall and his clowns. Those shits would be running around, all over the place acting like they own the joint. You're just doing a job. That's why I like you."

"That's me," I said. "Your average blue collar supervillain. I'm hoping that if you take another shot at Ultraweapon, you bring me along for the ride. I'd be willing to get my hands bloody on him, or at least say I was there when you killed him."

He laughed and then discarded a stack of hundreds. "Tracker in there. As for Ultraweapon, I've tried a couple of times, but haven't gotten him. If I ever go after him again, I'd have to be sanctioned by Devious and the Overlord first."

Sanctioned? Is this like the mob where you have to go to a boss for permission?

"Really? That's the first I've heard about that."

"I'm guessing if they ever think you might have a shot at killing old Lazarus, they'll let you know whether you can." *He could be messing with me. Then again, maybe not. Vicky would know. I'll ask her.*

"Looks like we're done here," Eddie said and zipped up the three bags. "How long is it going to take for you to get your plasma cutter rebuilt?"

I shrugged. "Three days." It would really take two, but I didn't want to fall behind on Vicky's quota. I was only getting sixty grand per robbery—fixed fee.

"All right, bring all this back to my warehouse and I'll meet you there."

I followed Eddie out the door and he transformed into his full electrical form and zipped into the streetlight. I took off with the burnt out shell of my cutter dangling from one side and three duffel bags full of cash in the other. In a way, I looked up to Eddie, but at the same time, I knew he was scum.

• • •

My arrival at Eddie's temporary base was greeted with the sight of his topless girlfriend trying to get him out of his clothes. His crazy-ass flame was hot enough, but she had a penchant for the nose candy and that kind of turned me off, even though I could appreciate her plastic surgeon's attention to details.

"If you want, I'll just take the money and go," I offered.

"You could always stay and I'll do you both," Susan, Sammy Joe, or whatever her name was, countered.

Eddie had bragged that she was some kind of nympho, but seriously?

"Have to pass," I said. "My girlfriend wouldn't like it."

"She never has to know," the woman retorted and pulled her top back on. "Too bad this one works alone, Eddie. I kind of miss all the guys. Try and find some better help next time, or at least someone who owns his balls. Finish up your business, Edward, and then come join me."

The nut job walked out of the room and left me with the equally psychotic male.

"Is she always like that?"

"Yeah, pretty much," he said. "Your pal Maxine got ahold of her a long time ago and something strange happened that she never talks about. I'm kind of glad I spend half my time in my lightning form sometimes. Sally is just a hardcore freak."

That's her name! "Nice," I said, while thinking that it was anything but. Vicky was more my speed. We could do things like talk to each other.

It wasn't like I was down on the female species. I just knew that my line of work wasn't conducive to attracting the really sweet ones. That's what made Vicky special. That's why I...

Oh shit! I almost thought the L word!

Eddie pulled a small bag out from under his table, while I wrestled with my new moral dilemma. "I already have your fee ready, Mechani-CAL. Get your plasma torch ready and get back with me and we'll do this again."

I took the bag from him and dropped it in my cargo box, not even bothering to open it. In this, I could trust him. He couldn't carry anything in his lightning form, so I was kind of necessary for his next set of jobs since Seawall and his band of miserable goobers were out of action.

"Nice doing business with you, Mr. Pulsive. See you in a few."

That's when the wall across from me exploded. On the other side was The Discus and She Dozer.

"You two are coming with us!" Discus said.

"Activate shields! Power to weapon systems! Bring flight systems to standby," I ordered and spun to face them. K-Otica and Spirit Staff broke through the north door and Eyelash came out of the room dragging a struggling Sally in her ocular whips. The woman held a stick in her hand and one of the bags from the bank glowed.

They must've hit up The Grand Vizier or Mystigal for a tracking spell.

"Guardians!" Eddie hissed after shifting to his form. "I'm gonna enjoy this!"

All the power died in the warehouse and, from what my scanners could tell, the surrounding blocks.

"They're boxing you in Eddie," I warned. "They cut the power to the area."

"Who wants to die first?" Eddie said and made globes of energy in his hands. I was tracking Dozer and the Discus, guessing my cohort would go after K-Otica and her beau. Eddie didn't like to be beaten, especially by a woman.

I fired first, because someone had to and I really didn't care for stupid posturing. Discus shielded most of it, but it still was enough to send him backward. Dozer hurled a crate at me, and I smashed it with my fist rather than wasting energy on it.

Eddie's globes of power sped toward the other two Gulf Coasties. Spirit Staff stepped in front to block them, but he never had to. Instead, the balls stopped short and simply disappeared. I spun and looked at Pulsive, but he was just as stunned as I was.

"We brought a friend, scum," She-Dozer said. "Why don't you come on in and introduce yourself?"

Helping Discus come back through the hole I'd sent him out was a man standing about six five and built like a Greek God, literally. The large Z drawn with lightning bolts on his costume left no doubt who we were dealing with.

Zeus! We are so screwed!

Eddie lost whatever remained of his sanity and started throwing everything but the kitchen sink at the Olympian. Zeus swatted it aside like Eddie was shooting nerf toys at him. With a wave of his hands, Zeus froze Eddie like a high-voltage statue.

Near panic, myself, I threw everything I had at him. My blasts were a little more effective than Eddie's nerf bolts. It might have amounted to a slap on the face or a really good noogie, but I wasn't sticking around for it.

"Activate jets!"

About the only thing I could be grateful for when the Olympian turned on me was that his blast knocked me farther away from him. It still cost me almost half my shielding. My jets sent me careening through the back wall with K-Otica in pursuit.

The Olympian couldn't fly and none of the other Gulf Coast Guardians could either, so my continued freedom hinged on being able to out fly her...and the helicopters converging on the area from all directions. There were six in all and they weren't police choppers either. I had either National Guard or regular US Army Apaches coming after me. Four of them were coming in from the waterfront, determined to prevent me from doing my patented "swim away" escape. In the distance, two coast guard cutters circled, daring me to try them after running the Apache gauntlet.

That had been my first thought, but now I had to abandon it.

The lead copter's chain gun started spitting out munitions and I dived low and headed back toward the city. Their firepower outclassed me, but if they wanted to use it, I'd make them do it over a populated area.

K-Otica barred my way, floating with a wide smile on her face, and I realized that I'd have to go through her. Assuming she was at her peak, she was faster than I was and her energy bolts were stronger, but I had shields and she didn't.

An absolutely stupid plan, formed in my head. Vicky would say that those were my best kind.

"Divert weapon power to shields," I said and turned toward her. "Maximum acceleration."

The woman flexed backward and unleashed her concussive energy; I only made quick course corrections that kept me from the worst of it. Only twenty feet separated us when she caught on to what I might be doing. She tried to go vertical, but I was at my top speed and she had only just started accelerating.

I angled up slightly and rammed the superhero. Her hand glowed and she tried to bring her power to bear, but I reacted first.

"Taser charge! Taser charge!"

Twin jolts of energy stunned the injured woman and she collapsed like a rag doll in my arms.

I held onto my newfound hostage and turned to face the helicopters, daring them to open fire. They seemed suddenly reluctant.

"Shields at fourteen percent. Structural integrity at eighty-one percent. Weapons at six percent."

Engaging my external speakers and transmitting on police bands, I said. "K-Otica and I are going for a little trip. I don't want to hurt her any more than I already have, but that's on you fellows."

With that, I turned northwest and headed toward Baton Rouge.

• • •

Thirty minutes later, my hostage came to. Her pained screams were the first thing I noted.

"How badly are you hurt?" I asked and slowed down. I'd gone down to the tree line to avoid pursuit.

"Ribs are killing me. I don't think they're broken, but they're definitely bruised." I could see her thinking about trying her powers and elevated by another fifty feet.

"If you're not at full power, I'll probably drop you. It's about eight stories down right now. Sorry about the ribs. Didn't really have much choice."

"You always have a choice," she muttered. "You just keep making the wrong ones."

"Probably," I agreed and watched her smooth her skirt and try not to look like she was checking for her communicator. "Not much we can do about it now. I ditched your tech on the outskirts of New Orleans."

"What are you going to do with me? Dump me in the swamp?"

"According to my maps, there's a fire station three miles up the road. I was going to drop you there and get my ass out of here before your friends show."

"You won't get away," she said. "Eventually, you'll slip up and get caught just like your buddy back there."

"Hopefully not anytime soon and Eddie's a world class douchebag. Maybe you fine, upstanding people can figure out how to hold onto him this time. It's just my opinion, but society would be better off if you could."

Karina seemed somewhat surprised by my statement and couldn't think of a comeback to it.

As we approached the fire station, I asked, "You're not going to try anything funny when I put you down?"

She said she wouldn't. Instead, she tried when I was only about ten feet off the ground. I got a nice face full of pretty colors, but not much else. Her temperamental powers must give her fits.

Even with the visor, I was still blinking it off when I unceremoniously dumped her on the ground. The money I'd gotten from Eddie was still there, but all of it and then some would be consumed by repairs to my suit.

Grimacing in pain, she looked up at me from the ground and stood while some of the firefighters who'd been polishing their engine came around for a better look.

"You got lucky this time, Mechanical."

"Mechani-CAL," I said slowly to correct her. "At least make an effort to say my name right, Karina. Gotta run. I'm sure these strapping young men can look after your injuries. See you around sometime."

• • •

"I got you a present!" Vicky walked into the bunker in the side of the mountain where I was working, two weeks after the debacle with the Gulf Coasters, and announced herself.

"Hey, V," I said. "You're a sight for sore eyes and sore everything else! Gimme a minute or two to finish up this one. How's work been treating you?"

One of the bots was powered up and my "helper" for the day. I'd tried doing the installations in the armor, but the connectors were too difficult to manipulate in the suit.

"It was a good week. One of my plans was put into motion and the results have been favorable. How's the refit going?"

"We probably have about three hours left," I answered. "And a crap ton of old plasma rifles. Got any idea what you're going to do with them."

She laughed and said. "I like your mercenary attitude, but they're spoken for. I believe they're being sold to a rebel group in Central Africa. Good thing I brought some reading material along with your really, really cool gift."

"Quit teasing," I chided her and watched as she set a couple of her trashy romance novels on the desk.

"You know you love it, Cal. I heard your tops on the Gulf Coaster's Most Wanted list. Congrats."

"It's a dubious honor, at best. They've been on a tear lately and have caught most everyone else. Hell, I think Rodentia is number three and when he's high up on someone's list; they must be scraping the bottom of the barrel. More importantly, am I still on top of your Most Wanted list?"

"Maybe," she said, playfully. "Then again, you might be on the bottom if I decide to be on top."

I laughed and finished attaching the connectors. The panel would get sealed up later. There was flirting to be done.

"All right beautiful," I said standing up and stretching, before closing the distance between us. "You have my undivided attention."

She started to fish around in her bag before I stopped her. "I want a kiss first."

"You're just a big softy, aren't you, Mr. Stringel?"

"Only around you," I said and heard Bobby's voice in the back of my head. *Damn, Cal, you got it bad!*

After kissing for few minutes, she pushed me back. "If we keep going, you won't have the energy to properly thank me for your gift later."

"All right, whatcha got?"

She pulled out a thumbdrive and handed it to me. I connected it to the bunker's system and opened it up. "Drawings? Let's see what they...holy shit! Is that what I think it is?"

"Joseph got his greedy little paws on Patterson's Direct Neural Interface; don't ask me how. I convinced him to let me have a copy of the schematics and that the one you build would be better than any that those turdburgulars who work for him could do."

"Wow! No more voice commands." I'd heard rumors that Patterson's people had finally developed one, but there it was in front of me like the Holy Grail of human to computer interaction.

She grinned. "Just think and the suit responds. You'll have to wire up your old armor when you give it to me, but I thought this would make the perfect start to your Mark Two. Unless you don't want it?"

"Do you know how much I love you right now?"

Her lips froze in the middle of what she was about to say. "Wait! Did you just say..."

"I guess, I did," I confessed. I'd been planning on a way to tell her in some grand fashion, watching fireworks or something like that. In the middle of a bunker filled with robots for witnesses and the scent of machine oil in the air hadn't really occurred to me.

Then again, we kind of have an unconventional relationship.

"Well, then, I guess I love you, too," she said, practically glowing. "Cal, before we do anything else, turn off the robot. It's kind of creepy."

I've never issued a shutdown command faster in my life.

My estimate of three hours to finish the installation was off considerably, but Vicky didn't have me around for my excellent time keeping skills.

Life was good.

Chapter Twelve

The False Promise of a Better Tomorrow

The end of the pilot upgrade program was celebrated at the Branson estate with considerable fanfare, or at least as much expensive takeout food and two people relaxing in a hot tub could account for. Unfortunately, the money wasn't there for the follow-on phase and I would have to wait for the next year's budget. On the plus side, I'd already been to the other three bunkers that were slated to be upgraded next and had a good idea of what I was up against.

"So, when do you start working on the Mark II? Or are you going to add to your resume of being the most wanted villain in the American southeast?"

I kept massaging her shoulders and said, "The money from your boss will let me finance the new suit without having to rob a bunch of banks. I think I'll lay low for a bit rather than press my luck. Let 'em think I've gone into retirement or something so they let their guard down. That's when I'll bust out my new armor and open a can of whup-ass!"

Vicki laughed and said, "Don't forget to upgrade my armor."

"Actually, I was thinking that I might build you a new suit from scratch and simplify things."

She turned her head and gave me an interrogating look. "Are you saying the suit is too complex for me?"

"No. I'm saying that integrating that direct neural interface with the current controls on the Mark I would really be a pain in the ass. After all this time in it, I know where I made a bunch of mistakes."

"Such as?"

"Well, there are redundant circuits that I built into the armor that have never had to be used. Also, I really screwed the pooch when it came to power distribution throughout the whole upper half of the armor. Looking back, I could make that same suit better, and for less money than before. It's helping me with the design of my new armor. I think the question really is do you want that old thing, or how about I set you up with a custom build especially for you?"

Her silence made me wonder if I said the wrong thing. I was this close to panicking when I saw the expression on her face. Vicky's smiling face had been replaced by what I've come to call her "all business face." It was something I only saw on the times when we were talking as employer and employee instead of boyfriend and girlfriend.

"How much of a cost savings are you talking about, Cal?"

I stopped massaging and scratched my chin. "Twenty-five or thirty percent. Maybe more if I substitute my power capacitors for the cell that runs the weaponry. It would also depend on the quality material I use and what your performance expectations are. So are you going to tell me what's going on in that diabolically, beautiful mind of yours?"

Looking very pleased with herself, she said, "As you might have heard, I am on something of a hot streak lately and I have got a decent amount of pull right now."

"Go on," I said as she pivoted to face me and slung her arms around my neck.

"What if, instead of another run of pulse cannons, I talk the boss into letting you build him a platoon of low-cost Mark I powersuits? You're right about the limitations of the Pummeler suits. I think I can get Joseph and the boss to approve your design as long as you keep the markup within reason; say no more than twenty percent."

"Twenty?" I asked. "Isn't this the part where you try and haggle me down to ten and we settle for something around fifteen?"

Her smile returned, more radiant than ever. "I can sell the boss on twenty and maybe a year or so after you deliver the suits, I'll put in my two weeks, and then you and I trade your junkyard in for a nice villa in Belize or Costa Rica. I hear it's very nice down there. How's that sound?"

It sounded pretty damn good. Like some kind of hybrid of an accountant and an engineer, I ran the numbers. Six or seven suits in a squad and two squads in a platoon meant at least a dozen.

Twenty percent on that is more than I've made in all my bank robberies! That would make me filthy, stinking rich!

"Do you think we could pull it off?" I asked, daring to hope.

"If you can make it, I can sell it. Now, here's my question, could you just walk away from all of this? You've been obsessed with Lazarus Patterson. We leave the country and you might never get your revenge on him."

The question made me stop and think. My little threat to Barton sent Promethia's forces scrambling. I'd probably cost them a pretty penny. Their little schemes had made me forfeit my twenties. I'd left Patterson's employ to become rich and I was now poised to become wealthier than I'd ever imagined and had a woman by my side who cared deeply for me.

Unlike Patterson, who trades his latest fling in when the shine begins to wear off, I wanted to see where this went.

"Yeah, I could let it go. Not for the money, or Costa Rica, but I'd walk away for you."

Smooth, Cal Stringel, very smooth.

It was obviously the right choice of words from Vicky's perspective. After several long kisses, she whispered in my ear, "Good. We have a plan now. I still want your old armor, because it belongs to you, just like we belong together."

Apparently, I'm not the only one with the right moves today.

The world was a crazy place where a perky criminal mastermind and a powersuit wearing schmuck could find each other, but that was fine by me. The two of us had the beginnings of an exit strategy and the start of something I never thought I'd get.

Looking back, I should've known better.

• • •

Over the course of the next nine months, I fell into a pattern that left me little time for anything else. I'd alternate days working on the designs for the streamlined Mark I suit and building my Mark II. Life was good; hell, I even did karaoke with Tweedledum, sometimes. The Mighty Biz would have cringed at our rendition of *Just a Friend*, but I thought our version of *You've Lost that Loving Feeling* was rather catchy.

Vicky listened to us do it live on my thirty-first birthday and asked if I knew the reason I was the one playing the drums in my past bands— wench! Loveable wench, that was true, but still a wench.

"When is it going to be done?" Vicky asked. On the rare occasion she came to the junkyard, she'd become an ad hoc assistant. For obvious reasons, we usually met at the estate near Branson Missouri.

"Next week is when I probably start doing my shakedown runs. It's got a solid ECM on it, so I shouldn't have to skim the tree lines anymore out of fear of showing up on radar systems. My top speed is now around two hundred and fifty miles per hour."

"Yes. Yes. I've heard it all before," Vicky chuckled before lowering her voice an octave and trying to imitate me. "Three times the shielding of the original suit, fifty percent greater lifting capacity, thirty percent more armor coverage over the vital areas, improved scanning suite, and let's not forget the icing on the cake, the twenty percent reduction in force blaster's cycling time for increased firepower."

"I guess I must say that a lot," I observed.

"Maybe once or twice, but it's all good. So, you decided on your first job in the new suit, yet? Preparing to storm the headquarters of the Gulf Coast Guardians perhaps?"

I spent a moment rolling my eyes at her before walking over to the large flatscreen mounted on the wall and bringing up some video footage. "See this?"

"It's a truck weighing station," she said and tried to sound serious. "It looks pretty difficult. Are you sure you can take it?"

"Do you want to hear my plan or not?"

"Sheesh! Just trying to have a little fun with you. Look at me, I'm a big stick in the mud," she said with a mock pout.

I gave her my best "talk to the hand" gesture and said, "The stop is near Kingston, Tennessee."

"Okay," she said, slightly more interested. "Is it the Army base or Patterson's robot assembly factory?"

"As if you have to ask?"

"Go on. I'm starting to like this."

I figured she would. "Anyway, on the second Thursday of every month a Prometheia semi has to stop here on its way to the assembly plant. I figure that it's either full of powercells or synthmuscle. Either one I would need for our platoon of suits, and it would drop our overhead and increase our profits."

"Your plan has promise," Vicky said in a thoughtful manner.

"So, I stun the driver and the worker, steal the truck and take it to a warehouse, unload it and then ditch it."

"Don't forget..."

"...to kill the GPS and check for one's hidden in the cargo. Got it covered, Sunshine! If it's full of synth, it'll be enough to build our suits and keep this one running for the next decade. We both know the stuff that Devious and the Overlord make isn't as good, no offense."

"It's not like I make it," she said and shrugged.

"If it hurts Patterson and helps me, I'll call it a win-win."

"What about security?"

"There might be something, and the trailer, but the only people who would be in a semi full of robot components would be..."

She finished my statement, "...Someone who also makes robots and all those people are west of the Mississippi. They would try to steal it earlier. Okay, I'm sold. You have my blessing."

"Is this the part where I kiss your ring?"

She examined her empty hand and said, "Call me crazy, but this woman don't see no ring."

What did she just say? Does she know?

In my usual eloquent manner I said, "Uh..."

"God, you're so easy! Relax, boy toy—I'm not pushing you."

She's teasing me, but I've got to be cool. Vicky doesn't know I do have a ring for her, but I'm not ready to give it to her, yet. I need a good answer...something witty. I know!

"Well, I haven't had the chance to go out and steal you one, yet."

Vicky returned to her mock pout. "So, I'm not worth buying a ring for?"

"Be honest, if I bought you a ring instead of stealing one, you'd think less of me."

"Yeah, you're right! I just wish I didn't have to go to headquarters for this big pow-wow. I wanted to celebrate with you when you pulled your first job in the suit."

I didn't know where the Evil Overlord's Omega Base was except that it was somewhere in the west. The dude has a pathological hatred of Lazarus Patterson that dwarfs my own. The clone armor that his clone developer builds for him is usually painted with Patterson's latest schemes. More than once the Overlord has gone on a murder spree after initially pretending to be Ultraweapon.

It didn't mean Vicky's boss was better than me; he just had better toys.

"I'll call you on Thursday night and let you know how it went."

"You'd better," she warned and finished gathering the schematics for my low cost powered armor into her portfolio. Finishing, she smiled at me. "These are like printing your own paycheck, Cal. We're going to break the bank together!"

She paused and looked around. "I know I'm going to get on that plane and realize that I've left something important here."

"Maybe you're thinking about me?" I offered.

"No, I meant something useful," she deadpanned.

"Harsh!"

"Aw, did the big bad supervillain get his wittle feelings hurt? Maybe Aphrodite over there can keep you company."

She pointed at the old pinup that graced the workbench; of the Olympian Bobby gave me a few years back. *Eternally Yours my ass!*

I crossed my hands over my heart and said, "But she's the only woman who could ever steal me away from you."

"Sure," she drawled. "That's what I love about you; you have such a vivid imagination! Now, we'd better get going to the airport. I'm going to make us millionaires!"

• • •

A little over a week later, I was kicked back on the couch with a laptop connected to a SecureSat link speaking to Vicky and admiring my creation. Quite honestly, I couldn't imagine me ever topping the Mark II. I was wearing some damn fine armor. Unlike my original suit, I could be in and out of it in only five minutes—a thing of sheer beauty.

"The job was so easy that I could have done it months ago with the Mark I. The most difficult part was unloading the tractor trailer. It's going to take me three more trips to bring the rest of the stuff back, but I wanted to call you first and give you the good news."

Her face in the browser window brightened at the news. "That's awesome, Cal! So, don't leave me hanging, what did you get, and how much of it did you get?"

"Well, among other things, I now have fifteen spools of synth, six class C cells, and what appears to be a prototype frame for a Warbot variant. The serial number indicates that it is a D309XA."

Vicky wolf whistled and said, "Nice! That's more than we need to wire up the whole platoon. My people would be interested in looking at that frame. Things are actually moving along here. That means I can probably slip away from all this tomorrow and come out for a quick celebration of your first job in the Mark II. Joseph looked over your designs and he gave his blessing. He is going to take me to his sit down with The Man himself on Tuesday morning to present the plan."

Things are definitely going our way, I thought. "In that case, I shall prepare for your arrival. Are you coming here, or do you want me to meet you in Missouri?"

"Either," she replied. "Which works better for you?"

"If you're coming here, I can take my van back up to Tennessee tonight and pick up my next load."

"Do your thing, loverboy. I'll come to you."

"All right then, I'll catch a few hours of sleep and then get back on the road."

"Drive safely, Cal. I'll see you tomorrow afternoon. Love you."

"Love you, too, V."

I looked over where I had arranged the Mark I suit. When she came down the steps it would be the first thing she saw. The armor was down on one knee and had its hand thrust forward with a small black box resting on the palm. Sure, it was probably the cheesiest proposal ever, but for a pair of armor groupies like us, it worked.

Tomorrow, my life's going to change!

• • •

"We're interrupting the music for an important announcement. This is a breaking story from the Newswire service. Both Reuters and the Associated Press are reporting that the Olympians and the West Coast Guardians, supported by robotic assets of the military and Promethia, are at this time laying siege to what is widely believed to be the main base of the self-styled Evil Overlord. The base is located in an area near several prominent resorts in the Cascade Mountains. The governor of Washington State has declared a state of emergency and issued a shelter in place order for three of the counties in the affected area. All citizens are to remain off the streets and elements of the National Guard are currently manning checkpoints along all roads. Commercial and private air traffic into the Pacific Northwest is being diverted. Additionally, all planes and helicopters in both Oregon and Washington State have been grounded by the FAA. We are being advised at this time that the President will be speaking to the nation at the bottom of the hour. Stay tuned for more reports as this situation develops."

My blood ran like ice through my veins and I found it difficult to breathe. Somehow, I eased the van off onto the side of the road and put it in park, not wanting to believe what I'd just heard. With my finger, I stabbed at the selector and cut over to the AM stations and started searching for a news station instead of the classic rock station I'd been listening to. It didn't take too long to find one and I listened to the talking heads regurgitating the same information I'd just heard, but with their opinions interjected.

While the fools yammered on, I took stock of my situation and the options. I was still two and a half hours from my base. The Mark II was in the back of the U-Haul moving van I'd rented. I could abandon the van on the side of the road, but it would be discovered. Plus, I didn't have the fuel to make it that distance. I'd always assumed Omega Base was in Nevada or Colorado. Washington State had never crossed my mind. Frantic, I checked my cellphone for any message from Vicky only to find nothing. I couldn't even call her without the SecureSat link on my laptop.

The last time I'd been this lost was in the ambulance after the Bugler had thrashed me and I was strapped to a gurney under the watchful glare of a police officer as the EMTs tended to my injuries.

She'll be okay! She'll be okay!

A tap on the window brought me back into the present and I wondered how long I just been staring at my phone. A black state trooper was tapping on the window. Shaking out of my funk, I tried to clear my thoughts and rolled down the window.

"Is there a problem?" the man asked, slightly suspicious.

The gears in my mind struggled to turn and failed. I stared at him with probably the stupidest expression he'd ever seen.

"I said, is there a problem?" his head cocked to one side and I tried to shake the cobwebs from my mind.

Finally some words managed to tumble out of my mouth, "No...no officer. I just heard on the radio about that thing going on out west and I have...my girlfriend is out that way...hiking in the Cascades. I was trying to figure out how to get hold of her."

He gave me a nod and a reassuring smile. "I'm sure she's fine. Just give it a few hours. Everyone and their brother who knows anyone out there is probably trying to call right now, so you're probably not going to get through."

"You're right," I said, praying that he was, but finding it conflicted with the growing sense of dread.

"All right, then," the trooper said. "Take however long you need and focus on getting where you need to go in one piece. You won't do your lady friend any favors if you get into an accident worrying about her."

"I'll do that, thank you."

"Anytime, drive safely."

As he walked back to his patrol car, I breathed a sigh of relief that I'd talked myself out of that one. One of the last things Vicky had told me was to drive safely as well and I wanted to believe that was a sign from above that she might be okay. Everything was spinning out of control and I was helpless to do a damn thing about it.

• • •

By the time I reached the junkyard, there were reports of a massive explosion that had rocked the site of the battle. It was strong enough to measure on the Richter scale and the people who pretend to know began wondering if it might stir up some of the dormant volcanos in the region.

I didn't have to speculate. Someone, probably Overlord himself, blew up his base rather than let the secrets inside be captured.

As stupid as it sounded, I tried calling, anyway, while Tweedledum unloaded the U-Haul. When that didn't work, I left an email in her VillainMail and sent the Wireless Wizard a rambling plea to let me know if she accesses her account. I even went to the forum where I first made contact with her and left a posting for her there.

Desperation can drive a man to do many things.

For hours I waited, trolling boards on both sides of the internet looking for any information I could find. I wasn't alone. Everyone was searching for information. It was all the televisions would show. My mad scramble for anything connected to Vicky wore me down faster than any fight I'd ever been in, and somewhere around the eighth hour of continuing coverage, I collapsed into a fitful sleep.

When I woke up three hours later, I decided that if she got out and was still free; she'd try to make it to her place near Las Vegas. That's where I would go. If she'd been captured, I'd need to be closer than I was now to bust her out of jail.

Extending the U-Haul through next week, I tanked up on both coffee and gas and hit the interstate. My suit was in the back and I had a remote control back there to activate Tweedledum in guard mode. I spent my time searching through the news stations as they faded in and out of the static. There were some survivors, but lots of bodies. Several sources were estimating that the recovery effort would take weeks.

Naturally, Patterson, his team of pet assholes, and his butt buddies, the Olympians, all survived. Although, the presence of First Aid might have helped some of the others survive, so I'd give the world's greatest paramedic a pass.

When I heard that smug bastard Ultraweapon speaking at a press conference, I shut the radio off for a solid hour. He had the perfect life and mine was crumbling. I didn't give two shits about the money; probably one of the only times I could honestly say that. All I wanted was to see Vicky again and give her the ring in my pocket. I'd spent most of my adult life in pursuit of the bigger, better, paycheck and now it was the farthest thing from my mind.

Against my will, scenarios spawned in the back alleys of my mind, whispering the ways I could have stopped Vicky from boarding that plane. The rational part of me said that there was no way Vicky would have let me talk her out of going. Even giving her the ring would have only bought me maybe an extra day before she'd promised to come back early to celebrate. The drive became a haze of "shoulda, coulda, wouldas."

Unfortunately, the rational part of me would have also realized what a long shot driving to Vegas was, so I'd ignored it for the most part and the recriminations lasted through most of Texas before I walked myself back from the crushing weight of my guilt.

• • •

My heart skipped a beat when I turned into her development. There was a mystery SUV in her driveway. As I pulled in front, I saw it had Oregon plates.

She's alive! I dared to hope.

With no other thought able to pierce the fog of my delirium, I grabbed the key to her door and sprinted to the entrance. My left hand worked the doorbell as my right fumbled to jam the key into the lock. Bursting through the door, I shouted, "Vicky! I'm so glad you're..."

"Who's there?" A distinctly unVicky-like voice demanded with a hacking cough. "Hands where I can see them or I'll shoot."

The entryway was the only part that was lit. I could see a shape slouched in Vicky's recliner. The overpowering smell of alcohol assaulted my sense of smell.

That was about the time I realized that my pulse pistol was still in the duffel bag in the passenger seat along with the remote to activate Tweedledum. *Idiot!*

"I'm Cal, a friend of Vicky's," I said, keeping my hands in the air.

"Stringel? Is that you?"

"Yes, and you are?"

There was a clatter as a pulse pistol dropped to the table and the hand fumbled in the darkness for a second and turned on the light.

My eyes adjusted and I saw a man in the chair. He looked awful. Where his left hand should've been was a mass of white gauze covering the stump. He looked like a person who'd been pulled out of a house fire and then resuscitated. At his feet were several empty bottles of liquor.

"It's Joseph," he said, realizing I didn't recognize him.

Without the gun pointing at me, I relaxed enough to say, "Ducie? Are you okay? Is Vicky?"

"She was farther behind me in the escape tunnel. She didn't make it. For what it's worth, I'm sorry," he said slowly, driving a stake into my heart.

I slipped to the ground and stared at the carpet, letting the tears fall.

He gave me a couple of minutes before saying, "I know she cared about you. It probably doesn't make you feel any better now, but you made her happy."

"Thanks," I choked out, and tried not to think of anything else at moment. "How about you? Is there a reliable doctor I can take you to?"

"No, I've got maybe two weeks left at the outside. I'd never go away from the base for more than seventy-two hours. The machinery there keeps me from aging rapidly and dying and there's nothing else like it. It's why we don't have clones of everyone running around. I'm a..." he trailed off into a coughing fit before finishing, "high maintenance type."

"Damn, that stinks."

"Tell me about it. The only person we've seen so far who can make a stable clone is that Mexican who works for the Gulf Coasters and the process we have doesn't work on super powered people for more than a few minutes. Ha! The Overlord can't even clone himself!"

"How'd you get here?"

"Grabbed a jetpack and somehow got it working with my mangled hand. It had enough fuel to get me to Oregon and I stole a car after that. As for coming here, Vicky was always nice to me whenever I came to town, so I reasoned I'd spend my last days honoring her memory in a drunken stupor."

A bit of jealousy crept into my mind and I wondered how close they'd been, but I banished the dark thoughts. Vicky was gone and the Merchant of Death had sold himself some of his own product.

"She was something else," I said, surprised at the ease of the way I could say that. *It's probably just denial speaking.*

"That she was. I looked your design over for the cheap powersuits. Good stuff, Stringel. I might've gone with plasma or sonic for lower energy costs, but that's just splitting hairs. One of them would wipe the floor with a squad of Pummelers. You might want to keep that in your back pocket for down the road. You've got an eye for efficiency."

I appreciated the compliment coming from the dying man. "Is there anything I can get you?"

"Two cases of scotch—good stuff too, not some cheap shit either—and something to eat. She wasn't exactly stocking the cupboard here. There's an electric can opener, so you don't have to worry about if I can get it open."

"Yeah, I can do that. I'm going to go grab my bag from the front of the truck. After that, I'll get some sleep and get my head clear. I'll go shopping when I wake up."

"What're you planning?"

"I'm not sure. I've got my new armor with me and I'm going to go get her body. It's the least I can do. After that, I just don't know."

"Vicky was talking about your new suit. I'd like to see it tomorrow, if you don't mind. She said you'd made a number of improvements."

"If you're offering to eyeball my Mark II, I'll take you up on it, but you'll probably need to be sober."

He laughed hollowly, and said, "That's part of my rapid aging process. I can't stay shitfaced for very long."

The walk outside seemed shorter than when I'd first arrived. I'd back the van up to the garage tomorrow and help him out to look at the armor.

Even the optimist in me had given up on Vicky, but I could still bury her and say goodbye.

That wasn't going to be the hardest part.

Every day after would be.

Chapter Thirteen

Banned from Vegas Through No Fault of my Own

It was a struggle to open my eyes. Only one of them seemed to work. I coughed, but that only served to antagonize the rawness in my throat. I smelled vomit and scotch and was fairly certain I was the source of both. The odor taunted me and demanded I blow chunks again.

Instead I rolled away from it and my head slammed into the leg of a coffee table. That gave the rest of my noggin momentary relief from the throbbing pain by concentrating that agony on one small area.

I'm never drinking scotch again, ever!

It was either getting light out, or starting to get dark. *Dammed if I know.*

Somehow, I pushed my body upright and looked at the disaster area that was once a clean living room. Instantly, I thought that my girlfriend would be pissed...and then I remembered the reason I was in Vegas to begin with. Brushing aside the pain that recollection caused, I tried to reorganize my jumbled memory. I saw there were several more bottles than I recalled scattered around the room, along with a half-eaten grocery store pizza from Vicky's freezer. I didn't have time to process much else because the need to reach the bathroom became my number one priority. Lumbering into the hallway, I managed to reach my porcelain destination just in the nick of time.

After heaving my guts, I went back to the first thing I remembered which consisted of walking back in with the intention of going to sleep in Vicky's bedroom, but Joseph convinced me to sit down and have a few drinks with him.

That's how bad ideas are born. The clone is gonna give me no end of shit when he sees, but I still can't hold my liquor, I thought. *Where is he anyway?*

Once I rinsed and spit to get most of the taste out of my mouth, I did a cursory check of the two bedrooms and neither was occupied. So I went back to the living room and peeked through the curtains. Both the moving van and the SUV were still there, but the moving van was now haphazardly backed into the driveway. That triggered a brief memory of the two of us going out there so I could show off the Mark II.

Maybe he is passed out in the garage.

He wasn't. In fact, the garage door was still open; so was the back of moving van. Tweedledum was still deactivated, but he'd been left on all fours, doggy style, with a sombrero on his head and an empty bottle of scotch in one of his hands. Normally, the absurdity of seeing that would've made me laugh. Instead, my mind had sobered up rather quickly. It was what I didn't see that caused my sudden anxiety.

Where's my damned armor?

The panic sent me back into the living room, I found my laptop was on and connected up to the hidden portion of the Internet that the Wireless Wizard provided, at a ridiculous fee, for criminals. Next to the computer was the empty pizza box with items scrawled on the outside.

Ducie's Bucket List—The Powered Armor Version
1. *Storm my favorite bars any bar.*
2. *Seize the Lagavulin distillery on Islay. Too damn far! Seize the Excalibur hotel. That dragon is asking for it!*
3. *Tour the Guinness factory in Dublin. Also too far—tour something else Irish or Alcoholic.*
4. *Grow an evil twin goatee and destroy enemies. Barton in California. The facility in Los Angeles.*
5. *Go see the real Joe's house.*
6. *Blow it up.*
7. *Kidnap mother so she can see the Grand Canyon. She's never been.*

Pushing aside the empty bottles, I stared at the list. There was also a paper towel with a contract between the two of us. It was a barely legible forty-eight hour rental agreement for one set of powered armor in exchange for a quarter of a million dollars.

The clock on the computer said it was PM and not AM. I'd been passed out for something like sixteen hours. I wanted to throw up all over again.

• • •

It took a few minutes to process what was happening because of my pounding headache, but I fumbled my way through the necessary commands and started accessing my main computer back in Mississippi. The telemetry from the suit would be there. I could use it to find my suit and the clone.

He's at the Grand Canyon! At least he isn't in jail. How much of this list did he do?

There were also six new messages for me. The first was from Swamp Lord. He was a man who lurked in the bayous of Louisiana. He was one of those types who were sometimes a hero, sometimes a villain and didn't really give a rat's ass what the world thought. He could change his body into swamp air, really foul smelling vapor. It made him impossible to hold onto. Swamp Lord had bought a few things from me and was decent enough, if you could get past the body odor.

The subject line of his message was, "Congrats on the EPIC Drunken Rampage."

It had a pair of video clips attached and as much as I didn't want to do it, I clicked on the first one. It was someone watching the animatronic show at the Excalibur hotel. Just as the dragon comes out and starts breathing fire, my suit half lands and stumbles around, almost falling.

The crowd and the actors scatter, but whoever this moron was, he kept recording.

"Begone foul beast!" Joseph's voice booms over the external speakers as he turns my force blasters on it. The robotic dragon wasn't really constructed for anything more than entertainment value and pretty much disintegrated. The resulting explosion didn't do much for the side of the hotel either.

Joseph then pointed to the crowd and demanded they kneel and acknowledge him as their king. They did as he asked. Next, the drunken fool selected his "queen" and requested a kiss from her. The rather attractive woman seemed reluctant, but a second demonstration of the force blasters encouraged her compliance. Fortunately, he flew off without taking her hostage.

At least he has good taste. Shit! Whatever reputation I had is going to be ruined. Hopefully, the next clip wouldn't be as bad.

The second one was a collage someone on the internet had put together of my armor performing a simulated sex act on top of the Stratosphere, and at a couple of other Vegas landmarks. There was also the aftermath of the armor challenging Vegas Vic to a fight. The iconic cowboy sign had fared only slightly better than the dragon.

Below Swamp Lord's congratulations was an email from a Canadian villain who called herself Lady R.

You sure looked like you had the moves on top of the hotel. Why don't you bring your sweet little mechanized ass up to the frozen north and I'll rock your world! XXX

I wanted to groan, but even the sounds of my groans made my head hurt.

Rodentia was next, whining about not taking him along to do Vegas in style.

Blazing She-clops commented, *I thought what happens in Vegas stays in Vegas. Whatever, Stringel! Live your dream! You own it!*

The next time the one-eyed freak asked me to build her something I was going to charge double.

Another message from a villain I didn't know gave me props for knocking Blackjack and Slot Machine down a peg. That sent me in a panicked search for reports elsewhere and I proxied out to the real Internet and found news stories on the local TV websites. Sure enough, old Jojo had thrown down with the Sin City Sentinels.

Minor Supervillain goes on a Major Rampage

In the text of the story, I found the time of the next item on the list and called up the suit's video from my main computer. Joseph had arrived at a brewery and demanded a tour, along with more scotch, becoming upset that the place didn't make that particular drink and began trashing the place. The local hero duo of Blackjack and Slot Machine tried to capture him there and a brief fight ensued. It ended with Joseph chucking a small brewer's tank at them and leaving them a yeasty mess before flying away. Slot machine's blaster cannon had hit the suit a couple of times and I immediately checked the current suit status. Shielding was at only fifteen percent and armor integrity at sixty. Half my shield generators were shot and several minor systems were down.

Already, my mind was adding up the damage and it sounded like more than the sum Ducie had promised me!

Besides, I haven't even fought a hero in my suit yet, and he just fought two!

Quickly, I cross referenced the status with what the values were at the time of the fight with the sworn protectors of Sin City. Whatever happened, it was after that fight. The blaster cannon had only pounded my shields and chipped away at my armor.

Ducie, I typed, after installing a chat program into the HUD remotely. Voice coms would take much longer and I was out of patience. *What are you doing in my suit?*

Watching the sunset, Stringel. Can you come get me? The flight back from LA took the rest of my fuel. I don't want to spend the rest of my rental period hoofing it back to Vegas.

I tried to figure out how he managed to fly to the west coast and then to the Grand Canyon while staring at his list and typed. *Refresh my memory. What exactly did you do in LA?*

The reply came back on my screen as the chat program gave Joseph's dictated reply. *I greased that bastard lawyer that you insisted on, if that's what you're asking. Funny, after all this time of being called The Merchant of Death, that's the first person I'd ever directly killed. Dragged his screaming ass out onto his balcony and tossed the idiot off and yelled, 'Pull.' It was just like shooting a clay pigeon. However, your targeting system is out of calibration; you might want to check that.*

"He killed Barton! Everyone's going to think that was me!"

Joe's house? I asked.

You mean Joe's crater. Too bad he wasn't there. I'll be sure to send him the picture though.

My day wasn't getting any better. The real Joe Ducie was one of the few people I still respected.

What's this about the Los Angeles facility? You didn't attack Ultraweapon's headquarters did you?

Didn't do as much damage as I'd have liked, he responded. *Blew a few holes in the place; probably killed a few more people, but they had a pair of warbots on the site. You need better shield generators by the way. Still, I did manage to land a few shots on them.*

That explained the damage and the added body count didn't do much to brighten my mood. Thank God Patterson had run off with Aphrodite to Hawaii for a celebration.

You trashed my armor! I'm supposed to be going to the Pacific Northwest.

Don't get your panties in a bunch, Stringel! I'll cover the repairs. It's not like I'll need the money for much longer, besides, the way I see it, you owe me.

His audacity made me blink. He'd caused hundreds of thousands of dollars' worth of damage to my creation and had the nerve to say I owed him!

How so?

I've got my contact looking for Vicky's body already and he'll contact you when he gets it. He's identifying all the dead for the Overlord. You going up there will just screw things up more than they already are. Sure, I wanted to kill someone, but it was your guy I killed, so quit your bitching!

The clone had several good points. The only part about Barton's death that truly bothered me was that it'd be pinned on me. If I was ever caught again, the murder would mean I would never be offered parole.

Guess I will have to make sure I don't get caught, I thought.

Returning to the keyboard, I typed, *Did your boss escape?*

He always does.

Technically, he was the one who destroyed the base. Instead, he got away, the heroes got away, but Vicky and a whole bunch of others didn't. That really rubbed me the wrong way!

So when can you be here, Stringel?

Hang tight, Ducie. I need to clean myself up and then it'll take me a little while to get to you. Stay out of sight, and try not to blow anything else up since you can't fly away. Do you need anything?

Bring me more of the nectar of the gods! I'm starting to run low. Powercells and fuel. Also, some burritos and a fresh set of clothes.

I acknowledged his request and went to grab a quick shower while wondering how I was going to get the smell of his alcohol out of my armor. The death of my girlfriend still dominated my thoughts. The fact that I would soon be wanted for murder was a sudden and unwanted distraction.

Whatever reputation I'd made for myself was a lost cause. I sincerely doubted that many people would take me seriously and somehow I didn't think I'd be very welcome in the city ever again. When it came to Las Vegas, they say your luck will eventually run out. My luck ran out, got some friends, and came back to beat the crap out of me. About the only thing left was to change the way I look at things and be more like Swamp Lord and not give two shits what anyone thought.

In for a penny, in for a pound, I declared and pulled up the video of Barton's house. If I was going to get blamed for it, I might as well enjoy it.

• • •

Standing on a hill with a nice view of the Gulf of Mexico, two weeks later, I held two urns. Joseph's contact got as much of Vicky's body as could be identified and Ducie went with me to retrieve it. He made it back to Mississippi with me and three days after that he died, looking forty years older than when I found him in Vegas.

The cagey bastard showed me how to fine-tune my shield generators to get more performance out of them. Sober, he'd been as sharp as the real Ducie and driven to be the better of the two. Drunk, he was a riot and I was forced to lock him out of my armor for fear of a repeat performance.

"It's quiet here, Joseph. You can keep Vicky company. The two of you always got along. Thanks for the money and the tips on fixing my suit. It almost makes up for pinning four murder charges on me and making me swear off hard liquor from now on."

I spread the ashes and then reached into the cardboard box and removed the first of the five bottles of scotch he'd never gotten to and upended it.

"I don't know if there's a heaven for clones," I said, starting on the second bottle. "Then again, you and I both know you're not headed there. Odds are we'll see each other again."

Less amusing thoughts waited for me with the second urn. Vicky was the first person I'd ever truly loved. I'd put the ring on one of her remaining fingers before using the plasma rifle for a cremation job on the cheap.

"Originally, I planned to bury you. I couldn't decide whether to do it here in Mississippi, or in Missouri. Naturally, I cheated. I'm spreading half here and tonight I'll fly out to the place in Missouri to spread the rest. Actually, I was going to keep a little bit just in case I ever do make it to Costa Rica. As nice as it sounds, it wouldn't be the same without you. Hell! I'm taking the Mark I armor to the base in Alabama, because every time I look at it, I think of you."

Stopping for a minute, I found the words were getting more difficult. Talking to her had been easy. I'd never bantered like that with anyone before. Her wit and my sarcasm fed off each other. Now, it was like I could have food, or I could have drink, but not both.

"I hope you don't mind the arrangements. We never really talked about things like this. Besides if we're being honest, let's face it; out of the two of us the one who was going to die in the middle of a super powered battle was supposed to be me. So I can say without reservation that I'd never in a million years have asked you about funeral plans."

It felt good to get that out and I began to spread the ashes a little away from where I put Joseph's.

"You'd have laughed over that whole insanity in Vegas. You'd be giving me a ration of shit over how easily I let him into my new armor when you had to work on me for months to get into the Mark I. I can hear you now, 'I should have just gotten you drunk!' Yeah, I'm an idiot."

The anecdote was an attempt to calm me down and deflect with a little humor. She always said that my sarcasm was a defense mechanism, that if I could find a way to power shields with it, that I'd be invincible.

"You brought out the best in me and I was ready to walk away from all of this for a chance to be with you. I'm too chickenshit to follow you right now and I'd like to think you'd want me to push on, even if I don't know what I'm pushing toward, anymore. The best of me left with you and I doubt that I'll ever see it again. What's left will do what I always do; get by."

Bitterness echoed through my being at all the things left unsaid. I just stood there like a slack-jawed fool unable to string another sentence together.

Defeated, I turned away and whispered, "Be seeing you, V."

Chapter Fourteen

A Pain in My ASH

Between the repairs to the Mark II suit along with the suggested improvements from the late Joseph Ducie, it took me over three months to get it back to what I considered fully operational. Shield generator tuning was less of a science and more of an art; that explained why I'd never paid that much attention to it. Part of my jealousy about the super powered people was that they could just recover after a fight and still have their abilities. I had routine downtime for regularly scheduled maintenance and, on top of that, there would be periods, like now, of emergency repair where I'd be out of action for weeks or months.

It was part of the reason there were only a few people in the armored suit club. A lot of work and money goes into keeping the suit functional. It's a hobby for the rich or the obsessive; since I didn't have enough money to hire my own squad of engineers, I knew what category I fell into.

Maybe I should try and pick up magic—not that crap Joey's girlfriend in college was into—but the stuff that the Grand Vizier and Mystigal do. Swamp Lord probably knows a few of those voodoo types. Maybe he could hook me up? Nah, they'd probably want to steal my shadow or something. Magic would make my life easier, but it's a little late to turn my back on science and embrace hocus pocus. Plus, the only dead language I ever learned was COBOL.

Patterson usually kept at least one spare copy of his suit around in case he needed to, "spring back into action." I had a second suit, but I sent it away. The justification was that if I ever lost the junkyard and had to use The Pig Sty as my base again, I'd have a suit there waiting for me. Of course, that wasn't the real reason I didn't want to see the Mark I anymore, but I figured that if I kept telling myself that lie long enough, I'd eventually believe it.

Nothing short of the world ending would get me back in that suit.

The Gulf Coasters had taken the lead in the "Search for Stringel." The clone's outing in my armor had left Barton and three other Promethia employees dead and I was fairly certain a defense consisting of explaining that the clone of Ultraweapon's chief test engineer got me drunk and took the armor out for a crime spree, stood as much chance of working as I did against Imaginary Larry. Their last public release hinted that I was a coward, hiding and waiting to see if the investigation would go away. They'd even publicly hired the now retired Biloxi Bugler as a consultant, because he was an expert on fighting me.

They were taunting me and playing to my ego. For the most part I ignored it, along with the emails from several villains saying that the JV squad of the Guardians was calling me out and that I should man up and go fight them.

With a few odd exceptions, the villain community wasn't really a supportive bunch. They were more like a collection of drunken asswipes, armed with a thesaurus of insults as vast as the Internet. If it wasn't me, and I had free time on my hands, I'd probably be joining in.

As for the Bugler, he'd made only one public comment. "Perhaps Calvin Stringel has seen the horror of taking a life and has gone into seclusion. Maybe when he emerges he will be a different man and willing to accept the consequences of his actions."

That actually annoyed me more than the calculated jabs at my ego from the rest of those butt munchers. He might be the lamest excuse for a hero that ever threw on an outfit, but he was one of those true believer types—a Jehovah's Witness for the superhero community or something like that.

Frankly, I was more interested in Lazarus Patterson's contribution. He'd sent a squad of specially trained Promethia security to assist the Gulf Coasters. They were called the ASH team—Armored Suit Hunters. They were equipped with tech designed to take me down.

Any tech that could take me down could also be repurposed to take Ultraweapon down, and that was what made them more interesting than the super team I'd already fought.

• • •

"I'm glad you were able to make this meeting, Mr. Stringel. My predecessor spoke highly of your work. I hope you didn't have any problems finding this place," the man greeted me, doing a credible job not to be fazed by my Mark II armor.

"I've been here before," I said sticking to a short answer and trying to divorce the happy memories of my time at the Branson estate. I did have a small bag of rose petals, in my cargo box, to spread under the one tree where Vicky and I used to eat take out and pretend that we were picnicking. Neither of us had been very good cooks.

"Good," Paul West replied and gestured. "Then let's head inside and discuss how we plan to move ahead with the capabilities at our disposal."

I nodded and followed him into the conference room. It had a stuffy nature to it and Vicky loathed the neutral tones. Her meetings were either conducted at the breakfast table or in the hot tub. It was another item that separated her from jerks like this professional suit.

Vicky had also told me about the defenses in the room. The fact the stuffed shirt was bringing me in here could also mean that he was worried how I'd react and was taking precautions.

West took the worst qualities of someone you'd expect from middle management and somehow combined it with the sleazy salesmanship seen at car dealerships around the country. He had short, meticulously trimmed hair, no evidence that he'd ever had any facial hair in his life and a suit so laden with starch that my armor was probably more flexible.

Completing my initial assessment of the man, I decided that even if he wasn't Vicky's replacement, I wouldn't like him.

"So, what can I do for your organization?" I asked, remaining standing. None of the chairs in this room could have taken my weight anyway.

"As you can imagine," he began. "With the loss of human life at our base, there's been an increased focus on our automated assets."

It was a polite way of saying that they were short on warm bodies and were going to introduce even more robots. Considering Vicky and Joseph were part of those losses, his casual way of glossing over it didn't help improve my opinion of the man.

"My proposal to you is twofold. Primarily, I am recruiting for new people on his Engineering team."

Surprised at his opening move, I interrupted him. "You're offering me Ducie's job?"

West paused, almost aghast that I'd said that. "No, I'm afraid that position has already been filled, but you would be working under that individual.

"Who exactly would that be?"

"I am not at liberty to disclose that information, Mr. Stringel."

I didn't think he would. "I see. What kind of salary and benefits are you offering?"

West stated a number and went through a spiel. It was good, but hardly enough to make me forget that hundreds of people with similar packages were blown up when their boss decided they were worth a chance at whacking the heroes attacking his base. Too bad he underestimated Hera's forcefields. It was barely enough to keep my armor running. Money was tight, even after Joseph's bequest, but the biggest consumable in the armor was synthmuscle and I had an abundance of that, enough to keep this suit running for years.

"What would I be doing?"

"Robotics and weapons development, I'm told.

His answer was exactly where I figured this was going. I decided I'd head this crap off at the pass. "So, what you're really saying is that you don't want to pay the markup on my cannons and it would be less expensive for you to just bring me in house. Can we just skip the part where we pretend I'm an idiot?"

Naturally, there were some in this world, and some who've departed this world as well, who would argue that I wouldn't be pretending.

West paused to collect himself, before continuing, "Let me assure you, Mr. Stringel, no one believes that. We wouldn't be offering you employment if that was the case. You are obviously a good engineer. You wouldn't have been on the Ultraweapon team if you weren't."

His answer didn't reassure me. In fact, it did the opposite. "Would I still be able to use my suit for my own personal gain, or would I be giving that up?"

"Initially, no. A posting to one of my employer's many bases worldwide usually prohibits such outside activities. With a few exceptions, most are not allowed out of the confines of the base for the first eighteen months of employment, given the secretive nature of our business. I'm sure you understand the need for that."

It sounded wrong, even if I was a bit of a shut in. I still had the option to go places, just not the desire. Plus, I could see a villain simply deciding one day that all his employees were really just slaves and would work just for the sake of some food and not being killed. Labor laws didn't exactly apply in this vocation. The offer was getting less tempting by the second. They should've come and gotten me when I still worked at that brake and muffler shop back in the day.

The idiot I was back then would have jumped at that job...and have been pulled out in several pieces from that destroyed base. The idiot I was now had more reservations than the Native Americans had these days—just not the casinos.

"Would I be allowed access to the copy of the Ultraweapon armor in your employer's possession?"

"Perhaps that could be possible down the road, but for the foreseeable future, I doubt it. I don't have any authorization to allow that. Any access would have to be granted by The Overlord himself. We are interested in you for your exceptional skills as an engineer, and not as a supervillain."

"I should be flattered," I replied. "But I'm not. I'm sorry, Mr. West, but I am going to pass on this offer. I'd much rather retain my independent contractor status. Since your employer is appreciative of the weapons I can provide, perhaps we can discuss a larger run of pulse cannons. The assembly line I possess is in standby, but can be online within the week. My capacity is currently one hundred and fifty units per month, and if you are willing to commit to a thousand units, I am willing to lower my markup from twelve percent to ten percent out of respect for our past business dealings."

He looked disappointed, and I wondered how far he'd try to drive the price down. His next words disappointed me. "That won't be necessary, Mr. Stringel."

"Guess your new people fall on the plasma side of things then."

"Actually, no. Our new chief of development is impressed by your design and the simplicity behind it. She has assured me that we can reverse engineer that technology and have a production facility able to deliver three times your capacity within ninety days."

"So, your offer is, work for us or we're going to steal your design. I'd expect this from Patterson's people, but I thought you operated differently. I guess not."

He disliked my tone and became combative. "You were paid quite well for those cannons. Quite possibly better than you should have been, but that may be a reflection of Ms. Wheymeyer's personal opinions coloring her business sense. Speaking frankly, we can and will reverse engineer your design. Having you onboard would make the process easier, but you are overestimating your value and suffer from the delusion that you are irreplaceable. The fact is you are extremely replaceable."

Yeah, I'd about had it by then. "Oh, when you frame the offer that way, I guess I'll have to change my answer."

There was a split second of a smile where he thought he had me before I leaned forward and gripped the edges of the cherry conference table with my gauntlets and snapped a piece off. "My answer was just no. Now, it's hell no!"

Paul crossed his arms and tried to look unimpressed. "Is your display supposed to frighten me? You're a joke in that suit of yours. Maybe a decade ago that would have caught people's attention. It's been evaluated by our new people and our old people and been found wanting. Further, if you were stupid enough to harm me, I can assure you that there would be no hole deep enough for you to hide in, Stringel. My employer would see to that."

"So, you're worried that the lasers trained on me from the corners of the room and that statue, which is really a modified Type A robot wouldn't slow me down enough for you to hit the escape hatch hidden behind that cabinet three feet from you? But you're right, I don't want to offend your employer, but I have no interest in signing over my livelihood to him."

That actually did slightly unnerve the man and he stammered, "Patterson's people are already looking for you and are apparently looking to test out methods of stopping an armored opponent. The Overlord is offering you his protection because it is in his best interest that their prototypes are never put to use. You've already seen the place where you'll end up when they catch you, because if you think you can win, your delusions must be greater than I've been led to believe."

For a moment, I considered chucking the table at him and seeing if The Overlord would accept my apology that it was an accident. Considering it was impossible to lie to the man without him detecting it, probably not.

Instead, I shrugged and said, "I can handle Patterson's little security force and the Gulf Coasters."

"If you ever manage to develop into a credible threat, Ultraweapon will personally put you down. His people have watched all the available footage of your suit and have trained to it. You're outclassed and the odds are stacked against you, but you don't even care do you? My predecessor filled you with the idea that you're something special, when you're not. I guess you really are an idiot."

Ultimately, he wouldn't have pissed me off nearly as much if he had just left Vicky out of this.

"Oh, I care, West," I replied. "As far as being outclassed, I'm not the only one in this room who is outclassed by the competition. Vicky could have sold me on the deal and made me glad I took it. Hell, she was so good that she could sell the Ebola virus to Africa and made them think they got the better end of the deal! You? You're just a sad, sad imitation who now has to go back to one of the most powerful people in the world and explain how you couldn't make this happen. I bet you served up all the latest buzzwords about how you're a dedicated go getter, who doesn't accept no for an answer. You're a kingmaker, the rainmaker, and the showstopper rolled all into one, but you're as phony as the orgasm the last woman you slept with faked. My girlfriend never talked much about her work, but she gave me the impression that your boss has a low tolerance of failure, so I wouldn't want to be you, Paul. I wouldn't dare harm you, Paul. He'll end up doing that for me when he figures out that you can't deliver on your promises. Tell the Overlord if ever gets back into the cloning business, he ought to make one of Vicky so you can see what real talent looks like. Now, since we're just wasting our time, I'm going to show myself out."

As I turned, he said, "You're making a big mistake, Stringel. I'll make sure you never work for our organization again. You'll never be more than a bottom feeder."

"Please," I said dismissively. "I've made so many mistakes that this isn't even in the top twenty. Piss off, West, and don't ever lose the protection of your employer, because killing you wouldn't bother me at all."

I didn't want to linger, but I still made time to spread those rose petals. Odds were that I wouldn't be able to swing by this place again anytime soon.

Taking to the air for the trip back over the mountains where I'd stashed my van, I thought about the way I'd handled myself. Vicky would have chided me about burning a bridge and that there were any number of ways that I could have walked away without the hostility.

Vicky made me a nicer person and the absence of Vicky made me much less. I was fairly certain that I didn't like the person I was becoming, but even if I wanted to stop it, I wasn't terribly interested. Since I couldn't embrace her, apathy was the next best option.

• • •

The depressing thing over the next two months was that I'd put in for a couple of "rent a thug" jobs and been turned down. It seems Joseph's damage to what little rep I previously possessed had a lasting effect. I'd been offered one South of the Border, but didn't like the sound of it and passed. Other than a couple of weapons gigs, things looked pretty bleak.

Deciding I needed to enhance my value, I knew it was time to go after the people who were supposedly chasing me. Defeating the Gulf Coasters would put me back on the hiring radar.

Gulfport was a nice town. Close enough to New Orleans for the Guardians to get there in a hurry. It made a nice place to lay a trap. I just needed to make a couple of things and set the stage.

I hit three jewelry stores on the first night, for old time's sake. Also, with my connections on the various message boards, I could move metals much easier than when I was ManaCALes. Plus, it was unexpected and would probably make them wonder why I was messing with something that seemed beneath me.

Naturally, they came running out the next morning and were crawling all over the scene. I'd tapped into a nearby store's surveillance system that used weak passwords—SAFEfromU?—seriously? It was kind of amusing watching Discus and Eyelash play amateur detectives, while Dozer looked her usual strong and useless self. K-Otica, if tabloids were to be believed, was on maternity leave—good for her, though Spirit Staff was still active on the team. It made me wonder if their son was going to be an erratic martial artist with bizarre skills. Good for her. Out of the team, Karina was the one who bothered me the least.

Several of the ASH team wandered around, doing their best "I'm a badass" impression. I counted eight total. Six had those new hoversleds I'd been reading about, which made up for the missing flying superheroine. The other two rode around in a Promethia armored van, because that's what looks cool.

Dozer and Discus also arrived on those hoversleds. I'd heard that the East Coast team was using them, but this was the first time I'd seen the Gulf Coasties with them.

I tried not to be nervous, figuring that my new *harder edged* attitude on life and death would have gotten rid of the jitters.

It didn't.

Preferring to put my plan into action slightly more rested, I considered letting them go on their merry way, but it came back to the old saying of "shit or get off of the pot." I'd gotten more than my fair of shit, so it was time to give a little back.

I flew from the abandoned waterfront warehouse to the entrance of a bank about two miles from where they were. My guess was that the ones in the van would drive over, but the rest would run or use their nifty little Promethia issued toys. They'd been checking out the other crime scene for a couple of hours and would be getting bored, or hungry. I figured I'd make them run a little, spread them out a bit, and take them in manageable chunks for a while, because twelve against one seemed a tad unsportsmanlike.

Kicking in the doors, I watched the lunchtime line scatter as I walked up to the teller windows. They had a nice big sheet of bulletproof material separating us. I reached under the little slot with one hand and yanked. The owners of the bank hadn't sprung for the armored suit proof glass and a whole section of it came away.

Pointing my hand and making the discharge nozzle of my force blaster glow, I pointed at the nearest teller, a man, and tossed him a bag.

"You! Fill! Now!"

He caught the bag and looked sufficiently frightened. I pointed at a female teller. "You, get your purse and toss it in the bag."

The woman looked confused. "Why?"

"Because, if J. Crew here tosses in a tracking device or a dye bag, I'm going to need to come and kill someone. I've selected you. Old J. here looks pretty heroic and I'm sure if I told him to toss his wallet in, he'd do it, but you've got a ring, probably a couple of rugrats, and look friendly enough; he's not going to sign your death warrant. Are you J. Crew?"

The horrified man dumped the bag out onto the floor and I watched the dye pack explode all over his khakis and the cash.

"Smart kid," I said. I waited another minute while he filled and the woman brought her purse.

"Just your wallet ma'am. I don't need the whole thing; don't want your cell phone or the GPS inside of it. All this goes well and I'll drop it in the mail in a couple of days. If it goes poorly, well, then I'll return it in person. Neither of us wants that now, do we?"

It was actually kind of fun inspiring this kind of fear. I gave it a minute more before saying, "Alrighty, that's enough! I figure my friends a few streets over will be here soon, so I need to go and greet them."

Grabbing the bag and dropping it in the cargo pod, I guessed I had between thirty and fifty grand, lame really, but it seemed wrong to walk away empty handed. If the place had bought one of the magic trackers, it would be in the vault, because the drawers in the front would only be given to run of the mill armed robbers. They'd get dye bags and electronic tracking devices, not the voodoo that youdoo.

Jogging out through another one of the windows, I added to the property damage and ran over to the cars stopped at the light. I pushed a Ford F-150 over onto the hood of a VW and, so the people on the Chevy side of the Ford versus Chevy rivalry wouldn't feel left out, I roughed up a Tahoe as well.

Fair is fair, I figured. Watching people flee.

I also figured that at least one of the Coasties would stop to check for injuries, like the predictable heroes they were. Patterson's crowd was probably instructed to ignore any civilians and proceed to the target. They were here to test weapons and not save lives and I got that, but wondered if the do-gooders understood the distinction. Somehow, I didn't think so.

My onboard systems detected the first three flyers inbound and pulled the grenade launcher off my back and sent a few rounds of tear gas into traffic to add to the confusion, finding that people milling around made this more interesting. The launcher was one of those six-round types that the police and military, along with the criminals, have. It was disposable as far as I was concerned and the serial numbers had long since been removed.

The first three flyers circled about thirty feet from me. They wore standard Promethia security garb that consisted of a protective vest, with an internal forcefield emitter, over coveralls and a kevlar helmet. It cut down on their mobility, but offered a decent amount of protection. It looked like they could drive the sled with one hand while the other operates a weapon from a pintle mount. The arrangement didn't exactly allow for the greatest amount of accuracy, but they looked fairly comfortable doing it.

Whatever they were shooting was colorless. The impacts on my shields were registering something and that bothered me, so I stayed on the ground, but began dodging and tossing some force blaster shots to make them interested.

What are they shooting at me? Surface temp is spiking. I swept the low end of the spectrum first. *It's not radioactive, or infared. Wait! Got something around two point five millimeter wavelength and one hundred and sixty-five gigahertz. MAZERS! They're trying to nuke me with microwaves? Oh, hell. No!*

I couldn't picture Patterson coming up with this bucket of nastiness. That meant Joe was angrier than I thought about the thing with his house; like he really spends time there anymore! I reinforced my shields, deciding not to let them cook me alive and began returning fire in earnest.

Clipping one of the sleds with a level three burst, it yawed wildly, but had shield generators of its own, probably calibrated specifically for my force blasters.

Hadn't been expecting that! Let's see how they...what's that?

The two newly arrived sleds were making a beeline toward me about twenty feet apart. My scanners picked up a sizeable energy mass directly between them, some kind of energized net and they were releasing it!

I didn't take the time to consider if it was a suit style taser or something worse. Instead of triggering my jetpack and trying to fly up, I did my best powersuit belly flop and triggered a four second burst from my flight system.

It definitely scratched the paint job, but the net hit a tree and exploded. *Plasma web, not a taser then. They're definitely trying to kill me.*

"Surrender now, villain!" Discus' voice boomed.

"Your buddies don't look like they're interested in my surrender, Graham!" I yelled pulling myself off the ground. The microwave assault began anew. "You might want to ask them about Patterson's orders."

I didn't wait for him to answer and went airborne, wondering what the top speed on those sleds happened to be. The two who'd tried to drop the plasma net of doom were hovering and connecting a second net to their sleds.

Let's see if their shields can handle this! Maximum burst!

One of the pilots saw my torrent of energy coming at them and jumped. That's when I realized these two didn't have shields or had to drop them to hook up their net. The blast ruptured the magnetic plasma bottle and that willow tree from a minute ago was avenged in style. Both sleds detonated. The one who saw it coming was blown onto the upended Tahoe. His partner was vaporized. I high tailed it toward the warehouse near the waterfront. Things were a bit stickier than I'd hoped for and it was time to bring in my assistant.

Guess I can't hide behind the—I've never killed anyone defense anymore. The other one's not moving either, scratch two. Screw 'em. They're practicing for the Overlord. He wouldn't show them any mercy.

The final hoversled arrived on the scene as I departed. It had a dish mounted on the front of it. Care to guess where it was pointed? My ECM systems screamed missile lock and my scanners detected a launch farther back.

"Missile launch detected," Vicky's voice said in my ear. It was one of the few sound bites she'd recorded for me. She'd giggled, trying to stifle a laugh when she did. It wasn't the way I wanted to hear her again.

Must've come from the van. Launching missiles in the middle of a city. What could possibly go wrong here?

The sleds weren't as fast as I was, but the missile was gaining on me— something I wasn't too keen on. I skimmed the rooftop of a building and used my blasters to blow up the air conditioning unit on top of the building sending a hail of improvised chaff skyward.

Something caught the warhead and the weapon exploded. I felt sorry for the people who might be in the offices just below us, but considering the wash of the detonation tossed me off course and took a ten percent chunk of my shields with it, I was more concerned about myself, thank you very much.

Regaining control, I flew toward the warehouse and decided that the sled with the tracking gear was my priority target.

Flying into the open skylight, I rocketed to the far end and landed on the rafters to wait for my quarry to arrive. From there, I sent the activation code to my understudy. Tweedledum waited in the center of the warehouse, poised for a fake last stand. He had some decorative plastic injection mold armor over top of his frame that made him look decidedly like the Mark II armor. His "force blasters" were just plasma pistols modified to look like my weapons. They might even be more effective against the shielding the hunters were using.

I cut my systems and only had to wait about thirty seconds as my stand in moved toward the entrance. The missile sled arrived first with the microwave ones right behind. Patterson's people obviously had more practice on the sleds than the superheroes, or the Gulf Coasters stopped to help people like the good little protectors of society they are.

Dum fired away, to little effect. He did score a couple of hits. *They probably think I have some kind of double barreled action going on in my gauntlets.*

The robot was holding up pretty well against the microwave attack. His internals were less susceptible to cooking than mine. Even so, I guess I should have used something more sturdy than plastic.

"Missile launches detected," Vicky's voice said once more.

Dum didn't try to dodge. Instead he stopped firing and turned his head toward me and I felt a momentary pang of regret for putting him there.

When that half of the warehouse went kablooey, I felt a little sad, but relieved at the fact that I was still alive and able to feel that way about an oddly defective robot.

It's almost tempting to just fake my death and slip away. Patterson would think his anti-armor weapons were da bomb.

"Maybe some other day," I growled and kicked on my systems. On my comms, I heard the ASH team calling up the van so they could confirm the kill over an open channel. Discus was ripping the man a new ass for using that kind of weaponry over a populated area. Strangely enough, I agreed with him.

I went out through the broken ceiling and used the smoke cloud to cover my approach. Thermal imaging was a bit of a wash, but I could make out roughly where they were.

Like an avenging angel, well I guess I can't really say that term would apply; I broke through the wall of smoke and found myself staring into the disbelieving eyes of the guy who'd fired three missiles at me today. He was hovering and that was the last mistake he'd ever make. I rammed him. Sure, the shielding helped and did a number on mine too, but the impact separated him from the sled and he did the three story two and a half twist into the pavement. I gave him points for sticking the landing, because he didn't make a big splash.

The others were screaming over the open channel. "He's still alive! Negative impact! Hunter One is down!"

The two remaining sleds tried to reposition. I hit one with a level five and his shielding collapsed. His sled went down, with him fighting for control. I circled around and engaged the remaining ASH, who had turned to flee back toward where the Guardians were.

I clipped him and forced him to land on a building near where the first missile had nearly gotten me.

As he ran for the door leading back into the building, I landed between him and it.

"Don't do it, Stringel!" A bolt of electrical energy smacked against my shields and Discus leapt off his sled, executing a nice little combat roll. He came up between me and the ASH agent, already creating a pair of protective energy discs.

Nice move! Almost makes me wish I'd taken up gymnastics, I thought before saying, "Are you regretting taking Patterson's help yet, Graham? This isn't going to look good on the six o'clock news."

"You bear as much responsibility for what just happened as they do," he replied and threw his discs. I dodged one, but his aim was too good for me to stop both.

"Yeah, but I'm the villain. You need to ask yourself who they are," I shot back, both with my answer and a level three at the ASH running toward the fire escape. Predictably, Discus jumped in front and ate my blast with a freshly created set of discs. It still had to hurt. As cool as Graham's power was, it meant getting hit way too often. I'd still take his abilities if I had the chance. Combined with my armor and my shields, I would be unbreakable.

Continuing, I said, "I've seen all I needed to see here. Patterson's weapons aren't much better than anything else out there. Send them back with their tails between their legs and I won't..."

From out of nowhere, She-Dozer landed on top of me and hit me...hard. It was so hard, it knocked me off the side of the building. I'd gotten cocky and arrogant. Bad things usually happen at those times in my life and this was no exception.

Activate flight system! I directed the suit over the warbling of the master alarm. *Silence master alarm.*

Checking my almost depleted shields, I flew back over top of the building. Discus was climbing back on his sled and Sheila dropped into a fighting stance, daring me to come at her.

I started to and stopped myself. My internal monologue sounded a lot like Vicky. *What the hell are you thinking, Cal? The suit is already dinged up.*

"We're done here for today, Guardians," I announced. "Next time you won't be nearly as lucky."

I flew away, knowing that I'd already done too much damage to the armor for one day and that I should've gotten more than I did from that bank. I'd also lost Tweedledum, which meant a little more work around the junkyard for me until I could steal a replacement. Patterson's suit hunting weapons couldn't really be turned back against him—at least by me. I didn't have a team and a mobile launching platform to go after Ultraweapon. The microwaves were a neat trick, but I could solve that by installing a variable frequency output module on my shield generators, so I could shift it against attacks calibrated for my shields. My guess is Patterson's suit already had those.

The only good to come out of all this was my ruse would make Joe, and his boss, believe those weapons were less effective than they actually were. The deaths and property damage would be blamed on me, but Promethia would take a hit in the public eye and I couldn't picture the Gulf Coasters being so willing to let Lazarus send another team of hired thugs down here.

• • •

Arriving back at my base, I sent Paul West a quick note asking if he'd been able to pull his head far enough out of his ass to catch my performance today. I added that if his people wanted my footage of Patterson's weaponry from the battle to make me a decent offer.

Today, I'd killed several people. The first two had been mostly by accident, but the third one was intentional. I thought it would be some major revelation, that I'd come out the other side a different person. Instead, I seemed to be pretty much the same apathetic asshole that I'd been this morning.

Had I checked out on the human race?

Vicky probably could have helped me through it. All those jokes about a rolodex of hitmen made me wonder how many times she'd put it to use. But she wasn't there to help me reflect, so I just went on about my business and wondered if I was on the verge of becoming a homicidal lunatic like Eddie.

Two hours after I sent the message, I saw a new one in my inbox. It wasn't from Paul though. It was from Major Disaster, the spokesman for General Devious. It appeared that I was back on the hiring radar faster than I'd imagined.

Mechanical,

Congratulations on your fight with the Gulf Coast Guardians and the Promethia team augmenting them. As you may know, I am the aide de camp of General Devious. The General has decided that it is time to take the fight en masse to the superheroes once and for all. HORDES, or, Heroes Overmatched by Rampaging Destructive Executioner Squads, is intended to be an army of supervillains and you are being offered a place in it. Based on your capabilities and the mutual dislike of Lazarus Patterson you and the General share, she wants you to be part of the team that attacks the West Coast Guardians.

I overlooked the slight on my name and continued reading with interest. The message went on to list the fee I would be paid. It was decent, but I was already sold on the idea. With a team at my side, maybe I could bring down the mighty Ultraweapon once and for all!

Chapter Fifteen

HORDES Spelled Backwards is FAIL

It took two months for Devious to actually assemble her army. When most people think about villains, they believe we're more organized and always have our next plan ready. They actually believe that the reason we are more successful is that we don't have all the red tape following us around.

That's a load of crap if ever there was one. Yeah, there's less bureaucracy, and God help me if I ever have to deal with what heroes have to deal with, but our side of the fence has problems of our own!

Compared to the others, my apathy was pretty minor stuff. All seven of the deadly sins were pretty much on display here in a convention center in the middle of Iowa.

Yup, Shriners, Avon, and this week a supervillain army, all use our facilities. They should use our event in their marketing.

Since the rooms didn't have chairs that would accommodate the armor's frame, I remained standing near the back, with my faceplate open. Scanning the crowd, I tried to identify as many as I could, while at the center of the stage, General Devious had floated in the latest version of her throne, now with hovering capabilities, and addressed the audience.

Looks like Eddie is out of prison again, I noted while returning to our conventions "opening speaker."

She was in her mid-fifties, still attractive in a MILF-like way, clearly enjoyed cosmetic surgery or used her telekinetic powers to give herself the right amount of lift here and there. Her uniform was crisp, blonde hair perfectly in place, and so professional looking that I could see her running Fortune 500 companies or even whole countries. The General clearly had the charisma. In contrast, I thought of Maxine Velocity—the wild child who had something different about her costume or hair style every time she arrived at my workshop.

"The heroes look at most of you as a regional threat. Perhaps that does not bother you, but it should. I am proposing that we take this to the next level. It's time for us to set aside our differences for the common cause of defeating the heroes and driving those government bootlickers into the ground! Alone, most of you struggle against the superteams, but look around; we have all the numbers we need right here. We know where their headquarters are located. They're sitting there, openly defying us, and saying that we could never possibly organize an attack. Once we have eliminated the heroes, torn down their icons, and sent the common people scurrying into their homes like fearful church mice, then we can begin whittling away at the politicians. The world is right there, waiting for us to become its master."

From the reactions around me, the crowd was lapping it up. I'd like to say that I remained totally suspicious and did not for one instant imagine myself in an estate surrounded by beautiful women because we were the ones in charge.

Still, something didn't seem quite right. My neural interface picked up on my concern and brought the shields up on low. Surprisingly, the enticing mental distraction abated right before I got to the lovely journalists in little black dresses wanting to jello wrestle to see who gets to interview me. Too bad I didn't hold off on it for a few minutes.

Ah, the old subliminal sales pitch. Well played, General. Think I'll just keep my defenses active until she's done.

Without her added mental push, the speech was just your typical graduating class style inspirational variety, albeit with psychopathic undertones. The idea sounded promising.

"We will deploy skirmishers to engage the hero teams and keep them occupied and unable to assist each other. While that happens, the bulk of our army will descend on one major team at a time and obliterate them. Those in the skirmishing teams will be fighting heroes from different areas of this country who are less familiar with your powers; to give you an advantage."

She yielded the stage to Apostle, who was serving as Master of Ceremonies and hovered back to where the Overlord stood in his armor. While the man at the microphone went over today's agenda, I watched her in quiet conversation with the other heavyweight on stage.

When I saw that her lips were still moving, I checked and sure enough Overlord had his shields up. I lowered mine, but kept alert for any signs that she was still working the crowd.

No trust issues there, eh, Cal?

Frowning, I went back to her base plan and realized that her line of thinking was a two-way street. We would also be less familiar with the heroes we'd be fighting. I spent several minutes on how I could match up, if I was suddenly up against the East Coast Guardians, tossed together with an assorted group of villains trying to take on people who actively train together.

For someone coming down to fight the Gulf Coasters, would they be anal enough to memorize which nodules on the belt Discus wears charge his force discs with which energy or element?

Even someone like Eddie might be shocked, well, bad pun there, if Graham snuck up on him with the equivalent of a water balloon. They could really use something like Patterson's Threat Index team for this. Wonder if I should suggest it?

You just did, Mr. Stringel, came the reply in my head accompanied by a whimsical laugh.

I probably was turning pale at the moment. *Hello, ma'am. What brings you to my little corner of the world, today?*

She was still speaking with the Overlord, but was looking in my direction and had a half-smile on her face that sent a chill up my spine.

You're one of the few who picked up on what I was doing during the speech and are actively thinking about the negative aspects of our strategy. Most of the others are already getting bored or indulging in the little fantasies I encouraged. Would you care to know about the depraved imagery Rodentia's flea infested mind is practically screaming?

I thanked her for the kind offer, chuckled, and tried to decide if I should raise my shields again.

Oh, don't be such a spoilsport, Calvin, she broadcasted. *I'm not trying to exert any influence on you at the moment.*

Maxine said you had a penchant for lying.

Everyone says that, young man.

Could you lie to the Overlord and get away with it?

Apostle was wondering the same thing earlier. If memory serves correctly, he postulated that if we could harness the mental energy of me lying to the living truth detector and Overlord trying to catch me that we could...

Solve the world's energy problems forever? I offered.

Actually, he wanted to weaponize it in some manner, but your way could work as well.

Both of us laughed at that, and I saw the Overlord's armored mask turn toward The General.

Oh, you're busted! I thought and pondered how to mentally smirk at someone.

Please, she responded coolly. *You make the assumption that I care what he thinks. He only agreed to participate out of fear.*

Fear? He's got the biggest criminal empire of them all. But you're right; he lost badly and still needs to prove he has the goods.

From the stage, I saw the woman's Cheshire grin. *I agree with your point, but would offer two additional reasons. First, he's afraid that I might finally get the little billionaire and will try to muscle in to make sure he's the one. Second, without his pet clone, he's lost his great equalizer. His armor is on the verge of being unable to keep up with the innovations by Ultraweapon's people. Two years from now he could be as far away from Patterson's armor as you are from his.*

That was pretty mean spirited. *Harsh! No need to rub my face in it.*

Would you prefer I lied to you, Calvin? Only moments before, you were accusing me of telling falsehoods, so I was trying to be honest with you. I'm hurt.

She was seriously screwing with me, but it was funny. *Touché*, I conceded. *But what if I get Patterson before either of you do?*

Are you trying to make me burst into laughter up here, young man?

Hey, it could happen. Ultraweapon could be so busy fighting you two off that there's an opening for me. Stupider things have happened.

Yes, I suppose if that ridiculous oaf Gunk were here, he could clog up Ultraweapon's exhaust ports with that vile concoction he expectorates, and Lazarus' suit could explode. That would be far more insane than you landing the killing blow.

Without thinking, I imagined it, or perhaps she helped paint the mental picture. It was pretty amusing.

Rather vivid, Calvin. Thank you for the imagery. Of course, if you, or poor Gunk for that matter, did actually manage to kill Lazarus, you'd die soon after that. Either I, or my so-called friend seated next to me, are adamant on that fact.

It'd be worth it, I answered.

Oh, in that case, I wish you good hunting.

Thank you, Ma'am. I've always been fascinated by your chair.

Are you offering to upgrade it for me?

Only if the price is right, but a Direct Neural Interface would free up your hands and...

Yes, my people tried that already, but that technology seems to inhibit my powers and the amplifiers built into the chair.

Perhaps, but remember that gulf that exists between my armor and the set next to you? I'm fairly certain that same gulf exists between your engineers and me.

She steepled her fingers and considered it. *An intriguing proposition and it's refreshing to see some brash confidence for a change. I'll consider letting you work on it after I've killed Lazarus. It's been a pleasure speaking to someone with such an inventive mind and a willingness to say what is on it.*

Thank you. I guess. My response was tempered with the knowledge that people around her all the time are probably scared to have a free thought.

True. Most men seem intimidated by a telepath who knows how often you're staring at my tits.

With all her proper language, her casual use of that last word caught me off guard, which probably was her plan all along. For the record, I hadn't, but now she pretty much forced me to. *They do look nice, but the fact you can rip me apart with your mind kind of trumps that.*

Good, you're respectful as well and have an interesting mind. Pity you're not better looking or I'd be tempted to borrow you for tonight.

I flushed, falling for her flattery, which set me up for the sting of her insult. She was toying with me, but not in the Hillbilly Bobby "make fun of me and slap me on the back really hard" way, but more like a cat swatting at a mouse a few times with her paw before pouncing on it.

Yes, I suppose I am toying with you, General Devious confessed. *Now, go ahead and ask me what you've been wanting to but couldn't figure out how to phrase it.*

Since you brought it up, I said. *Was Maxine really Patterson's half-sister? How much of the story she told me was true?*

Yes, poor Maxine. At this point what difference does it make?

Well, I guess it would make a difference to Lazarus, but I'm guessing you're planning on telling him that he killed his half-sister at some point when you want to distract him; even if it isn't true.

She ignored my statement. *I warned her she wasn't ready, but she went ahead anyway. I sense you also cautioned her. Ask yourself, Calvin, do you believe you could face her as you are right now and prevail.*

I didn't have a bedazzler built into my suit, but now considered that maybe I should.

Don't bother with the expense, she advised. *Hermes now wears polarized glasses that will prevent copycats and I think you'll find that the other heroes who rely on super speed have taken similar preventative measures.*

Annoyed that my invention was now obsolete, I admitted that Maxine would probably win in a fight between the two of us.

Then we agree on something.

Yes, General Devious, we do. But you still didn't answer my question.

Her laughter returned. *I told you to ask the question, but I never said that I would respond. I try to limit myself to a small number of truisms each day, just to remember what it feels like. I've already reached my quota speaking with you today. Now, if you'll excuse me, my aide is attempting to contact me about something rather inconsequential, I suspect, but I've already kept him waiting long enough. Thank you for providing such an entertaining diversion. We should do this again sometime.*

Leaving me with that last statement, I wondered how much of her last statement was a truth, or a lie. I raised my shields back to that minimal level and decided most of it was a lie.

What really surprised me was that the assault would happen at the end of our little get together. The head honchos wanted to prevent word of our plan from getting out to the heroes and the government; and any of us that might have been having second thoughts about this were not going to be given the opportunity to back out.

For my part, I didn't want to walk away. If I had to settle for just being in the same area when Lazarus Patterson bought the farm, I could live with that.

As long as he didn't.

• • •

On the way out for a break after a briefing, I was at an automated buffet line when a man walked up to me. It was Eddie, obviously free from prison.

"Stringbean, my man!" he said and tapped the armor on the back. "New threads I see? Looking...well, sharp isn't the word, but I'm glad to see that when the nineties called and said they wanted their powered armor back, you answered the phone."

Clearly, he hadn't changed very much; Eddie was still an asshole.

Ladling some mashed potatoes onto my plate, I rolled my eyes at him. "Nice to see you, too, Eddie. The prison still has a problem holding you, or it's getting much easier to escape."

"A little of both," he said, and grabbed a plate. "It's the technology. It's everywhere these days. Everywhere! They were giving this politician a ten cent tour, and like, the dude gave up all his stuff, but forgot to take out his little hearing aid. It was pretty damned cramped in there, but as far as I'm concerned; it really is a miracle ear! I made a really big mess when I popped out. Now that I am, I owe those Gulf Coast bastards for bringing in the Olympian. You in?"

"Maybe," I replied. "Let's see how this all plays out first. "Which group are you in?"

"Skirmishers. You?"

"The main body," I answered. "What's being in the skirmishers like?"

"Not just in, bro. Leading the group. Goin' to see the sights in the Big Apple!"

"Good for you," I said, fearful for the population of that city. "Who's assigned to your team?"

"Rodentia," he said. "Can't seem to get away from that little punkass! But there're millions of rats in the city and that oughta count for something. There's that one crazy assed Swedish dude, CyberThor. Keeps saying this is the dawn of Ragnarok, but he's pretty powerful."

"I've heard of him," I replied. The guy experimented with synthmuscle cybernetics, despite all the warnings, and to no one's surprise, it kind of drove him a little insane. Combine that with a deep rooted passion for Norse Mythology and you've got a pretty dangerous piece of Eurotrash with delusions of godhood. His hammer was pretty much one giant capacitor. If I ever added a melee weapon to my armor, I just might have to steal that design, but getting into a slugfest means that my suit would be taking damage and I'd rather not go that route.

"Also, got this Canuck Lumberbitch named Lady R."

Curious, because of her one email to me after the Ducie clone rampage, I asked, "Is she a looker?"

"Oh, hell, no!" he exclaimed. "We're talking two bag territory, with both of them going over your head in case one falls off. Why? You looking? I could put in a word for you with Blazing She-Clops, if you don't mind a gal with an eye patch."

"No, not really," I answered, taking stock of the women in the villainous world. Many were knockouts, but also whackjobs. As a rule, the better looking they were the more dangerous they were, just like General Devious. Even the ones who weren't gorgeous were still lunatics and anything between me and one of them was bound to end badly, probably for me, especially if that one had a psychokinetic eye. In the case of She-Clops, looks could actually kill.

Call me shallow, but most of villainesses weren't really long term or even short term relationship material. Vicky was slightly better than average looking, with the total package of confidence, wit, and charm. Fortunately, she only worked for a supervillain and didn't have all the hang-ups associated with being one. Of course that made me wonder about my own hang-ups and that was a little too deep for a buffet line.

Damn it! Just thinking about her still hurts.

"All right man, but if you change your mind, let me know. If I didn't already have my girl back, I'd be tappin' that."

Eddie, I decided, was best taken in small doses. I remembered a time when I thought it would be cool to be like him. Fast forward several years and he reminded me of those guys who you thought were kings of the campus in college, but hadn't really adjusted to life after that.

"Did you have to break her out of jail?" I asked, starting to look for a way to gracefully exit this conversation without pissing him off.

"Nah, she gave them the old sob story about being my prisoner and being afraid for her life. The only thing they charged her with was aiding and abetting and she beat that since they couldn't exactly prove how she was aiding me."

"Good for her," I said, even if I didn't care. I'd finished loading my plate and would have to go somewhere I could pop a gauntlet off and eat something that didn't come from my feeding tube. "It was good to see you again, but I gotta chow down and then do some stuff before the next meeting."

"Try not to get caught or killed," he said. "See you on the flip side."

"Same to you," I replied and went off. I wasn't lying about having to get back on time. Unlike other conventions, there might be real consequences if you arrived late to a panel.

• • •

The skies above Los Angeles were filled with terror, smoke and the usual smog. The ground below wasn't much better as three robot armies, police, National Guard, gangs, everyday joes, mercenaries, heroes, and villains all clashed in a chaotic mess of epic proportions.

Combined, Devious and Overlord brought more bots to the party than Promethia and the National Guard. Billions of dollars in war machinery were slugging it out and this was likely to become the costliest battle in history, in terms of money spent.

With any luck, I'd be able to haul away some of the debris afterwards. Bless my little mercenary heart.

There were some moments when I had difficulty finding just one target to shoot at. Our side was disorganized and haphazard, but we had the numbers and didn't really care about collateral damage. For now, I busied myself with destroying Promethia's robots and tried not to think about the carnage that might be taking place elsewhere. I saw a pair of Navy helicopters toting a warbot, so I flew toward it and fired at the harness while taking fire from the attack chopper escorting the Navy birds.

I suppose I could have just downed the cargo choppers, but generally speaking, I didn't like killing defenseless people, even cops or the military.

On the other hand, the two bastards in the National Guard Apache weren't exactly defenseless and as far as I was concerned, it was game on.

My bolts broke the harness and the Type D warbot took a six story plunge into a parking lot. The leg assemblies buckled under the impact.

So, I didn't exactly defeat it head on, I thought. *A win is still a win.*

"Missile lock. Missile launch detected," Vicky's otherwise pleasant voice interrupted my moment of glory.

Opening the throttles on my jetpack, I accelerated away from the air to air weapon. It didn't appear to be the kind with advanced countermeasures, so as soon as it got on my tail, I threw my arms backward and unleashed a level three pulse directly into my rear arc. It was something I figured out after fighting the ASH team and learning from the mistakes I had made.

The resulting explosion vindicated my self-improvement program. The Apache crew didn't appreciate it and started sending thirty millimeter greeting cards in my direction. I banked and dived away, sending my own little "how're you doing" to the overly enthusiastic National Guardsmen.

Gotta hand it to the pilot. He's not half bad, I decided as the copter danced away from my bolt.

A trio of bullets rattled my shields and knocked me around a bit and I fired blindly; almost scoring a crippling blow. Instead, it ripped his chain gun off the mount and sent it spinning out of control.

My lucky shot must've spooked the pilot and he decided that maybe he shouldn't try to bag his first supervillain today and it was time to run away.

I started to pursue, but saw something that didn't just grab my attention; it put it into a stranglehold. Over the LA Coliseum, two specs zipped around in the air as tiny flashes of light could be seen.

It's Patterson and Overlord! That's where I need to be.

Forgetting all about the helicopter, I plotted an intercept course, determined to get Ultraweapon, and tried to will my flight system to go faster.

Crossing the distance, I scanned the channels to see if I could hear their conversation.

"...reposition units...request evac from...The Grand Vizier and Mystigal are attacking General Devious. She needs assistance!...Die Patterson!..."

Wait! That last one.

"When are you going to learn, Jerimiah? You're a delusional fool if you think you're going to win!"

The Overlord's name is Jerimiah? Yeah, I'd go with The Evil Overlord too.

"Want to know why I wear the armor, Lazarus? I'll tell you. Do you remember your old buddy Prophiseer? I choked one last vision out of his worthless husk before I killed him. It was that you would die at the hands of another man in armor. That's why I'm eventually going to kill you."

"I wouldn't put any stock in his words. He had a spotty reputation at best. Besides, you're in last year's model, Jerry. You and Devious need to join a support group."

Getting closer, I could see them better and tagged the Overlord so I wouldn't accidentally shoot him. *That would be awkward...and probably fatal for me.*

"Support this!" The Overlord screamed and launched a barrage of energy. It was pretty damned powerful.

"Impressive," Patterson grunted, weathering the storm and returning fire. "But The Olympians have already taken care of your little band of idiots in DC. Apollo's Chariot is already on its way and you know how fast they can be here. The clock's ticking asshole. You know what? I'm done playing with you!"

Ultraweapon turned his full fury on his rival and Old Jerry was suddenly on the defensive. The onslaught got that little voice going inside my head saying that it might be a good idea to just go somewhere else, but then I realized that he might not have enough juice left to stop me and I diverted extra power to my weaponry.

Fire force blasters! Maximum discharge!

Twin bolts of avenging power lanced from my arms into the back of the Ultraweapon suit. My heart was pounding so hard that I could hear the throbbing inside my brain. Seeing him spinning through the air tasted like vindication.

Now to finish him! I thought and willed my blasters to cycle faster.

Elated, I drew closer and prepared to deliver the final blow when Ultraweapon's flailing descent halted abruptly and he spun on me.

"What the...? Stringel? Is this some kind of a bad joke, Jerry? You invited this worthless gnat?"

His arms pointed at me and I saw the glow of his force blasters just as I was trying to issue the command to fire.

"Die!"

I'd never been hit so hard in my life. Twice at close range and two more times while I fell. The first two stripped away most of my shielding and sent me in the other direction like a batter connecting with a hanging curveball. The next one slammed into the armor's plating during my descent and I couldn't breathe. With the wails of every alarm I'd installed in the suit going off like an angry drunken garage band at three in the morning, I dropped from the sky. The fourth would have probably killed me, but I'd corkscrewed and my somewhat intact rear shielding took the brunt of it before I went face first into the stands of the stadium.

● ● ●

When I came to, almost everything was offline, except the alarms. Amazingly enough, I wasn't dead. The faceplate was cracked and the feedback from the interface made me feel like I had a skull fracture... or maybe I did.

Ten fingers and ten toes, I thought. I could still feel them. The rest of my body was in so much pain that I almost wished I was paralyzed. I could see the blurry timestamp on my HUD and tried to do the math. It took a little longer than I'd expected, but it looked like I'd been out of action for at least twenty minutes.

The automatic repair systems had kicked in. The suit's left arm was dead and I was pretty sure the arm inside of it was broken as well. The legs were okay. Flight system was at forty percent capability with only one of the two tanks online, so I'd need to conserve my flight time. All the front shield generators were burnt out and the rear ones were hanging by a thread. Frontal armor was breached in three separate areas.

I used my one working arm and forced myself to stand, or to do a close approximation of standing, and tried to get my bearings. Neither Patterson nor the Overlord was anywhere to be found. I'd been left like a hunk of garbage to be found by a cleanup crew. It was pathetic. I was pathetic!

One step at a time, I worked my way to the exit of the empty stadium burdened by the weight of my complete and utter humiliation.

In the sky, I saw the blazing visage of Apollo's Chariot. *As if things weren't bad enough already!*

Instead of giving up, crawling into a hole and dying, I flew north out of the city, staying low and trying to look as inconspicuous as a semi-mobile wreck could. Spotting a slowly moving freight train coming from the Port of Los Angeles, I decided to become a technological hobo and hitch a ride back east.

Knowing my luck, I'd figure out a way to screw that up!

I broke into one of the cargo cars and found an empty spot to sit down and feel sorry for myself.

That was one thing I was actually quite good at.

Chapter Sixteen

Maybe the End of the World isn't Such a Good Idea

At some point in the nearly two years since I took the slow train out of Los Angeles, I stopped caring about everything. Yeah, I'd always been a bit short when it came to the milk of human kindness, but ever since the *gnat* had been swatted away by Ultraweapon, I'd lost pretty much all interest in everything and anyone.

Sure there'd be moments like those first few weeks when I'd gotten back to the junkyard where I'd work at a fevered pitch on an idea for the Mark III suit that would prove to the world that I wasn't a third rate Ultraweapon imitator, but it would never get anywhere. All I had to show for it was reams of half-finished schematics, part of a torso assembly and an arm that would be the start of the brand new suit.

In truth, the three things I'd completed consisted of my junkyard doggie and two self-destructs; one for the junkyard and one for my suit. For some inane reason, Hillbilly Bobby had insisted on one for the hole in Alabama, so I already had the design. Considering there was only one exit to the base, it seemed like a bad idea to me. As for my suit, I converted one of my cargo holds in it into a spot for an overloaded powercell that would take me out if I ever needed to call it quits. One thing I'd settled on during that train ride was that I wouldn't be going back to that prison no matter what, even if it meant blowing myself sky high.

The Junkyard Doggie, well, I ended up using that prototype Promethia warbot frame to make a surprise for anyone who decided to disturb me in my scrap yard of self-loathing. I'd used up the rest of my parts for pulse cannons, outfitting my robot and setting up some gun emplacements in the rest of Home Sweet Shithole.

Beer was my best friend and we welcomed each other with open arms. I still couldn't touch the hard stuff. *Thank you, Clone Ducie!* Hygiene and I weren't nearly as tight as we used to be. I'd grown a scraggily beard and let my hair get to the point where I could feel the grease on my scalp.

The problem was I couldn't stay motivated about anything except television and the internet. Most days, my suit sat around like the shell of the man I once was. If it could've talked, I bet it would have been begging me to take it out and do something.

I'd pull a robbery or two, now and then, just to keep the money flowing. My newfound drinking habit wasn't exactly cheap, but when I was running short, I'd always scrape up the initiative to do just enough to get by.

Cal Stringel—Just enough to get by! It could be my motto.

Most of my income was now coming in off special request builds. I still built a really nice pulse pistol and my jetpacks might not be the lightest in the business, but they got the job done.

I avoided any work involving the top tier villains and wanted nothing to do with The Overlord's organization or any of the others. In General Devious' case, it wasn't even possible. She'd been captured in Los Angeles and was now enjoying her stay in the Dakota Supermax wearing an inhibitor collar and pushing her wheelchair. Her fanatics had tried, and failed, to rescue her twice, while most of the others in her organization caught on with The Overlord, or someone else's forces. Hell, the only people who could get a job with the Overlord these days were people with a genetic engineering expertise. Right now was a terrible time to be support staff for a supervillain. That nugget told me Jerry had done a little giving up of his own about keeping in stride with Patterson's armor and started looking for other methods of conquest.

Part of me knew that I'd never catch up to Patterson's suit. He could hire a thousand people just like me to make his suit stronger, faster, and more lethal. General Devious' warning to not try and run with the big dogs kicked around in my mind, but then again, she was in a comfy prison cell right now and I'm the one still free—mostly.

As for Patterson, the man continued to live the life of Riley. If the gossip magazines and television shows were to be believed, his romance with Aphrodite had hit the skids and that was probably the only negative thing that could be dredged up these days. I guess I'd be sad, too, if the hottest woman in the world gave me the old heave ho. Somehow, I doubted Stacy Mitchell would ever give me the time of day.

It must really suck to be him, I thought and looked down at the jetpack I was finishing up for this one clown...I mean customer, who wanted to be able to rob high rise apartment buildings with ease. The number of jobs he'd have to pull to pay for the purchase and the fuel didn't seem to be worth it, but I wasn't going to argue.

To me, it was the equivalent of using my armor to knock over a gas station, but his currency helped pad my coffers just the same. I was beginning to think of myself as some kind of chipmunk hoarding my little pile of cash for the inevitable rainy day.

As I made the last minute adjustments to the equipment in front of me, I caught my reflection in the polished metal of the jetpack. The mangy beard and sunken eyes made me look like some kind of redneck TV extra. I had to think back for the last time I'd had a good night's sleep.

Oh, yeah, it was two days before Vicky died. I should probably at least shave and make myself presentable, or at the very least make an effort to stay downwind of him.

Looking over at Tweedledee's dormant head mounted on the computerized workbench, where I hadn't built a weapon in what seemed like months, I considered reactivating him just to have some company, but decided against it. In my mind, I heard Bobby's voice saying that if I was lonely, I should just get a dog.

Wouldn't be a bad idea, I responded to the imaginary voice.

Or, he continued. *You could always, I don't know, bust my ass out of jail!*

Bobby, c'mon, man! You know I ain't got the juice to pull that off. I'd need months of planning and, most importantly, I'd need Vicky.

I could help, Vicky's voice chimed in. *It sounds like fun.*

I'd take you up on that, if you were really here and I wasn't imagining this. It was further proof that I needed professional help, but the free flowing apathy kicked that can down the road for another couple of months.

That does kind of stink, she replied. *Why don't you stop listening to us and get cleaned up?*

She had a point, even from the dark corners of my mind. I boxed up the jetpack and turned off my equipment. Before I shut down my browser, I scanned the message boards and travel advisories. If I was going out later today, it would be useful to know the places to avoid if I didn't want to run into any superheroes. Just another service the Wireless Wizard offered. I had to hand it to the guy, he quit the villain business and just sold secure computing services to us. It was a good gig, and I was more than a little jealous.

Scanning the screen at one of the message boards, I saw a rumor that Patterson was trying to track down the Overlord's latest secret base.

Jerry, you better watch out, I thought. *Old Lazarus is trying to press his advantage before your next world domination scheme is ready.* In the old days, I would've been angrier, but I'd accepted my life as a D-List Supervillain. Hell, I'd probably write a memoir, if I thought it would sell.

Not seeing Andydroid or any of the Gulf Coasters in my travel plans, I closed out and went to make myself resemble a close approximation of a living being. It was hard not to reflect on the wasted potential of my life. My twenties could be summed up with: went to college, went to work for an asshole, decided to be a supervillain, went to prison. When I got out, I tried to be a better supervillain. Unfortunately, that didn't go over so well.

Now, approaching my thirty fourth birthday and celebrating almost a full decade of mediocrity, I was pretty sure that if I did write that book, it wouldn't be anything that I'd want to read.

• • •

The sale and delivery went off without a hitch, which was unusual. I was already on my way back from Montgomery. My limited warranty covered mechanical defects from operation only, not including damage caused by combat or use of this device during the commission of a crime.

It's all in the fine print, trust me. Then again, if there was a catastrophic system failure, I probably wouldn't have anything to worry about, but repeat business would suffer.

Making my way back, I caught some of the chatter from the news channels that something strange was going on, on the west coast. The first reports were something about zombies, but that shit hadn't happened since fifteen years ago in Haiti. Besides, something like this was more likely to happen in New Orleans instead of Oregon. Also, I seriously doubted that someone could pull that off under Grand Vizier and Mystigal's noses. For that reason alone, I discounted it and kept on flying.

Two hours later, I'd stopped discounting it and was staring at the television screen and trying to figure out what the hell was going on. This zombie plague, or whatever the hell it might be, was spreading, and a state of emergency was already declared for everything west of the Mississippi, along with Western Canada and Northern Mexico.

Just to be safe, I sealed up the armor, and hooked up the re-breather unit. I lined all the spare air bottles up along the wall. Running the numbers with the food paste, the water, and everything else, I could operate sealed for several months without having to worry about necessities.

It made me glad I listened to Vicky and took a shower this morning.

• • •

By six p.m. I'd seen the bugs for the first time. They'd gotten into a news station in Duluth while it was on the air and I'd watched the anchor and the attractive eye candy next to him try to brush them away before suddenly stopping and going all glassy eyed. The little critters were small; only about as big as a grasshopper.

"All of you will join with the hive mind," the two said at the same time. "There is nothing to fear."

Watching them stand up and walk away, didn't really make me feel reassured.

Yeah, the armor stays on.

I sat there watching the country go silent one state at a time. St. Louis had tried widespread insect fogging and supposedly the Olympians went there to assist the Silicon Sisterhood in stopping this, but I wasn't sure. Three hours later, the Olympians were broadcasting from their headquarters in the suburbs of DC that they had a solution, but would need all available heroes and villains to try and implement it.

I seriously considered it, but passed on that kind offer. If they were desperate enough to need a cellar dweller such as myself, they were in deeper trouble than the Buffalo Bills in a Superbowl appearance.

The message boards lit up for a few minutes after that announcement, with everyone trying to decide if they could get some money, pardons, or a chance to sleep with an Olympian for their participation, but shortly afterwards, there was a message from the Wireless Wizard that he was taking VillainNet offline because all the traffic on the internet was disappearing and he was running out of places to hide our collective bandwidth.

Deciding to be proactive for a change, I went ahead and went offline; amused by the panic spreading through my fellow supervillains.

Wow, end of the world and everyone is trying to figure out their angle, but take away their internet and that's cause for panic. What a bunch of idiots! As much as I loathed all the fake sincerity of all the heroes basking in the adoration of the public in general, my fellow supervillains annoyed me just as much in different ways.

I was actually relieved that it was bugs, as long as my suit was intact, I was bug-proof. I flipped around and began looking for channels that were still broadcasting.

It took three days before BBC Australia went offline, but that was the last English speaking station that I could find.

• • •

"...broadcasting in the clear on this frequency. Is anyone else out there?"

I'd broken out a beat up shortwave radio and was surprised to find someone still uninfected after almost two weeks.

Against my better judgment, or perhaps because I was starved for any kind of human contact, I flipped the transmit knob. "I copy. Over."

"We're running a sanctuary out of Louisiana. Are there more survivors with you? Over."

"I'd prefer not to say until I know who I'm dealing with. Over," I answered.

"Hold on for a minute and I'll get our leader. Over"

The line went to static for a minute before another voice spoke, "This is Swamp Lord, broadcasting in the clear to the person identifying themselves as a survivor. Over"

"Swamp Lord!" I said. "Small world! It's Stringel. Over."

"Unfortunately, it's getting smaller every day, Mechani-CAL. What's your situation? Over."

"Been sealed up tight for two weeks. Went out a couple of times, but only had to deal with some mindless cops and National Guard. They were searching through the area a couple of days ago, but I haven't seen them since. No one else is with me. How have you been holding up?"

There was a pause before I realized I hadn't said, "Over" and breached short wave etiquette.

"Those bugs don't do so well out here in the bogs. We got a lot of hungry critters who think they're tasty. Whenever I find them, I just suffocate them. I heard there're some pockets in the Everglades too and up in the Great White North where things are too cold. Over."

Swamp Lord's gaseous form would keep him safe, but his powers started fading when he wasn't in the wetlands and that left him kind of limited.

"That's more than I've heard. How many people have you got? Over."

"Three hundred and sixty two at last count," he replied. "We're starting to run low on supplies and could use you and your suit. Are you willing to do me a solid? Over."

My first thought was to ask what was in it for me, but I thought it over. What else was I going to do here? I'd watched more movies and listened to enough music to drive me to boredom. I could use some company.

"All right, I'll do it," I said. "But only because you and I go back. What are you short on? Over."

"Shit, Cal. You name it! Medicine and food are the priorities. New Orleans is a ghost town. The bugs pulled everyone out of there, but there're still a bunch of the critters waiting around the city and we can't go in. But you can. We're about thirty minutes north of there. You should be able to get everything and anything you need there. Over."

"Can do," I answered. "I'll be in the Big Easy tomorrow morning and will contact you then. Over."

"Can your suit transmit on this frequency? Over."

"I can modify it. Over."

"Good deal, Stringel. You're a real world saver. Over and out."

Hardly, I thought and turned the radio off. It would take me a little while to button everything up here; who knew when I would return.

• • •

After a few hours of sleep I flew up to the hill where I'd spread Vicky and Joseph's ashes.

"Sorry I haven't been up here, lately," I said, addressing them both. "Your employer's latest plan seemed to have gone tits up and things aren't looking good. Too bad neither of you were here to talk him out of it. I'm going to try and give Swamp Lord some help and see if I can do something useful with myself. I don't know if I'll be back, so this is goodbye for now. I guess I can't keep complaining about how my life sucks anymore, since I'm still free. I reckon if you were here, Vicky, that you'd be proud that I was going to do something, but yell at me for doing it *pro bono.* Joseph, you'd probably point out that it took the end of the world for me to get off my worthless ass and do something. Naturally, you'd both be right."

"Take care of each other and I'll see you when I can."

• • •

There's a certain level of nervousness when pulling a solo job. I'm always looking over my shoulder and worried about what might go wrong. Looting a pharmacy in the empty city of New Orleans just didn't seem like a challenge. Recalling all the pictures from Katrina, it was way different now. The cars abandoned in the streets, not even wrecked, made me feel like any minute a director would come out and yell, "Cut!"

My usual anxiety started trailing off and in its place were the beginnings of boredom.

That, in itself, should have told me that things were going to go horribly wrong.

I'd brought a pair of slings from my base attached to thick polymer bags. They'd hold five hundred pounds each without tearing and I was filling to capacity with canned goods. A glance over at the discolored, formerly edible goods in the non-working refrigerators warned me against opening those doors. True, I wouldn't be able to smell it inside my suit and hell, it might even smell better than the less than fresh odor I was putting off, but it didn't seem like a good idea.

If I ever got to that third version of the suit, I'd have to try and figure out how to fit a shower inside.

On my internal sound system I was rocking to the one and only Biz Markie when the bright flash outside illuminated the front of the store.

"Energy signature detected," the robotic voice in the suit warned me.

Power to shields and weapon systems, I thought and felt the suit respond to my mental commands. Cautiously, I worked my way up the seasonal isle and wondered who might be out there.

Maybe Swamp Lord got hold of some other supers. Good! They can help carry some of this shit.

That was the glass half full reasoning that I held onto as I headed to the front door. Outside I saw Apollo's Chariot, several hoversleds, and at least six of the Olympians. The glass went from half full to all the way to the top in a split second. *Hurray! The heroes are here. It's about time they showed up to start cleaning up this mess.*

Aphrodite, in all her glorious beauty and looking better than that pinup over my workbench, had her fingers touched to her forehead and must be psychically scanning while Athena stood guard next to her. Her probes wouldn't get through my shields, so I activated my chest mounted spotlight.

"Hey, guys," I started and was unsure of what to say to them. "Fancy meeting you..."

As the Love Goddess' head snapped up and I found myself drawn into her deep eyes, an energy spear smashed into the front of the store and sent glass everywhere. That knocked me out of my momentary fantasy all right.

"Capture him for the hive," Athena ordered and that mental glass I was thinking about earlier; don't ask what it was full of.

Shit! Shit! Shit! Fire force blasters! Maximum discharge.

My twin bolts of energy hit Ares head-on and did absolutely squat. Hermes had already circled around me and smashed my back with her rod with enough force to knock me into one of the bags I'd been preparing. Grabbing two ten pound bags of flour, I crushed them together as she drew close again. The cloud of flour would hopefully blind the speedster and give me a little cover. Something detonated on my shielding, an energy spear I guessed, or it could have been an arrow from Artemis. Either way, my shields didn't like it any more than I did.

Options! I need an option!

Hermes was a blur brushing her eyes clear and dispersing the cloud of flour like a dust devil. I was beating a hasty retreat toward the back of the store, firing wildly with my blasters as soon as they cycled through and trying to figure out if I should go straight through the roof or into the alley. Hermes would be on me like nobody's business if I didn't get off the ground, but up there Apollo's Chariot could easily outfly me. Getting away from it would be impossible!

Ares just grabbed the aisles and started pushing. He was going to bury me in a pile and trap me.

My only shot at getting out of here would be to damage the Chariot and fly to the water. I tried to remember if I'd seen Poseidon in the group, but realized that I hadn't stopped to take notes.

Activate flight system. Fire force blasters! I blew a hole through the roof and went out of it before the wall of debris Ares was pushing reached me.

There was only one thing in my possession that had any hope of damaging the Chariot.

Activate Self Destruct with twenty second delay.

I dodged one of Aphrodite's psychic bolts, along with an energy spear, but the archer hit me again. *Does that damn woman ever miss?*

Apollo's pillar of flame barred my way and the alarms in the suit warned me not to go any closer.

Detach self-destruct assembly.

I reached behind me and felt the weight of the class C powercell primed to explode and hoped it would be enough. I'd never played much baseball or football, so what I ended up doing was some half-assed combination of a fastball and a forward pass, but it looked like it would be close enough...until Hermes streaked in from nowhere and deflected it.

No!

The powercell bomb bounced to where several of the Olympians were positioned at the entrance to the pharmacy. Ares didn't hesitate to pounce on it as the weapon detonated.

The others were scattered like bowling pins by the force of the explosion. I didn't linger to see if I'd done any lasting damage to the Olympian and turned on the afterburners. They'd be after me in moments. Apollo was already heading for his chariot. Aphrodite and Zeus were mounting the hoversleds.

All I'd have to do is make it to the waterfront and do my swim to freedom. Just a few more miles.

"Energy signature closing rapidly," the suit warned.

I tried to evade, but I only managed to avoid a direct hit from Apollo. It was enough to send me crashing into a warehouse. Silencing the master alarm and looking at my depleted energy levels, I didn't like my odds, but was kind of in shock that I'd held on this long. Of course they weren't in full control of their faculties, so it wasn't exactly like I was getting them at the top of their game.

I fired my blasters and opened a hole in the wall, intending to go through it and stopped. Instead, I shot a hole into the next one as well and squeezed into a janitor's closet and hid, hoping they would think I went out the hole and chase me that way. The minimal shielding I had left should keep Aphrodite from detecting me. Zeus was another matter, but my power levels were so low that he might also miss me.

Doing a quick diagnostic, I heard a death knell in my mind. There was a breech in the armor on the back of my leg that I only now noticed. If I went into the Gulf, the suit would flood and short out. I wouldn't be coming out alive. I stuffed a wad of rags into the crack in my armor that would hopefully prevent one of those bugs from crawling inside and taking me over.

I heard movement outside, and peeked through the crack in the door. Hermes was rushing around the room and searching in a random manner. I gently shut the door and tried to figure out an option that got me out of here intact.

Nothing came to mind. I couldn't even locate any power to recharge my suit. I didn't want to go out like this, but even my self-destruct was gone.

I'm so screwed.

Cal Stringel's adventure continues in the smash hit, *Confessions of a D-List Supervillain*. Look for the third installment of the series in the fall of 2014.

About the Author

Jim Bernheimer is the author of several novels and the publisher and editor of three anthologies. He lives in Chesapeake, Virginia with his wife and two daughters while writing whatever four out of the five voices in his head agree on. Visit his website at www.jimbernheimer.com

Other Books by the Author

Horror, Humor, and Heroes Volume I

Horror, Humor, and Heroes Volume II

Horror, Humor, and Heroes Volume III

Dead Eye: Pennies for the Ferryman

Dead Eye 2: The Skinwalker Conspiracies

Spirals of Destiny Book One: Rider

Spirals of Destiny Book Two: Sorceress

Prime Suspects: A Clone Detective Mystery

and

Confessions of a D-List Supervillain

The best is yet to come!

CPSIA information can be obtained
at www.ICGtesting.com
Printed in the USA
LVHW080251120521
687191LV00022B/378